BIG CATS AND KITTEN HEELS

BIG CATS AND KITTEN HEELS

by

Claire Peate

HONNO MODERN FICTION

Published by Honno
'Ailsa Craig', Heol y Cawl, Dinas Powys
South Glamorgan, Wales, CF6 4AH

A catalogue record for this book is available from The British Library.

ISBN 978 1870206 884

Published with the financial support of the Welsh Books Council

Cover design: G Preston
Cover image: Getty Images
Printed in Wales by Gomer

For David

Trwy cicio a brathu mae cariad yn magu

Through kicking and biting love develops

(Welsh proverb)

1

"**So,** Rachel, just what do you do?" Marcia asked me, her bony bottom perched on the edge of the sofa. If she lost any more weight her skinny behind would actually puncture the leather cushions and all the stuffing would come springing out beneath her like squirty cream from an aerosol can.

"What do you mean 'what do I do'?" I asked, sipping my wine and popping another olive into my mouth. I didn't like her tone.

"Well, you don't ski." Marcia held up a manicured hand and stuck her thumb out, as if counting.

"That's right," I nodded, mimicking her by holding up my hand and sticking my own less manicured thumb out.

"And you don't ride," she counted.

"Right again."

"And you've never tried hiking, surfing, sailing, climbing, mountain biking…" She counted my non-activities on her fingers, each one an admission of my failures to do anything remotely exciting.

I nodded, lips now pressed together in a tight smile, clutching my wine glass in a stem-crunching grip. Marcia always had this effect on me. Why had I agreed to meet my pal Angela when I knew her new-found friend Marcia would be joining us? Why did Angela even like this brassy upstart – surely she could see what Marcia was like by now?

Apparently not.

Marcia had attached herself to my friend Angela after meeting her at the gym six months ago where they discovered they had a shared passion for bikram yoga, whatever that was. The gym is an alien place to me so right from the start I was excluded from their little in-jokes. I had nothing to add to their banter about that ugly man with the pink towel and the woman who never shaves her legs, so I just smiled and waited for the conversation to move on to something I could actually contribute to. Like the controversial reorganisation of our local supermarket or the poor choice of blockbusters at the video shop. But sadly neither topic was ever brought up and the gym-talk just increased and extended to include beauty spas, holidays and sports.

I was in danger of fading into the background almost entirely, at the rate things were going.

Marcia was busy pouring out a bottle of wine for us, winking at Angela about some no doubt secret joke they had between them. Probably at my expense. She was one of those people who got a real kick out of manipulating others – I'd seen her do it in the past few months and I had thought that she couldn't manipulate me, or at least that she had enough respect for me not to try it. But here she was, giving it her best shot. I took a deep breath and steeled myself. I could rise above it because I knew that deep down I was a strong and confident person and her previous victims had always been a little edgy. Well, they had been by the end of it. From the safety of a bar sofa well out of range, I'd watched Marcia effortlessly insult Angela's friends, belittling them so subtly that anyone not directly in the firing line wouldn't be aware that it was happening. But the strange thing was no one ever said anything about it to Angela. Maybe because Angela was never on her own. Marcia seemed to be hanging round her all the time lately and if you invited Angela out then there was a pretty sure bet that the bony-bottomed one would be tagging her scrawny arse along too. I had hoped tonight it would be just me and Ange but clearly Marcia had other ideas.

I was brought back to the present with Marcia laughing an exasperated little laugh and looking at Angela, who up to this point had been sitting back on her own leather sofa, checking out the bar menu. I put another olive into my mouth, trying not to look bothered. Ordinarily I would easily have laughed off Marcia's petty behaviour, but I was tired from a long day at work and I could feel myself having a sense of humour failing. Another deep breath in...

"What about something a bit less exciting, Rachel? What about ... jogging?" She cocked her head to one side and looked at me, clearly enjoying herself.

"Nope."

"You've never been jogging?"

"I ran for the bus once."

"Yoga?"

"No."

"Pilates?"

"No."

"Sp–"

"–No."

"But you didn't even hear what I was going to say!"

"Well, I wouldn't have done it anyway," I whined like a kid in the playground.

I was angry now. Angry that she was trying to play with me, angry that I could feel myself rising to it and angry that it must be so obvious that my Achilles heel was my recently lacklustre life. Marcia really knew how to get to people.

"Look, Marcia." I set my wine glass down on the table sharply – the crack drew looks from around us. "I just…"

I just what? What could I say? Come out and admit my life was dull and she was right? Cheers for pointing it out?

I decided to give it a go. "Look, Marcia, the answer's going to be no to whatever stupid sports thing you say because I just don't do crazy stuff like you. I don't paraglide naked off mountains or water-ski off the back of a flaming yacht. So what? Lots of people live their lives without doing crazy stuff like you. Angela doesn't do any of that! And, as it happens, I don't care that I'm not a sports freak, I think I'm perfectly normal. Now can we move on please?" I turned to the bar menu. Pasta or pizza?

"Well, you can't know Angela very well then," Marcia said softly. "She does do 'crazy stuff', as you call it, and it's you who's the freak, my love."

I flung down the bar menu. "How dare you call me a freak?"

"You implied that I was a freak just for being an active,

normal person who enjoys perfectly normal, healthy interests. Personally, my love, I don't think it's normal to vegetate in front of the TV every night like a pensioner, but then that's just my opinion. You really should try to incorporate some exercise into your life. It might help with…" She smiled and her eyes flicked down to my waist. Heart pounding in anger, I watched as she calmly reached into her handbag and, pulling out a lipstick, she touched up her lips. She looked at me, eyebrows raised, waiting for the next move.

"Girls, girls." Angela leant forward on her sofa and laid a placating hand on Marcia's and my knees. "Neither of you is a freak. Marcia, you are – perhaps you're a bit sportier than the average person, and Rachel, well, you're not sporty! There. That's all there is to it. Now who wants to go halves on a pizza with me?"

"Yes but I do *do* stuff," I whined again. "Marcia's implying that I don't do anything remotely sporty and that's not true. I'm not boring. I'm not a slob."

"Oh honey, don't take it like that," Marcia purred, feigning disinterest by examining her lips in a compact. "I never said you were a slob, that's just untrue. I just wanted to know what sports you particularly liked." Snapping the compact shut she sat back and folded her arms, a smug look on her face. "That's all I was asking for, nothing else. It just seems to me as though you don't get up to very much. That's all. Did you walk here from the bus stop, for instance? I mean, that's exercise isn't it? It's practically hiking," she laughed.

"Oh just fuck off, Marcia!"

There, I'd said it. Now everyone around us was looking in our direction. The laid-back ambience of the Bay Canteen had been broken by the bickering children

11

in the back. Or rather the bickering child, because Marcia was looking completely relaxed and in control and it was me ranting and raving.

"I was only asking," Marcia said sweetly, sipping her wine and watching me from over the rim of her glass.

"Sure you were!" I bit back.

"Oh come on Rach!" Angela said, "Marcia was only trying to find out what you do."

"It's obviously a bit of a touchy subject for you," cooed Marcia.

"It is NOT a touchy subject for me!"

She'd done it. She's pushed and pushed and here I was. Just like the others she'd worked on before me. Looking ridiculous for no obvious reason. Worked up over seemingly nothing at all. My heart was thundering in my chest. I was going to go home before it got any worse. How could I compete with a person with so much experience of manipulating people?

"Angela, I'm off," I said, jumping up and grabbing my handbag. "I've had enough. I'll call you next week." I bent down and kissed her cheek. "Sorry hon," I whispered into her ear.

"Actually, Rach," Angela suddenly looked uncomfortable, fiddling with her wine glass, "I'm away next week…"

"Oh." I didn't know she had holiday booked.

There was an awkward pause before Marcia gave her little laugh again. "Oh, didn't Angie tell you? We're going horse riding in Northern Spain together. It's going to be amazing, isn't it Ange?" She squeezed my friend's knee. "Two crazy sports freaks riding in the Spanish countryside!"

I stood rooted to the spot. Angela made a move to

rise up from her chair. "You're not going home too, are you honey?" Marcia said, putting her hand on Angela's shoulder, gently but firmly, effectively keeping her on the sofa. "The night is too young for you to hide away at home on your own! Good then, I'm going to get a bottle of wine for us, and now Rachel's decided to leave us we can plan what we're going to get up to in Spain. I've bought some guidebooks with me. OK with you?"

"Oh, er," Angela faltered, looking at Marcia and then back to me. I stared back, open mouthed.

"That's if you're still thinking of going off home now, Rachel." Marcia turned her attention to me, still standing at the table. "We'd love you to stay, if you want to change your mind."

I felt as if Marcia had physically hit me.

They were going on holiday together. Marcia and Angela. Horse riding. It turns out that I didn't know my friend much at all. And now Marcia was telling me that I could stay and talk to my friend if I wanted to.

How had this happened?

"White OK?" Marcia rifled through her purse and when Angela wasn't looking she shot me a look that said, "Are you still here?"

I could feel tears prickling at the back of my eyes.

"Don't go Rach –"Angela made another move to get up from the sofa.

I opened my mouth to say something, but there was a lump in my throat. I turned and headed for the door, pushing past the people who were still turned in our direction, watching me lose it, waiting for what I'd do next. "Well, where did all that come from?" I could hear Marcia saying as I walked away. "She's got some real issues, don't you think?"

13

2

I did not have Some Real Issues.

I stomped briskly through the streets and back to my flat, pounding out my anger on the pavement.

I did not even have One Real Issue.

Marcia was a spiteful, thoughtless, self-centred, scrawny old cow and I wished more than anything I had kicked her skinny arse all the way from Cardiff Bay to East Anglia. And possibly further.

Bitchy, scheming little health freak.

How did she do it? How had she picked up on exactly the one aspect of my life that I was most unhappy with and used it against me? I hadn't talked about my boring life to her – of course I wouldn't be that stupid. And besides, I rarely got the opportunity to get a word in edgeways; she usually hogged the conversations with her long list of "crazy stuff" that she bragged about endlessly whenever I had the misfortune of being out with her. I regularly had to sit tight and listen to her rattle on about weekends spent hiking in Chamonix, mountain biking in the Lake District or sunning herself in Portugal. So how she had found the time to learn one single thing about me I don't know. It must have come from Angela – she knew how I'd been feeling lately. But surely Angela wouldn't have shared my innermost thoughts with Marcia, would she?

Would she?

I stomped on.

Maybe Angela did share my secrets with Marcia? Maybe I was wrong to hope that Angela would respect my confidences and keep them to herself? Perhaps she had no loyalty to me, after all, where was the support this evening? She'd let herself be manipulated by Marvellous Marcia and she'd not even had the nous to realise what Marcia was doing. How could she be so blind and why on earth was she actually hanging out with that undernourished, scheming, petty ego-freak? Angela wasn't like me; she had lots of friends to choose from in the city because she'd lived here all her life. So why chose to spend such an increasing part of her time with Marcia? What was it about Marcia that was so appealing?

I knew the answer all too well.

It was her energy. Her God-awful in-your-face zest for life. What had she done now, who was she with, where had she been? Every time I saw her she had notched up another series of fantastic experiences which had served to move her further and further from the dull and plodding life that I was living. But while it just irritated the hell out of me, Angela and others lapped it up, eager to be drawn into this manic lifestyle themselves.

Never mind. I took a deep breath in and slowed my pace. Even in my red-hazed anger I could see that it was a beautiful evening and ten minutes after I'd stormed out of the bar I was calming down. The pavements were still wet from the rainstorm, reflecting back an orange sunset. It was beautiful. I'd arrived at the park. Away from all traffic and noise I finally slowed down to an amble and, as far as I could, began to enjoy what was left of my evening.

OK, so Marcia was right. I was going through a bit of a crisis. Just a bit of a crisis and certainly nothing dramatic. It was about being a bit dull, a bit quiet. Hitting thirty and feeling as if I was sixty. And it certainly wasn't helped by being in the presence of Marvellous Marcia.

It had been a hard couple of years. Leaving London behind, with all my friends and family, and moving to Cardiff. The job was tough, the hours were long, but I did enjoy it and Cardiff was a great city to be in. But there was something missing. Somehow I had gone from drunken nights spent with friends at poky Soho bars and clubbing in shiny high-heeled shoes to long hours climbing a career ladder, owning a shoebox flat crammed with Ikea furniture, hiring out videos and microwaving meals.

Since I'd moved from London it had been an effort to meet people. I'd met Angela through work and she had taken me under her wing almost straight away. She'd introduced me to her circle of friends and I've been slowly building on that ever since. But maybe she was tired of me now? Maybe I wasn't sparkling enough for her? Maybe I was too flat, too still, compared to her effervescent other friend. Was I losing the first friend I had made in this city? The real key to my social life to date here in Wales?

I hoped not.

It's not as if I've been maudlin about the whole moving-out-of-London thing. I have tried my hardest not to think too much about my change in lifestyle since I moved west; to put on a brave face and realise that things will pick up. Eventually. But if I have a great weekend or a particularly good time at work and I think things are looking better, within half an hour of meeting Marcia I feel completely crap about myself again. Would other normal, mortal people feel the same in her company? Was she a particularly super-active sort of person or was she typical of what people in their early thirties were doing? I found myself, begrudgingly, wanting to be like her. To be her. I wanted to swan around and live the life she did with the horses and boats and snowboards. To go exploring in an off-road vehicle; I hadn't even been inside one, let alone take it down a steep-sided mountain. I hated to admit it, but although she was a malicious, brassy-haired, snub-nosed little cow, Marcia was nevertheless everything that was sophisticated, stylish and exciting. She was somehow at the core of everything, knew all the right people and went to all the right places. If she were a magazine she would be *Tatler* or *Harpers*. Me? Given my current mood, I would probably be more like *People's Friend*.

Or *TV Quick*.

I'd felt the rumblings of my Dull Life Crisis for a while now. Months, I suppose. But I can honestly say it was right there, right at that moment in the trendy bar with its matt chocolate walls and sparkly chandeliers that it had really hit home. I was in such a dull old rut that I didn't even have a boyfriend – I'd left him behind in London. I'd finished with him because, and this makes me laugh now, I'd thought he was too boring. Compared to me now he would look like bloody James Bond. Maybe I should give him a call...

No!

No, I wasn't desperate. And he was boring. Deeply,

fundamentally dull. Whereas I was certainly not dull, I just hadn't adapted to my new not-twenty-now, not-in-London-now lifestyle. It would come. Surely this DLC was a result of my circumstances? Surely it was because I'd uprooted from my established life in London, not because I was thirty and was genetically programmed to become dull and boring and shun all kind of excitement now that my twenties had past?

Wasn't it?

I was a fun person, I was friendly, and I would find some new and exciting road to go down. And maybe I'd go down it in a sports utility vehicle. As for men, well, I'd never had a problem there. Long black hair, curvy and tall, while I wasn't exactly beating them off with a big stick, I'd had my fair share of attention. I was just finding that at thirty a lot of the good ones were taken. Blah blah blah. It's such a cliché but it's true. Everyone knows it. That's why it's so clichéd.

Before I knew it, I was automatically rooting around in my bag for my keys to the front door of the building. Home. It was nine o'clock on a Saturday night and it looked like another night with my two friends Mr Remote Control and Mrs Takeaway Menu. At least they were always there when I needed them and wouldn't abandon me to go horse riding in Northern Spain.

Goddam it.

3

Apparently the first step in curing a problem is to realise that you have a problem in the first place. So with this in mind I decided to enter in my diary that the official start to my Dull Life Crisis was that evening in the bar with Marcia. I underlined it, just to be sure. My diary was one of those that tell you a supposedly interesting fact for each day, and on the start of my DLC it read, "Good King Wenceslas died in 929."

Really? Had he really existed? Had he really looked out on the feast of Stephen and was there really a poor man gathering winter fu-uu-uel?

Oh my God. I was so boring I actually found it interesting.

I flicked on. A few weeks later an entry read, "In 1922 Charlie Osbourne started an attack of hiccups which lasted 68 years."

Now that was interesting, surely? Even Marcia, if she'd had the time to read a diary, would have found it interesting. Wouldn't she?

I closed the diary and threw it down on my pile of *Tatlers*. In truth there was no official start to my DLC – it had been coming on for a while now. For it to be so obvious that Marcia had picked up on it and used it against me, that implied it was pretty serious. I was projecting my crisis to those around me. I could no longer pretend I was happy doing what I was doing. Or rather not doing what I was not doing.

For a while I had been soul-searching, wondering how I was going to fill my life with something more fulfilling than getting up, going to work, coming home, eating and sleeping. The trouble was that anything more fulfilling seemed a lot of effort and the plain truth was that I wasn't interested enough to join a sailing club, motivated enough to attend a reading group or bored enough to take up an evening class.

I just didn't care enough about anything that would push me out of my smotheringly comfortable existence.

I'd fleetingly wondered whether my way out of feeling dull was to sex up my day job: that I should look at changing that and the lifestyle would follow. After all, being a project manager for a national network of lawyers was not the most exciting of jobs. But the pay was great and I loved my apartment, which had cost an arm and a leg. Could I really do some trendy sort of job in television and earn twenty quid a week? No. Besides, I actually enjoyed what I did and I was good at it.

But there was one glimmer of hope on the horizon. One thing I could look forward to. Pencilled in my diary at the end of next week, on the very same day that "The

American novelist Ernest Hemingway shot himself in 1961" was "Louisa's hen weekend – Brecon Beacons."

That would be exciting.

Fun even.

At the very least I was probably going to have a better day than Ernest Hemingway had had in 1961.

Louisa was a good friend from university who I missed dearly as she'd never yet managed to get a weekend free to visit me in Wales since I'd moved, although she kept promising me she would. She had stayed in London and was busy flirting her way to the top of an independent estate agency. Louisa was good at flirting; a real professional, but all done with perfectly good humour and not at the expense of anyone else. She had flirted outrageously with our hideously ugly and foul-breathed lecturer and had (shock!) come top in our year of degrees. She had smiled and giggled and won over the interviewer for her first job and had taken off from there. Starting with representing bedsits and studios in Kilburn, she'd gone on to selling apartments in Marylebone and eventually houses in Fitzrovia, placing millionaire businessmen in millionaire properties. Good on her. She was using her good looks which she had in abundance, and why not? As she said herself it would be a shame to waste them, because one day they'd be gone and then where would she be? Plain and poor. And it didn't bother her fiancé James either. He knew the flirting was all a show and there was never anything more to it than harmless fun. Besides, the two of them were deeply and madly in love and their wedding was going to be the event of the year.

But first we had the hen weekend.

According to the scarily efficient nine-page dossier that a girl called Laura, the Hen Weekend Organiser, had put together (not including additional two-page calculation of costs) we would be horse riding, hiking, spending a day in a luxury beauty spa and all this in the setting of the beautiful Brecon Beacons. By the end of the weekend I could happily see Marvellous Marcia again safe in the knowledge that she wouldn't be able to count my failings on quite so many of her manicured fingers. Horse riding? Done that! Hiking? And that! Spa-ing? That too! Maybe I would take to one of these activities and realise that it was for me and hey presto, I would have something more exciting in my life than a fact-a-day diary.

I picked up the diary, opened it and drew another line under The Official Start of my DLC. This was where it ended.

4

The morning of the start of the Hen Weekend began bright and sunny and, unlike poor Ernest Hemingway, my spirits soared. I was desperately looking forward to the long weekend and the opportunity to see Louisa again. At last it came to five o'clock and I sprinted for my car. Pinned to my dashboard was a postcard that had arrived this morning and which would spur me on to make sure I got the most out of the weekend:

Hi Sweetie – Hope you're feeling better after the other night at the Canteen. Marcia doesn't know what happened and is feeling really bad that she might have upset you. Riding here is amazing! Plenty of breathtaking views and saddle-sore nights! Staying in Parador up in mountains for next four days. Three pools, spa centre and fancy food! Luxury! Marcia wants a word so bye bye from me.

See you soon (Debbie's party on the 18th?)
Ang xxxxx

Feeling terrible that you got so cross the other day
: (Let's meet up and make up. M x.

Well sod Marcia.

And sod Angela too for being so insensitive.

Beside me on the passenger seat was a two-page set of directions from Laura the Hen Weekend Organiser – the same girl who had recently supplied me, with the nine-page Hen Weekend Dossier. Back when I'd lived in London I'd met Laura once at a dinner party that Louisa had hosted. From what I remembered, Louisa had been right to put her in charge of organising the weekend. Not that it was "organisation" per se; it was more of a military operation. When I'd taken the phone call from Laura about the weekend, she didn't tell me what was planned, she briefed me. She used frighteningly serious words like "precisely" and "sequentially" during the conversation, and gave times as o-eight-hundred-hours. It was no surprise. Although by day Laura was a primary school teacher to the future urban ruffians of Hackney, at weekends she was out with the Territorial Army, learning to jog ten miles with a rucksack filled with dumbbells and honing her ability to take the pin out of a grenade without breaking a fingernail. Very useful for the day job. She was a good laugh, though, and when drunk she came out with the most horrendous stories about the army, so I was very much looking forward to seeing her again and hearing more tales along the line of surviving on nothing but your own wee for two days in 40 degree heat.

I cast my eye down her directions – they were

horrendously detailed and scary-sounding but in reality it was pretty simple. Point the car north, go west a bit at Abergavenny, and then I'd have to consult the directions a bit more. There were lots of "take a 90° right at High Barn farmhouse [OS459 567]" and "take steep track [1 in 4] up Coed y Bere lane [OS 456 577]." Maybe I should be a bit apprehensive if this was a sign of what was to come? Maybe the TA-trained Laura had gone all-out with the weekend plans and had some army-style horse riding planned for us all? Perhaps it wasn't going to be as much about having fun and relaxing as I imagined, but more a regimented exercise in hen weekending? Would there be weapons involved? Scary stuff, but then again potentially useful with the Marcia-situation: arrive at Bay Canteen, lay down M16 and see then whether she's up for any more belittling and manipulation...

Well, it was too late to worry about my weekend now. I pointed my trusty VW Golf in the right direction, threw the postcard into the passenger foot-well, picked it up again, ripped it in half, threw it back in the foot-well and I was off!

The journey up in the late afternoon sunshine was pretty uneventful, although I was practically chewing the steering wheel in frustration at being caught on a single-lane road behind the slowest vehicle in Wales. The driver of "Barry Llewelyn's DISCOMANIA!! - mobile disco and lightshow" was one of those motorists that sticks to 40mph on the open roads and a good 10mph below the speed limit elsewhere. Just in case one of his vinyls gets scratched. God knows what his performance at discos was like. Nevertheless I dutifully followed behind him, gnarling my teeth every time I had to slip down to second gear, which was often.

I finally lost it around Abergavenny when, on a 50mph stretch of road he slowed down to 17mph because there was a sign saying there was the possibility of sheep on the road. I slammed my fist down on the horn, which let out a pitiful "weeeeeep". I expect Marcia had a car horn that would have cleared the road. Damn it.

I was in a hurry because Laura had made it absolutely clear on page five of the dossier (section 7.2) that bedrooms were to be allocated strictly on a first come first served basis, apart from Louisa the hen, of course, who would get the best room in the house. And when I spoke to her on the phone Laura had said something vague about all the bedrooms being great except ... perhaps ... one ... and had left it there. So I was absolutely determined not to be the sucker who arrived last. Laura was not going to negotiate on which bedroom you deserved, given that it wasn't your fault you arrived late.

Thankfully Barry the DiscoSnail turned off after Abergavenny and I sped away, shouting obscenities in his direction.

Finally at around seven I pulled up on the gravel driveway of the place that would be home for the next three days.

The Hen House – as Louisa had referred to it – was stunning. I'd never stayed in anything quite so grand in my life. It was surrounded by oak woodland on three sides and a field of sheep on the fourth, with a river just visible at the bottom of the field, sparkling away in the early evening sun. The place was like a miniature redbrick castle, three stories with odd shaped leaded windows irregularly punched into its old walls.

The minute I'd come to a halt the front door opened

and I instantly recognised Laura as she strode out. She raised her hand at me in a serious sort of half-wave, half-salute before coming over to the car. She'd cut her hair even shorter than when I'd seen her last; now it was barely above a grade 2, short and spiky and not at all softening her features. It was obvious she didn't spend much time flicking through the beauty section of *Cosmopolitan* searching out this season's best lipgloss.

"Rachel!"

"Laura! Hi! Good to see you." I climbed out of the car and shook the hand she'd extended to me. It was a firm and brisk handshake not unlike the ones my father always insists on giving me every time I see him.

"How's the legal world?"

"Oh you know. Ticking over. How's the youth of Hackney?"

"Bastards the lot of them. Anyway, got many bags?"

"Er, six…" I went over to the boot and opened it up, hoping to hide my sheepish expression and not appear too much the duffer.

"Six bags? Christ. Right, let's divide them up and get you inside. I'll give you a tour and show you to your room." She hauled up four of the heaviest and turned to walk back to the house. "You're the last to arrive, I'm afraid."

I smiled a tight smile and grabbed the last couple of bags.

Damn that disco man.

The Hen House wasn't posh exactly. To be posh it would need to be formal and impressive, and while it was definitely impressive it could never be described as formal. There was a sort of a shabby opulence to it that enveloped me the minute I stepped inside. It was the sort of place, in fact, that I imagined would have belonged to a very rich but very Bohemian family – people who had children called Tanzibar and Coco and were actors or writers or painters. People who walked around barefoot and dined on couscous and home-grown salads in the garden during the summer.

The artists or writers or whoever they were who had lived in the house had decorated the rooms in gorgeously striking limewashes of orange and scarlet and lime. The bright chalky walls were covered in old gilt mirrors that were barely able to show you back your reflection, while here and there ancient formal oil portraits hung next to quirky bold paintings of nudes. Everywhere was a riot of colour from the vibrant paintings to the multicoloured rugs and patchwork throws.

The furniture was a fantastic jumble of antiques, rough-cut dark wood pieces from India and eclectic junk shop finds. Enormous Venetian chandeliers hung from the exposed beams in the downstairs rooms and in some of the bedrooms.

But not in my bedroom.

How could the people who lived in this house have ever left it? It was amazing. If I owned it I would never have left it. Laura said, having flicked through the house's information book, that the owners had relocated to Carcassonne in the south of France. I wondered what they did out there? If there was a Tanzibar and a Coco, what did they do now they had moved? Did Tanzibar break in wild horses, riding barechested across the southern French plains while Coco pursued her career in modelling and commuted to Paris? Who knows? What was certain was that I would never live the kind of life that someone who owned this place would live; it was totally alien to me with my project-manager job and Ikea-decorated apartment. But for one weekend only, this bohemian life and my very ordinary life would come wonderfully close, and I could pretend, for a few days, that I was the sort of carefree creative type that lived like this up here in a beautiful and remote Welsh valley. And I could escape the oppressive Dull Life Crisis that was starting to smother me.

When I'd had the tour and dumped my bags on my (small) bed in my (small) bedroom, I went to join the others in the sitting room.

"Rachel, darling!" Louisa jumped up from her sofa and embraced me in an enormous bear hug. "It's been so long!"

"I know!" I hugged her back, my face covered in her long white-blonde hair. It was good to see her; I'd forgotten how much I missed her over the past couple of years. "I can't believe you're actually going to get married in a month. Are you nervous?"

"Me? Nervous?" Louisa laughed. "Come on, it's James who is the nervous one! But look at you – you look so tired. Why did you move out of London? I mean – Wales, for fuck's sake! How's it going? Working hard?" She examined my face, looking at the bags under my eyes.

"Oh, you know, busy."

"Mmm. I bet. Hey, I saw your ex the other day, he was shopping in Bayswater."

"Oh!" I was momentarily taken aback. "How is he doing? Still as dull as ever?"

"Great, actually. He was really busy so he couldn't chat for long. He's changed so much I hardly recognised him. He was telling me how Natalie – did you know he's got a new girlfriend? – anyway, how Natalie is the South West

29

regional finalist in kite surfing and she's got him into the sport in a big way. They've bought this really cool split-screen VW camper. He was off with Natalie to Newquay that evening. And he's grown his hair long, surfer style. It suits him."

Bugger.

"He was asking what you were up to these days. And he said 'hi'."

Bugger bugger bugger.

Why was everyone so bloody active and exciting? It was looking like Marcia was right in her assumption that it was me who was the freak with my dull old life. Perhaps Hemingway had a good point; today was a really good day to shoot yourself.

Louisa rushed off to the kitchen to rustle me up a cup of tea while I went to meet the other two hen-weekenders for the first time. Louisa had told me all about them, so I could pretty much work out for myself which one was the retiring Cathy and which was the boisterous Henna.

"I'm Cathy." The timid-looking girl held out her hand and I shook it. She had mousy brown hair tied up in a tight ponytail and wore very sensible clothes. Suddenly I felt a bit more confident with my lot. I was more dynamic and active than Cathy. I must be. Surely she didn't go kite surfing or scuba diving? "I'm a Doctor of Medieval English at Sheffield University."

"Oh Gosh," I managed. What on earth can you say to that? How interesting? No. How useful? No.

"So … er … you're Louisa's cousin, is that right?"

"Yes. On her mother's side." She gave a nervous laugh and sat back down.

"Henna," the girl sitting next to Laura on the sofa jumped up and introduced herself. "Journalist." She was a petite, slightly plump girl with neat black hair cut in a shiny bob. Just below her hairline was what looked like an enormous bruise starting to form, which every so often I saw her touch and wince.

"Henna writes for *The Times*," said Louisa, obviously proud of her friend. "She makes stacks of cash for writing one half-page article a week. In fact, Henna, have you worked out how much you make per word?"

"God, I don't know. Fifty pence or something, I think. Anyway, enough of that. Now we're all here – Laura, you're in charge, can we crack open the wine? Is that in keeping with your timetable for the weekend?"

The room went quiet and Laura, clearly not impressed at being the butt of Henna's comment, shrugged her shoulders. "I haven't timetabled drinks and snacks," she said in a brittle voice, "but now you mention it, perhaps it's a good opportunity for me to take you all through the Schedule & Rota that I've prepared for the weekend."

Henna winked at me, hiding a smile from Laura by turning away and smoothing down her sleek black bobbed hair to cover her fresh bruise.

Laura assumed her best Territorial-Army-Hackney-school briefing-voice and stood, legs apart, in front of us and, using the back of a wooden spoon as a baton, she took us through the Schedule & Rota edition 2 (we never got to see the mythical edition 1).

Although it was a scarily efficient piece of work, and didn't particularly inspire confidence in having a fun and relaxing time, it did at least mean that there were probably going to be no arguments over who would do what.

HEN WEEKEND SCHEDULE & ROTA
Edition 2

Friday

Arrival – 5pm	Bedrooms assigned on a first come first served basis. Debrief of schedule & rota + run through of inventory.	Laura to debrief
Dinner – 7.30pm	Shepherd's Pie (p.248 of cookbook) carrots Ready-made dessert	Rachel & Cathy cooking Laura washing up
Drinks – 9pm+	In main hall. BYO	

Saturday

Breakfast – 8am (sharp)	In main hall	Henna to prepare Cathy to wash up
Health spa – 9.30am – 4pm	Llangorse Manor Spa (25 min journey)	Cathy & Rachel to drive
Dinner – 7.30pm	Local pub?	Laura to source suitable venue

Sunday

Breakfast – 8am (sharp)	In main hall	Laura to prepare Cathy to wash up
Lunch preparation – 9am		Laura & Rachel
Horse riding – 9am – 4pm	Monmouth Riding School (23 min journey)	Laura & Cathy to drive
Dinner – 7.30pm	Chicken in white wine (p.233) Gateaux	Henna & Rachel Cathy to wash up

Monday

Breakfast – 9am	In main hall	Henna & Cathy Rachel to wash up
Lunch preparation – 9.30am		Laura & Rachel
Hiking – 10.30am	From Pen Coed Lodge onto Offa's Dyke Path (see OS Map below for route)	Laura to lead
Depart – 4pm	All responsible for ensuring lodge in same state as when we arrived	All

"Right, well as there's no time slot for it I might go and get some wine then." Henna made a dash for the kitchen. "Rachel, do you want to find glasses?"

"Absolutely."

It took an age to locate where the glasses were hidden, tucked away in one of the many, many cupboards in the palatial kitchen. When we finally got back to the sitting room the others had turned on the TV to get the local weather report. And it was then, at that very moment, that we all discovered just what we'd let ourselves in for.

Opinion on the news report was divided. Louisa and Henna agreed that it had to be the funniest piece of TV they had ever seen. In fact, Henna had laughed so much the wine she was drinking came out of her nose and she had to be calmed down by Louisa as she wiped the tears from her eyes. The quiet Cathy and the eminently level-headed Laura, however, said that it was absolutely disgusting (Laura), very frightening (Cathy) and that the interview should have been cut the minute things started to go wrong. And me? All I could think about was the look on Marvellous Marcia's face when I regaled her with tales of riding my enormous black stallion across barren moorland while staring death in the face.

The TV report had started normally enough, with the professionally smooth man in the studio introducing the evening news item. "It seems," the presenter was saying earnestly to the camera, "that sightings of big cats have been on the increase here in Wales since the 1970s and although no proof of the animal actually exists in the form of photographs or video footage, there does seem to be compelling evidence to suggest there are big cats living right here in the Welsh countryside. Experts say that these animals are not the native wildcats that once roamed our country – those were last seen hundreds of years ago. What we could have here is a non-native species like a lynx, leopard or puma. This could be because of changes to rare animal licences thirty years ago – many circuses were faced with a tough decision on either having their animals put down, or giving them a fighting chance and releasing them into the wild. It is suspected that the animal that was reported attacking livestock in the Black Mountains in South Wales was just one of those animals, or even the offspring of the animals, if a breeding pair were released. Siwan Parry is live in Tretower in the Black Mountains where the recent sightings were reported. Siwan, what's the mood like in Tretower this evening?"

The TV cut to a willowy, chic-looking presenter, clearly bitterly disappointed at being posted out into the countryside and having to wear enormous green

Wellington boots that clashed horribly with her fitted turquoise trouser suit.

"Thank you, Dylan, yes I'm here in Tal-y-coed Woods near Tretower where just this week there were sightings of what was said locally to be a big cat. With me is farmer Bryan Maund whose … horse … was …. attacked … supposedly by…" and she petered out. The cameraman zoomed out from her bewildered face to show, out of focus, a gruff red-faced farmer hobbling full-pelt downhill away from them. Then things became rather confused. There were screams and shouts, which must have come from the crew and then the cameraman dropped the camera. In the flash of an eye, as the camera dropped, the TV viewers saw the presenter being knocked down by an enormous black animal. "Get it the fuck off me, John! John!"

The TV then cut back to the studio.

The newsreader was staring aghast.

"Ngh!" He gripped the newsdesk and stared into the camera.

You could tell there were people shouting into his earpiece by the way he was flinching, but all he was capable of doing was opening and closing his mouth. The director then must have lost faith as the camera cut to the weatherman standing in front of a giant map of Wales, his expression much the same as his colleague.

"Aah – hello," he managed to say, looking around him at the studio for some direction, "well, it's, er, going to be a lovely weekend. Ahrm, yes…"

Laura turned the TV off and we sat stunned for a moment. Louisa and Henna were killing themselves laughing and saying, "Did you see her face, did you see her face?" They stopped when they saw Laura looking serious. Everyone looked at each other, not knowing what to say. The only sounds now coming from the crack and fizzle of logs on the fire and the tick tock of the grandfather clock in the corner.

"Tretower?" Louisa said. "Isn't that near here? I passed it on the way up. It's like ... it's like a mile away."

"Yes," said Laura flatly. I felt sorry for Laura – having been the one who had clearly spent so much time and effort organising the weekend, now all her plans looked like they were going to be ruined.

Henna suddenly grabbed her mobile and bounded out of the room. "My editor's going to love this," she sang out as she ran off, punching in the numbers.

"Well, I don't see how these rumours should affect us," Louisa placated the worried-looking Laura, "I mean, it's the health spa tomorrow, and the horse riding the next day is going to be on proper bridle tracks. We're not going orienteering any more, are we? These cat things probably live in the woods or something. Not near where we'll be going."

Cathy, Laura and I didn't say anything.

Eventually, Cathy, twisting her ponytail round and round her fingers asked in a quiet voice, "Do you think that was it?"

"What was it?" Laura asked, rather sharply.

"Do you think that animal was the big cat?" It was the question we'd all been wondering but no one particularly wanted to voice. What on earth had knocked the presenter down? Whatever it was, it was huge. Although in hindsight it didn't seem particularly cat-like. It had more of a lolloping gait, rather like a dog. But whatever it was, the fact that there had been sightings of big cats in the immediate area was pretty scary stuff.

Before anyone could answer, Louisa's phone started to ring. We all jumped.

"It's James!" she said, looking at the display. Her fiancé was having his stag weekend in the valley next to ours. Louisa had told us that the boys were having a weekend jam-packed with activities that would make even Marcia's eyes water. Despite my urge to be rid of my DLC, I was relieved our weekend wasn't as full-on as theirs, which included paintballing, go-carting, orienteering, paragliding, hiking and abseiling. At least the most ambitious activity I had to face was horse riding and really, how hard could that be?

Louisa left the room to talk to her fiancé and now Henna had returned, she, Laura, Cathy and I were all sitting in silence pretending to not listen in. Whilst actually listening in.

Louisa emerged from the hallway a few minutes later, looking triumphant and snapping her phone shut with a confident flick of her fingers. "James says they're staying put. They've seen the news report too, but the bloke who runs the bed and breakfast says it's all a hoax and the big cat story has been going on for years."

"Wouldn't he say that to keep his customers?" I offered.

Louisa shrugged. "Apparently this bloke said sightings have been reported for years but there's never been any proof," she answered, text-book style. "That's what the newsman said, wasn't it? Anyway, the owner reckons the animal was just a big dog that one of the lads in the village owns – the whole thing was probably a prank."

Oh well then, that was me convinced. I didn't say any more though, a) because I was already getting black looks from Laura and quite frankly she scared me, and

b) because it could actually be very exciting and I was half imagining reclining in my chair at the bar, popping an olive into my mouth and saying, "Well, Marcia, I was attacked by a savage leopard at the weekend. Olive, my love?"

5

I didn't think much of the threat, and I don't think any of the others thought much of it either. Well, perhaps except Cathy. She seemed to be particularly quiet and nervy. That evening, however, after having checked Laura's Hen Weekend Schedule & Rota (edition 2) I found myself in the kitchens with Cathy making Shepherds Pie for five. After a very few minutes I discovered that "especially quiet" and "nervy" seemed to be the order of the day with her. As we cooked our great vats of mince and peeled the three tons of potatoes and carrots that a meal for five seemed to require, we got chatting.

I liked Cathy, we were quite similar in the fact that we were more than a bit scared of Laura and her "it's ten o'clock – time to have fun! RIGHT NOW!" attitude to the weekend. And besides, next to Cathy my DLC didn't seem so very bad. Perhaps my problem was that I hung around with people who were too vibrant and exciting.

Maybe if I spent more time with quiet people like Cathy, people who kept themselves to themselves a bit more, then I wouldn't feel quite so bad about my own sad lack of excitement.

But for all her reserve and quietness there was definitely something rather bizarre going on with her. Every few minutes her phone would beep and she would frantically rummage around in her pocket, check the text and, with lips pursed, would push the phone back again into its hiding place. Over and over and over again. No one had asked her about it; we were all hoping she might volunteer the information herself, but so far that hadn't been the case.

She and I were chopping potatoes when it happened for about the tenth time during our cooking. She turned shaky and her knife clattered to the floor.

"Are you all right?" I asked, putting a hand on her shoulder. "You seem quite tense."

"I'm fine, I'm fine," she said, her left hand hovering over her jeans pocket where the phone was still hidden.

It was clear that she didn't to want to talk about it so I went back to chopping my potatoes and worrying about how I was going to ride a horse on Saturday without making a complete arse of myself. I could hear Cathy furtively stabbing the buttons on her phone, checking her message, the small intake of breath, and then the thrusting of the phone back into the pocket. Should I make more of an effort to see if she was OK, or was that prying? I was just deliberating how I should ask if she was all right without appearing intrusive, when she solved the dilemma for me.

"It's my fiancé," she said in a quiet, trembly voice. I turned round and saw she had tears in her eyes. "Or rather

… it's my ex-fiancé." She gulped back tears and put her hand on her forehead, taking a deep breath in.

I put down my knife. "Oh. When did you two break up?" I went to get her some kitchen roll.

"Last weekend," she sniffed and taking the kitchen roll she blew her nose loudly. "I think it was the wrong thing to do … I don't know … How do you know if they're the right one?"

"Mm." I nodded my head in some sage sort of way. "Tricky one."

"Urgh," she sighed, "I just panicked, I think. He was talking about the wedding and – I suppose I felt a bit claustrophobic and launched into this big conversation about how I was having doubts…" She talked quickly, sniffing back the tears.

"And were you?"

"Well, no, not really. He's just so wonderful and we get on really well together. I think its just nerves over getting married. Marriage didn't work for my parents, or his parents, so why should it work for us?"

"Why should it work for anyone?" I volunteered, slipping into the role of utterly sensible agony aunt. "But you won't know if you don't try. What's his name?"

"Heath."

"What does Heath say in his texts?"

Cathy sighed. "He wants to know where I am and why I'm not returning his calls. He says he doesn't know what's happened to me and," she let out a sob, "he's worried about me!" She burst into tears and I manoeuvred her into one of the wing-backed chairs and poured her a glass of wine.

"Why don't you give him a call?" I said. "Let him know where you are and that you're OK. Arrange to meet him when you get back?" I sounded very sensible and for a moment I felt another one of those pangs about being all grown-up and reaching thirty. At least I didn't wear flat shoes and support tights. Although I could certainly see the benefits…

"Yes," she sniffed, "yes, I should. I don't know why I've not replied properly to him. I suppose I thought I'd do some thinking about us this weekend, but now I don't think I need to think about us. I think we're OK as we are. What do you think?"

"I think," I said, struggling to understand what she'd just said, "I think you should go upstairs and give him a call."

"Yes, you're absolutely right." She got up shakily from the chair. "Thanks, Rachel." She walked out into the hallway, wiping her eyes with the kitchen towel as she went.

I turned back to my potatoes and jumped as Laura silently appeared out of nowhere, no doubt on a reconnaissance mission.

"Just making sure you're on target to serve dinner," she said, checking her watch before turning a concerned eye to the virgin, unchopped carrots on the work surface. "Where is Cathy?"

"Excused duty," I replied, unable to help myself. Was she for real? "Personal business."

Laura frowned. "Do you want me to draft in another person to assist you?"

"Not necessary. I'm on top of it."

"So we're on track to deliver?"

"Check!" I said. "Kitchen division is ahead of schedule and will be on target to achieve the objective." I even mock saluted her, which I immediately regretted because she might get annoyed at me for blatantly taking the piss. In fact, she beamed and heartily slapped me on the back, clearly delighted to have found someone on her wavelength.

"Excellent," she said, "good woman!" and went back to her position.

6

That night we drank. We drank like it was going out of fashion. We drank, in fact, like the dinner was so absolutely God-awful that we wanted to obliterate all trace of it from our systems. Which was actually pretty close to the truth. The lamb was tough, the mash was dry, the carrots and beans had gone very badly indeed and even the supermarket cheesecake didn't live up to the high expectations we had from the picture on the box. The bohemian, stylish setting of the Hen House was somewhere where you would expect to find pan-seared scallops and a Japanese mooli salad. I, however, had done a serious injustice to the ambience of the place by creating what could only be described as a 1970s school dinner. The only difference being the girls hadn't had the inconvenience of pushing a tray along a rail to get the individual portions slopped onto their plates – I'd done the slopping out myself.

In my defence, I had to cook for the five of us with practically no help as Cathy came back down from making her phone call in a worse state than she had been when I sent her upstairs and could only be placated with wine.

Still, the mood thankfully was not dented by my culinary disaster, everyone gave a toast to the "crap chef" and Laura hastily amended the Schedule & Rota so that I was excused from cooking on Saturday evening and was now responsible for washing dishes and therefore minimising any harm to the public. Edition Three of the Schedule & Rota was passed round the table and signed off and we all breathed a sigh of relief.

If more defence were needed, I had got pretty hammered on the rosé while I was cooking. Seeing Cathy pressed into the comfy-looking chair drinking wine had put me in the mood for some, so I'd joined her drinking while I carried on cooking. The problem was that the Hen House came equipped with the most enormous half-bottle goblets that completely disguised how much you were drinking. By the time the meal was served I was very much the worse for wear. I was so smashed, in fact, that I thought my Shepherd's Pie was actually delicious and even helped myself to a generous second portion while the others looked on in thinly disguised horror.

I didn't know it at the time, how could I when I could barely focus, but being pissed so early in the evening was fundamental to the entire success of my weekend. Things would have turned out *so* differently if I had abstained from the bottle while cooking.

However, I was completely ignorant of this at the time, and was happy to tuck into my brown, mushy slop with vim and vigour, occasionally stabbing the table as my double vision played tricks on me and made me think my plate was bigger than it was.

Whether it was my Dull Life Crisis kicking in and making me overly-sensible, or whether it was the shock my body got from the food I'd exposed it to, but some time into the cheesecake I started to sober up rapidly and realised that any more rosé now would probably be a very bad idea. And so, as the others drank their way through several bottles of wine, I kept to the water and eventually they all caught up with me. After they'd eaten as much as they could bear to eat – and watched me devour three portions of what I believed to be a really delicious meal – we retired to the sofas and gazed at the fire crackling and fizzing in the grate.

"How do you feel?" Cathy sat beside me on the plump velvet sofa. She leant towards me and looked at me critically.

"Fine," I said, taking a sip of water. "Full."

"Here." Laura came in from the kitchen and put a plastic washing-up bowl down beside me.

"I'm fine! Honestly, stop fretting, it was only a Shepherd's Pie."

"Yes, but what did you do to it to make it that bad?" Henna laughed. "I mean it was…"

Cathy's phone beeped and we stopped talking. She ignored it, preferring to stare into the fire as if she hadn't heard it. Henna watched her eagerly, sitting cross-legged on the edge of her armchair, fighting the urge to say something, in a journalistic frenzy to get to the bottom of the mysterious text messages.

It beeped again. Jumping up, Cathy grabbed the phone from her pocket and stomped out of the room. We watched as she left, pulling the door closed behind her, and listened to the tread of her feet on the stairs as she went up to her room.

"What is it all about? Does anyone know?" Henna bounded over to the wine and poured herself another goblet. "Louisa? Laura?"

"Yes please." Louisa downed the remaining quarter-pint of wine from her goblet and thrust the empty glass in front of Henna. "God, I don't know what's got into Cathy. To be honest, I'm a bit pissed off that she's all weepy because it's my hen do and she should be here to have a nice time, not sitting teary-eyed holed up in her room all the time." She accepted the full glass back from Henna and took a swig. "Oh, I don't mean it. I'm sorry for her. It must be her boyfriend or something, maybe they've had a big old bust-up? Rach, you were with her in the kitchen this evening, did she say anything to you?"

I tentatively put my empty glass forward for Henna to fill. She looked at me critically but filled it anyway.

"Erm, well…" I've never been that good at lying. "I think it might be to do with her fiancé."

"I knew it!" Louisa looked triumphant. "Shall I go and have a word with her? Get her to switch her phone off at least."

"No. Best to leave her, I reckon," I volunteered, "she'll come down when she's ready. Anyway, I brought a box of chocolates, shall I go and get them?"

I looked at Laura, who was obviously the one to ask. She nodded her permission and I dived into the kitchen, emerging a minute later with a gigantic box of chocolates.

"Oooh," Louisa happily took them off me. "Good! I'm famished." She ripped open the lid then looked up at me sheepishly. "Sorry, that was a bit unfair."

"That's OK." I waved it away. "The dinner was crap. I

accept that. It was all a ruse. I just didn't want to cook any more this weekend."

We passed round the box. "So what did James have to say about the stag weekend?" Henna asked as she siphoned off the majority of the soft-centres.

Louisa lined up a fistful of chocolates on the arm of her chair and set about choosing which one she'd have next. "Apparently they're just having a quiet night in tonight like we are."

Laura snorted.

"What?" Louisa frowned as she nibbled the crystallised ginger off a chocolate.

"You believe him?"

"Of course I do. I wouldn't be marrying him if I didn't trust him completely."

Laura, Henna and I exchanged brief glances over the tops of our wine glasses.

"Well, that's very noble of you." Laura poured the rest of the bottle into her glass. "I didn't think anyone trusted anyone these days."

"You don't know me and James then," Louisa said happily.

"Lucky girl." Laura gulped down her wine. "The only blokes I meet are the worn-down teachers I work with, who are so insecure I'd spend my evenings listening to their rantings, or the lads in the TA, most of who are married anyway."

"Really?" Henna asked. "I thought people in the TA were all single. I thought weekends in the TA were like a big Club 18-30 but with guns."

"Ha! No, there are lots of married men. And some married women."

"But don't their families mind them being away for the

weekend?"

"Obviously not." Laura shrugged. "Probably glad of the break and the extra money."

Henna pondered, staring into the fire. "Can I talk to you about the TA some time? It might make an interesting article, you know, women in the firing line and all that."

"Happy to help," Laura grinned, "but you won't want a photo, will you?"

"Not if you don't want to. I can always use a library photo of a woman driving a tank towards certain death or something."

"Sorry, guys." Cathy crept back into the room and sank into her armchair by the fire. Here eyes were pink from crying.

"Are you OK?" I passed her a glass of wine.

She nodded, taking a deep breath in. "So, what were you talking about?"

"Henna's going to make Laura a press hero," I explained.

"Oh well, that's nice." Cathy gulped down the wine. "Have you saved someone's life or something?"

"No. I'm just a woman in a man's job."

"Oh. Right."

"I know someone you could write about." I leant forward and helped myself to another chocolate from the table.

"Go on." Henna wobbled over to get another bottle from the oak dresser.

"Her name's Marcia and she's the scrawniest, most self-obsessed, little cow I've ever met."

"Sounds nice," Louisa laughed. "I should have invited her this weekend."

"I'm surprised she's not invited herself here. She seems

to be everywhere at the moment, invited or uninvited. But the thing about her is that she is the most active person I have ever met. Ever. Seriously she does all this amazing stuff." I finished off the wine in my glass. "I would love to know whether she's the weird one or it's me. Because she spends her time paragliding and surfing and skiing and horse riding and…"

"We're going horse riding," Laura cut in.

"I know. And I'm glad, but she does it all the time. And more. Is that normal?"

"What, you mean to do all those activities?" Henna considered for a minute. "Has she ever bungee jumped?"

I searched my brain, trying to remember exactly what was on that long, long list of Marcia's. "Yes! Twice. Once in New Zealand and once in Canada."

"Thought so. What about white water rafting?"

"Yup."

"Sky diving?"

I nodded.

"Sounds like an adrenaline junkie to me." Laura grabbed the bottle off Henna and poured herself another glass. "I see it all the time in my line of work."

"What, teaching in a primary school?" Louisa giggled.

"Seriously though," Laura continued, "they just live for the next thrill and the more they have the less the feel. It's tragic when you think about it. They go from one new thing to the next new thing and they're never satisfied so they take more and more risks just to feel alive and then WHAM!" She slammed her hand down on the coffee table and Henna choked on her wine. "They end up spread across the tarmac of an airfield."

"Fucking hell Laura, you didn't have to fucking do

that!"

Laura shrugged and turned back to me. "I think your friend should be pitied."

"She's not my friend. And I don't pity her. She's one of those people who spends all their time talking at you, like the best thing you could be doing with your time is to listen to her talk about herself. It's so selfish." I sat back, glad to have got it off my chest. "So you don't think I'm weird for thinking she's a bit overactive?"

"No way. She sounds a real piece of work. So why do you hang out with her so much?" Louisa asked blearily.

"I don't mean to. She's just sort of integrated herself into our group and no one seems to want to shake her off. I think they actually like listening to her."

"You need a new set of friends, honey." Louisa leant over and patted the sofa beside my leg. "Oh sorry, I meant to pat your knee." She tried again and this time managed to connect.

I emptied the rest of the bottle into my wine goblet. "I'll get another. Where are they, Laura?"

"Bottom of the pantry. Do you want me to give you a hand?"

"Oh come on! How much trouble could I get myself in to? I'll be fine."

I headed off.

7

I walked out of the sitting room, away from the warmth of the fire and the cosy glow of the lamps and into the hallway. It was noticeably colder out of the reach of the fire. And very dark. I scrabbled around in the gloom for the light switch, brushing my hand up the side of the doorway in methodical sweeps trying to find it. It was rather spooky all on my own after being so cosied up in the lounge with the others. My hand slid up the wall, higher and higher, before it connected with the switch. I froze. That split second before I flicked the light on, I heard a plaintive wail from outside. Didn't I? In that moment of darkness, I could feel my heart thundering in my chest, my hands suddenly clammy. But the bulb flickered into life and a peal of laughter erupted from the lounge. Everything was normal again.

"Wine!" Henna's voice commanded from the other room.

I paused, hand still on the switch. It was nothing. It must have been the wind in the woods or something. I hastily grabbed a bottle of wine from the pantry and flicked the light off again, heading back to the fireside and shivering despite myself.

Any unease I had melted the minute I saw the girls around the fire drinking and laughing. Louisa had reached her limit about half a wine goblet ago and was now telling whoever would listen about her fiancé James, who had very good career prospects.

"So what's a very good career prospect, then?" I set the wine on the table and looked around for the corkscrew.

"Well, you know he's in marketing," Louisa began. I nodded. I was sure the corkscrew had been on the dresser the last time I looked. "He's just moved from shampoo into the sanitary paper range and –"

"Sanitary paper?" Henna let out a peal of giggles. "You mean bog roll? James works in bog roll?"

"You can laugh." Louisa looked slightly mortified. "But it's actually big business."

I snorted. "Big business?"

Even Cathy was laughing, quietly clutching her sides as she saw Louisa's tight-lipped expression.

"I'll have you know James is revolutionising the sanitary paper world, actually, and they've already promoted him in the three months since he took up the job."

"Well, that's … that's really good." I wiped the tears from my eyes. "Has anyone seen the corkscrew?"

"What's the brand of sanitary paper, then?" Laura tried her best to bring order back to the conversation, despite having been the one to have laughed the loudest.

"He works for Mitcham Scolding," Louisa said guardedly.

Henna thought for a moment before breaking into a grin. "Don't they do that Absorb-O range? They do. Oh my God! Is he responsible for Absorb-O?"

"Yes actually and –"

Whatever she said was drowned out by our laughter. Laura fought the tears back but couldn't stop them. "Absorb-O. It's tough enough!" she quipped, the brand strapline from the adverts, mimicking the Australian accent. "Go put it to the test!"

"You're just jealous." Louisa was smiling now, taking it in as good a humour as could be expected when your fiancé works in toilet roll.

I checked the dresser and mantelpiece for the corkscrew. Where on earth was it?

"Change the subject!" Louisa banged her glass down. "Come on then. Cathy! You've been quiet all evening." Cathy looked up, mortified. "You stand up and recite those first few paragraphs of Chaucer's 'The Nun's Priest's Tale' in its original Middle English dialect. Go on – it's amazing! How do you know how it sounded all those hundreds of years ago?"

"I … I can't…"

"Yes you can!" Henna started a chant and we all joined in, "Chaucer! Chaucer! Chaucer!"

I stuck my hand up. "Before you start, can anyone tell me where the bloody corkscrew is, because I can't find it anywhere."

"Over there." Laura pointed vaguely to the bay window. "I think Henna left it on the table by the window."

"Ah, thank you." I headed over.

Cathy went over to just beside the fire, clearing her throat. "In appreel, whann soft-e wass they son," she began, spouting a completely meaningless string of words and staring straight in front of her in full lecture mode.

I opened the curtains and stepped into the cold and draughty bay. The corkscrew lay there on the table where Laura had said it would be. I picked it up and turned to go back when I was stopped in my tracks for the second time that evening. There it was again. A noise. Outside the window.

"Shh." I turned to the girls who were staring open mouthed at Cathy. I glanced down at my watch – it was just after midnight. We weren't expecting anyone else to arrive, were we?

I closed the enormous, red velvet curtains behind me to block out the light and stood in the cavernous, chilly space. I still couldn't see anything outside. Not even the fluffy white coats of the sheep in the field below. It was pitch black. The kind of black that really gives city-dwellers the creeps. People like me. Creeped-out, I peered through the leaded panes. Nothing. We were completely alone with this infinite blackness. The sheep were still in the field; as I could hear them bleating, kicking up one hell of a fuss. Did sheep usually do that?

"Is that normal?" I whispered to Henna, who had come to join me in the bay.

"Is what normal? Ooh, have you uncorked the other Wolf Blass? Can I have some?"

"That noise the sheep are making. I don't have a clue about sheep, but shouldn't they sound a bit more placid than that? A bit more 'baa-y'?"

"I dunno," she slurred, knocking back a slug of wine. "Laura," she yelled, sticking her head out of the curtains, "geddoverhere," and our countryside representative staggered in to join us in the bay.

"What?" Laura said, after seeing us with our noses

pressed against the leaded panes and laughing.

"Is that –" Henna gestured to the window "– the noise that sheep usually make?"

Laura listened for a moment.

"No."

Henna and I stepped back from the window.

"Oh," I said. "But it is sheep that are making that noise?"

"Oh yes. No doubt about it."

"Well, why?" I asked, wishing I were a bit more savvy when it came to the countryside. There was a whole other world out there that I had no idea about. Maybe I should start to get to know it – venture out into suburbia and keep on going for a bit? Maybe that was my ticket out of my DLC – get to be a child of nature. Perhaps I should start by watching those wildlife programmes that are on the TV all the time, usually hosted by an overenthusiastic Bill Oddie.

"They're scared," Laura said after listening closely to the sheepy noises down below us. "There's something out there that's frightening them."

Something out there. We all considered the words for a moment.

Something. Out there.

Frightening.

The curtains jerked violently aside and the three of us leapt up.

"Fucking FUCKING hell!" Henna threw a hand to her chest. "Don't do that!"

"What's up?" Louisa and Cathy had come over. Louisa was now drinking wine straight from the bottle, having bypassed the formality of a wine goblet completely. Henna wrestled the bottle off her and took a swig, swaying.

I closed the curtains behind us to block out what little light there was from the room. Now there was a crowd of us filling the bay window.

"This is cosy," Louisa giggled. "So why are we all here again?"

"Rachel thought she heard something…" Henna began.

"Well, it's bloody sheep, that's what the noise is," Louisa scoffed, "honestly, what a bloody townie. You don't get out much, do you? You moved to Wales, you should know what a bloody sheep sounds like."

"Actually, there aren't that many sheep wandering around in the capital city. And besides, I know they're sheep. It's just I thought I heard another noise as well as the sheep…"

"Another noise?" Cathy asked nervously, and the girls hushed up. "What, like a big cat sort of a noise?"

"I don't know. Maybe. Whatever it was the sheep sound like they're scared. Laura said so."

Laura nodded. "It's true. They sound scared."

"Which ties in with Rachel hearing the other noise," finished Henna. "The other noise scared them."

Louisa shrugged and stumbled back to the sofas saying, "Sounds like bloody sheep to me. Where have the chocolates gone? Henna, did you eat my chocolates, you fat cow?"

The four of us turned back to the window.

There was a face.

Less than a metre away from the window.

I screamed. My heart leapt into my throat. The girls at the window screamed too, and Louisa ran back to us. A man was standing in the shadowy field below the window. Right there – looking in at us.

I could feel my skin prickling. I felt sick.

"What the fuck!!" Louisa tore the curtains open.

"There's a man in the field of sheep!"

Through the twisted, thick panes of the old window, I could just make out that he was wearing a dark jacket and he was slowly walking towards us, emerging from the black until he was just directly under the window, his face lit by the lamplight coming from our sitting room. He could reach out and touch the old lead panes. My head was filled with horrible images: what was he doing to the sheep? Why was he here? What was he going to do…?

"Hello there, ladies!" he shouted at the window.

The five of us girls, crammed in to the bay, gaped wordlessly back at him. I could hear from the shaky breaths that the others were as frightened as I was. The shock of seeing a face look up at me from the night would haunt me for the rest of my life. However long that would now be.

No one said anything. En masse we all stared back like a pack of meerkats watching the hunter. I felt the urge to scrabble back from the glass and run to the safety of the cellar. But at that very moment, Marcia popped into my head. What would Marcia do in this situation? Run off to the cellars and hide? No.

I stepped forward.

"What do you want?" I shouted at the figure. His face was horribly distorted by the bubbles and folds in the ancient glass. I shifted my position, trying to get a better look at him through a less opaque patch of window: did he look violent, angry, honest, harmless? How would I identify him in a police line-up afterwards? If there was an afterwards…

"I'm sorry to scare you, love! Can I come in and use

your phone?" his muffled voice called out in a sing-song, lilting Welsh accent.

"Don't you have a mobile?" I shouted back.

"Good point," whispered Laura at my back, patting me on the shoulder.

"Not got it on me, see," the man answered, holding his hands up in a sort of a shrug.

"Pah! Unlikely," whispered Laura in my ear. "Ask him why he needs a phone."

I turned to her, temporarily forgetting my terror, "You bloody ask him, Laura!"

"You've made the connection, Rachel." She patted me on the shoulder again. "That's very important. Go on, ask him." The others nodded wordlessly at me. Meerkats, the lot of them. I sighed and turned back to the window.

"Why do you need to make a call?"

"It's my sheep. They're in danger. I need to get a vet here right now. Please love, let me use your phone."

I turned back again to the girls, huddled tightly behind me in the bay. Louisa and Henna, who were the most drunk of all the drunks assembled there, just looked green-faced and incapable of speaking at that moment. Laura seemed to have more of her wits about her and together with Cathy they shrugged their shoulders.

"It's up to you," Laura slurred.

"It's up to me?"

Why was it up to me?

"Please!" the man shouted from outside, "I won't be a minute. I just need to make a call to my vet, see."

"OK, OK," I relented, throwing my hands in the air. "Come round to the front door and I'll let you in."

"RACHEL!" Louisa gaped at me, horrified. "What the bloody hell are you doing? You can't let him in!"

"I'm making a decision. Nobody else looked like they would."

"What if he's a murderer? He could kill you. He could kill us! Maybe he's the big cat – yes! What if he's the Beast of Brecon like on the news? What if he goes around killing sheep and making it look like it was a cat attack?"

"What?"

We all looked at Louisa.

"Well," she began defensively, "I mean, maybe he's mad and … you know … he had this big trauma as a boy and … he has to kill as a way of dealing with the trauma. Fuck, I don't know. It's possible. Stop looking at me like that. At least I'm not the one inviting him in to the house."

"I'm not a killer, love. I'm a farmer."

We turned back to the window, having forgotten we had an audience just a pane of glass away.

I felt myself turning red with shame. "Yes, well, you can understand what we're worried about. It's not as if you've got the equivalent of a British Gas calling card or something."

There was a pause. "No, you've got me there. Hold on a minute though, I've got my NSA invite." Through the glass I could see him scrabbling around in his jacket pocket. He found whatever it was he was looking for and triumphantly held it up to the window.

"What's the NSA?" Laura asked.

I peered up to the glass and read the worn scrap of paper, "Cymru Wales National Sheep Association AGM 2007. Royal Welsh Show Ground Tuesday 29th July at 2pm. Well-known auctioneer Mr Bryn Davies from McSparrows has agreed to be guest speaker. All welcome."

Laura looked sceptical. "He could have written it

specifically to…"

I held up my hand to stop her and looked out to the man at the window. "Enough! Come round to the front!" I called to him and I walked out of the bay.

"Rachel!" Louisa and the others padded after me, still clutching their drinks for support.

I looked around the hallway as I walked down it to the heavy wooden door. "Laura, you grab that poker and keep it nearby. Everyone be on their guard. No, Laura, don't brandish it. Jesus Christ, we're not going to attack the man – he's probably harmless. This is rural Wales after all, not Manchester. Just keep the poker nearby, hidden or something. That's better."

Slowly I slid back the iron bolts and turned the key in the lock. My heart was still thundering in my chest and it was a wonder I could hear the scrape of the metal as I opened up the house to the man outside. I sincerely hoped I was doing the right thing here.

I pulled the heavy wooden door open.

"Oh…"

There was a clang behind me as the poker slipped out of Laura's hand.

This man was handsome. Very handsome! Dark-eyed and almost swarthy, he was tall and broad with a mop of thick brown hair and the most amazing cheekbones.

I looked round to see the girls clearly having the same revelation that I was having, marvelling at the Welsh Adonis on our doorstep. Suddenly I felt happier about the prospect of letting him in to the Hen House. He looked harmless enough. I know they say that about serial killers, but this man really did look like a nice chap. And really, so handsome. Surely no one so good looking could do anything really bad, could they?

He was still holding his scrappy invite which he now proffered to me.

I shook my head, ashamed to be such an untrusting townie. "Come in, then," I said, pulling my fingers through my hair in a bid to look more presentable. He stepped in to the porch and now he was fully lit I could see he was wearing a filthy jacket that had probably once been waxed, with well-worn jeans and T-shirt. And there was a broad gash of blood across his chest.

I stared at it.

"Not mine," he said, obviously seeing my expression of horror as he walked past me into the hallway, "don't worry. It's sheep blood. The name's Gwyn, by the way. Gwynfor Jones. I'm the farmer down yer in the valley." He pointed back up the driveway. "Sorry for interrupting you all. Party, is it?"

"Hen weekend." Louisa stepped forward in front of me and held out her hand, trying to balance and stay upright. "I'm Louisa," she giggled in what she probably imagined was a coquettish way and I inwardly groaned. What is it about alcohol that impairs all sense of judgement?

"Pleased to meet you, Louisa." Gwyn shook the proffered hand then, looking round at me again, said, "I won't be a moment, if I can just use your phone – it's quite urgent, like."

"Of course." I led him in to the sitting room. He followed and as he did the girls crowded round him, eager to be the one who walked alongside him.

"So are you a sheep farmer, then?" Henna sidled up to him and stared at him with doe eyes.

"Err … yes. I have sheep so that makes me a sheep farmer."

"Wow. That must be like a really amazing job. I'm a

journalist. I write for *The Times*. Do you get *The Times* here? Yes? Well, you might have seen my picture then, they always print it on my columns but I keep asking them to change it because it's taken from above and it looks like I have a double chin but I haven't. Look. See?"

"Oh right." Gwyn shot me a nonplussed look. I lifted my hand in a glass-tilting motion to imply she'd had the best part of a couple of bottles of wine. He nodded, smiling. Fortunately none of the others had seen this exchange, being too busy admiring his broad chest and tanned features.

I'd always had an image of farmers in my head based on those adverts for milk and cheese; hearty middle-aged fellows with ruddy faces and jolly, round stomachs full of beer. A bit like Santa in a Barbour. But this one looked more like the models from the aftershave commercials – all dark tousled hair and strong jaw line. A model in a bloodied waxed jacket and manure-clad wellies. Still…

"I like Welshmen," Henna whispered deafeningly into my ear. She overtook me and flopped down on the sofa nearest to the phone where the farmer would be sitting to make the call.

"It's good of you to invite me in," he was saying, looking round for the first time, "but my God, look what's happened to it!"

"What?" I asked, alarmed. Had we trashed the place already? We were rather drunk but surely we'd not spilt wine on the rugs?

"Phew!" He walked forward and went up to the fireplace where a few of the largest logs were still glowing in the grate. "The last time I saw inside this place was about eight years ago when they started the restoration. It was nigh on a ruin, it was. Now look at it, you'd never know, would you?"

"Know what?" Louisa asked, sitting down next to Henna on the seat second nearest to the phone, patting it lightly as an indication for Gwyn to sit beside her.

"That it had been a near ruin." He looked at me as he said it.

"Oh. No. Well, I suppose not really," I said, not really understanding what he was saying, watching his hair flop round his face as he brushed it away with a large rough hand. "So, anyway, here's the phone." I handed him the cordless phone and he smiled and sat on the opposite sofa to Henna and Louisa. Cathy immediately sat down next to him. Thwarted but not discouraged, Louisa jumped up from her sofa and glared at Cathy until she moved aside and let her take the coveted position next to the farmer. Hen's prerogative. She slowly lowered herself next to him, smiling in what she no doubt thought was a provocative way, but was actually pretty glassy-eyed and unsteady.

If it weren't so weird, it would have been funny, seeing Louisa and Henna turn on the charm like a plumber turns on the mains water. I was glad I was the more sober of them; at least it meant that someone took charge and I didn't seem to have done a bad job up to this point. I was quite pleased with myself actually. Perhaps tomorrow Laura would take me aside and speak to me about how the Territorial Army needs people like me, that I'd shown excellent leadership material and perhaps I should come along to their HQ or whatever they call it, and enrol.

That's what I could do to inject a little excitement into my life on a more permanent basis: join the TA! That would wipe the superior smile off Marcia's face when I entertained her with tales of weekends spent dusting and buffing anti-aircraft missiles and crawling on

64

my stomach through the barren wastelands of war-torn Dorset. Rehearsing violent warfare scenarios dressed in full combat gear, in places called Pippin Winterbury and Honeybourne Minster.

Actually, that sounded really crap. I could never be in the TA. After all, I wasn't even sure what sheep sounded like, so what good would I be trying to survive in the countryside? I'd probably die of a gnat bite on my first night away from a town. And as Marcia had so helpfully pointed out, I hadn't even been hiking or jogging in my dull and sheltered life. So to go from nothing to everything might be pushing it a bit. Besides, the uniform would never flatter my curvy figure. Camouflage only goes so far.

8

While Gwyn dialled the number, he looked round at the girls surrounding him, smiling sheepishly. "If I'd have known I'd be entertained I would have dressed for it," he said and ran a hand through his hair. How old was he? Mid-thirties? Phew! He was lovely. Louisa laughed at him, like he'd just said the funniest thing ever, and laid a hand on his thigh. I cringed. I really couldn't bear to watch.

It shocked me to realise that I had instantly been transported into a full-blown school-like crush. I wanted to sit on his lap. I wanted to run my fingers through his lovely Welsh hair. How long had it been since I'd felt like this? It must have been years. Nevertheless I was the perfect example of British reserve, standing at a distance, the others milling around him while I managed to exercise some restraint and not fling myself into the mix. They giggled and pouted and flirted while he smiled and leant back, a broad strong man looking ever so slightly overwhelmed by a gaggle of girls.

Invisible, I went into the kitchen and made a cup of tea for him. I couldn't imagine the girls would let him escape back to his sheepy field straight away. Besides he would probably have to wait for his vet to come over, so he might as well wait in the Hen House rather than in his dark field. If there was a big cat on the prowl outside then he'd have a much better chance of survival in here than out there.

Louisa laughed loudly. "Oh Gwyn, that is just so funny."

Well, a slightly better chance of survival.

I poked my head round the door to ask if he would actually like a cup of tea but he was busy dialling his vet's number and politely peeling Louisa's hand off the top of his thigh.

I went back into the kitchen. While I searched for the teabags and sugar I could hear the chatter stop while he was on the phone to the vet, describing what had happened. He was telling the vet that his sheep had been clearly distressed and making such a noise that he'd gone to investigate, finding one of the younger ones had been torn in two…

Torn in two.

I thought about that phrase while I boiled the kettle. Torn in two. Torn into two pieces. Torn. That wasn't good. For a brief moment my imagination got the better of me and I pictured Louisa's alternative scenario with the handsome farmer ripping a sheep in two with his bare hands, smearing himself with blood and laughing manically. Then, flinging aside the mangled carcass, he searched for the next kill, coming to the isolated house full of women to carry out more dark deeds, pretending to call his vet while lulling the girls into a false sense of security…

No. That was stupid.

The plain fact was he was far too handsome to be a bad man.

So did the "torn in two" imply that there was actually a big cat out there? At the very least there must be something out there that could tear a sheep in two? Urgh. What a horrible phrase. But now it was stuck in my head.

Torn.

In two.

That would probably explain why it was such an emergency and he had to call a vet straight away. If the vet identified it as a cat attack, what would happen? My thoughts went back to that TV report with the girl knocked down by the big black animal. Were we really really in danger? Should we be scared?

Would he want milk in his tea?

I considered it for a moment and then decided that he probably would. He didn't seem like a slice of lemon type chap and besides we had no lemons. I stirred in a generous spoon of sugar, contemplated it and then stirred in another one. These farmers probably had at least two sugars, like builders. See? I was starting to find my way around this rural unknown.

I headed back into the sitting room. Gwyn had come off the phone now and I handed him the mug. He lightly pushed Louisa's hand off his thigh again and took the tea.

"Thanks." He smiled at me and I felt myself blush.

"No problems. I put two sugars in. I didn't know whether I should…"

"Oh lovely," he said, taking a sip and really doing quite a good job at hiding a wince.

"Sorry," I grimaced, "I'm crap at making tea."

"She's crap at cooking as well," chimed in Louisa. "I'm not. I'm a really good cook. I bet you like your food, eh Gwyn?"

"No no, it's lovely. Honestly," Gwyn said, so obviously lying.

"Gwyn was telling us about the Hen House." Laura steered the conversation to something a bit more sensible. "He helped in renovating it."

"Really?" I perched on a dining chair as the sofas were taken up with the Gwyn Appreciation Society. Even the quiet and hitherto rather sedate Cathy was looking more animated than usual. And hadn't she undone the top button of her blouse? I was scandalised.

"There I am!" He brought me out of my thoughts as he handed me a scrapbook of the property. I glanced at its pages showing the old building in various stages of restoration. Countless photos of roof beams, dodgy brickwork and plastering.

And there he was, stripped to the waist, hoisting a giant rafter on his bare shoulders.

"Ngh!"

"What?" He looked at my expression, frowning slightly.

"Oh. Nothing. Just ... what a ... what a rafter."

"That's nothing. There were eight of those and three thirty-footers. Not that I carried them by myself. Anyway, this was at the start of the project, I guess, moving the old timbers out and cutting back the undergrowth".

Look at those arms! Look at that chest!

"Let me see! Let me see!" Henna wrangled the book

off me. I outmanoeuvred her and grasped it tightly. But Louisa had come from out of nowhere, standing close to Gwyn, and now leaned in to him, bending over the book.

"Who's that?" She pointed to a mean-looking old farmer who was gurning in the background, holding a large scythe in a very aggressive manner.

"That's old Tomos, lives on the next farm to me, down near the river. He wasn't a bundle of joy on the day. You can probably see that for yourselves. And that –" he pointed at the other farmer – "that's Elijah from over the valley, poor man, it's his flock that the predator's been getting. Well, until tonight. Now it's moved on to my flock…"

Cathy, who had been taking a sip of wine, choked and looked up at him. "You really think your sheep was attacked by a big cat?"

He sighed. "Folks have said there's been a cat round here for years but I never reckoned much to the stories. But tonight – well, my sheep's been torn in two and I don't know how any other animal around here could do that. No dogs or badgers or foxes would do it."

There it was again. Torn in two. I shivered.

Suddenly everyone fired questions at Gwyn. Were we in real danger? What did the cat look like? Had he seen the news report? What did he think of it? I couldn't help feel a bit excited by the whole thing, which was probably enormously misguided of me because it sounded like we were probably in quite a bit of danger. But right here right now we were entertaining a handsome farmer in the middle of the night, and everything seemed pretty good. Even the possibility of an impending mauling from a wild animal didn't seem so bad if Gwyn was on hand to rescue me.

There was a knock on the door.

Henna screamed.

"Jesus Henna, calm down." Laura glared at her. "A big cat wouldn't knock."

Henna took a deep breath, gave her a sarcastic smile and then wobbled over to the wine bottle.

"That'll be my vet." Gwyn made a move to get up but various remonstrations from Louisa kept him seated.

Seeing as no one else was prepared to answer it and leave Gwyn, I went, collecting the poker on my way and putting it within easy reach. Just in case. I knew it wouldn't be the big cat at the door because even I knew that a big cat could not knock on the door like that. Still, stranger things have happened. I could picture another one of my diary entries: "August 2nd: Five girls died in a savage cat attack in a Welsh valley in 2007."

For the second time that night I opened the heavy old door. There was no slavering black cat ready to pounce and there was no tanned, handsome farmer leaning against the porch. There was just a very tired-looking middle-aged man standing in the gloom.

"Roger Williams, vet," he muttered. "I had a call from Gwynfor Jones."

"I'm here!" Our farmer strode down the hallway to the door, a gaggle of girls trailing behind him. "Thanks again," he said to me and held out his hand. I shook it. It was large and strong and warm.

"I hope your sheep are all right," I said lamely.

He joined the vet in the porch. "Best be off. What's your name, love?"

"Rachel."

"Well, Rachel, thanks again. And I hope you enjoy yourselves. And be careful. You're not planning on going out into the wilds are you? I never set any store by all this

71

talk of cats before, but this, well, I'm not so sure now."

"We'll be OK. There are five of us. Surely it won't attack a group of five girls?"

"Be careful of the men round yer then," he laughed. "Anyway, I live up on Ty Nant farm just round the corner if you have any problems. Anything."

"Thanks," I said, heart pounding, my head suddenly filled with the unmentionable things he could help me with. I held on to the door for support.

"Don't get eaten or anything," I called out after him as he disappeared into the darkness.

"Right-o," he called back, and was gone into black night.

I closed the door and drew the bolts closed again. Oh my goodness. What a treat.

9

"I can't believe we're in so much danger." Cathy said quietly, perched on the edge of her chair, staring into the last embers of the fire.

"Never mind that." Louisa sat back into the sofa. "This is perfect! Perfect! Thank you for organising it, Laura." She leant over and gave Laura a kiss.

"I didn't organise the farmers or anything." Laura shrugged the kiss off.

"But what a bit of luck."

Henna examined the stem of her wine glass. "You're not actually planning to…"

"To what?" Louisa had a broad smile across her face. "Of course not, Henna, I'm almost a married woman! But I can find him attractive. It doesn't mean I want to get off with him or anything. It's just so nice to flirt with someone. God, it's been so long I thought I'd forgotten how, but it all comes back, doesn't it? All the old techniques!"

I hid my smile. "But you do want to get off with him, don't you?"

"Well, yes. Of course. But honestly Cathy you can stop looking at me like that, nothing's going to happen! Like I said, I love James and we trust each other and nothing is going to happen. It was just harmless flirting. That said…" She turned to Laura who was busy stoking the glowing logs sending embers flying. "You could try to build him into the weekend, couldn't you? I mean, it would be a shame to not see him again. He's the only person we've met round here…"

"And the vet," Henna added.

"You get off with the vet then." Louisa winked.

"Hold on." Henna leant forward, looking serious. "Are you saying none of us can get off with Gwynfor, even though you're not going to?"

Louisa laughed incredulously. "Look, no one is going to get off with anyone. OK? It's my hen do. It's about having a laugh with my mates before I get married. It's about *me*."

"So, can I just clarify," Henna put her glass unsteadily on the side table, "you'd be pretty pissed off if any of us were to get off with Gwyn?"

"Yes."

"OK." Henna leant back. "Glad that's clear. You're not going to have him, and neither are we. Seems a shame, though. Letting him go to waste."

"He might be married," I volunteered. "Although he wasn't wearing a wedding ring."

"Rachel, you looked!"

I shrugged.

"Look." Louisa folded her arms. "If anyone was going to get off with anyone it would be me, because it's my hen do. But I'm not because that's not what this weekend is about. It's about friendship and wine and relaxing. When you have your hen dos, then you can have hen's prerogative and do what you like, but this is my weekend. OK?"

"Fine," said Henna, pouring another glass of wine. "But can I leave him my number. For another time?"

Louisa rolled her eyes. "Yes. Whatever."

A log snapped in the grate making Laura jump back.

"I wonder what the vet said." She poked the log tentatively. "Whether it was a cat attack."

"Maybe we'll have to cancel the horse riding," Cathy said.

"We can't!" I pleaded. "What will I have to tell Marcia when I get back? I have to go horse riding. And besides a cat isn't going to attack five girls and five horses. We'll be fine! I don't want us to be put in mortal peril or anything, but I do really want to go horse riding."

Laura nodded. "Rachel's right. We'll be fine. Just stay out of the woods and make sure we're home by dark. We won't even know it's there. If it is there." She turned back to the fire.

"Well, I definitely think we should open another bottle of wine." Henna staggered up. "Rach, where are they hidden?"

"I'll show you." We walked into the kitchen, somehow made less scary when there were two of us. The wine was tucked behind the breakfast cereals so I crouched down and fished behind the packets of cornflakes. "There aren't many left."

Henna swayed in the doorway, hiccupping. "We can go into town and get some more tomorrow, I guess." She staggered towards the wall and tapped the rota. "That's if it's timetabled in our precious Schedule and Rota." She did an impression of Laura, arms crossed, looking super-serious.

I laughed. "That's as maybe, but there aren't any towns nearby. And anyway, you're right, it's not in the rota so you're not going to get away with it."

"Oh well, it's the pub tomorrow night anyway." She wobbled down onto her knees and shuffled over to me as I examined what was left of our much depleted wine stock. It was serious; we were down to the budget supermarket own-brands.

Henna sat back on her haunches, holding on to the door frame for support. "Rach, can I ask you something?"

"Sure." I sat back. "What?"

She hiccupped, looked over her shoulder and then, leaning forward, said softly, "What do you think of Laura?" Her breath smelt of pure Wolf Blass.

"Laura?"

"Shhh!" She theatrically put a finger to her lips.

I looked round and dropping my voice said, "She's fine. I met her a while ago so I kind of know her a bit. Why?"

Henna put her hand up to the enormous purpling bruise on her forehead and then looked at me meaningfully.

"She did that to you?" I looked at it in horror as Henna nodded. "Why?"

"She said it was an accident. It wasn't."

"Oh my God! What happened?"

Henna checked behind her again, wobbled and fell over. "She's mad. She is, honestly! Mad." She hoisted herself up by holding on to a shelf. "Everyone's going on about being scared of a big cat, but I reckon we should all be more concerned about who is in the house with us than what's locked outside."

I laughed.

"Seriously!" Henna said, "Listen to this then: Laura and I arrived at the Hen House at the same time and I guess we both had in mind what she'd said about the rooms being on a first come first served basis. So we both sprinted to the front door to be the first one in."

"And you collided?"

"No, she bloody nutted me."

"No way!"

"Definitely. She nutted me. I'd got to the door just before she did and she leant forward and nutted me right there on the doorstep. But Louisa was behind us and I reckon she knew what had happened, so Laura had to concede the second best room to me."

"Oh my God. I thought all the rooms were really good. Except mine."

"Mine's got an en suite and Laura has to share a bathroom with Cathy. But yes, they're all much better than yours." Henna put her hand on my arm. "I think you're really great not making a big thing about having that awful room. The others would kick up a stink. I would have done. But you just accept it."

"You mean I'm a pushover?"

"Unselfish," Henna corrected, pointing a finger vaguely in my direction. "Right. Help me up. I reckon this Aldi French wine should hit the spot."

"Yes. It will probably do that."

Henna giggled but then clutched on to my arm. "Hey, don't say anything about Laura nutting me, will you?"

"Of course not!" I winked and we headed back into the lounge.

10

It must have been about two in the morning by the time we stumbled off to bed. Laura instigated the move after blurrily consulting the Schedule & Rota and telling us we had to be up in six hours and off to the health spa an hour after that. Those beauticians were going to have their work cut out when they saw the state of us – I wondered fuzzily whether some sort of liver-focused massage would be on offer to help mend a part of my body almost certainly damaged after the volume of alcohol I'd consumed. Once the handsome farmer Gwyn had left, the five of us had found a renewed energy, which we diverted into the opening of a few more bottles of wine, which meant, in my case, getting pissed. For the second time that evening. The others weren't in a better state and there was much swaying and clinging on to bits of furniture once we managed to prise ourselves off the hugely comfy sofas.

After we staggered round the house locking all the

doors and windows, we each went our separate ways, all the other girls heading up the stairs to their beautiful airy bedrooms and sumptuous bathrooms, while I slunk off to bed in the kitchen.

In the kitchen.

Laura had been absolutely right about all the bedrooms being good except one. Mine. A miniature bed was shoved against one wall, a miniature chest of drawers next to it and a miniature window facing out to the front door. It was all a bit *Alice-in-Wonderland*; perhaps one of the wine bottles I'd emptied had carried a "drink me" label on it and I had actually grown into an enormous giant in a perfectly normal-sized room. But that couldn't have been as my six bags were perfectly in proportion to me and were piled up on the chest of drawers, ready to topple at a moment's notice.

As if the dimensions of the room weren't bad enough, to get to the room I had to go through the kitchens, so I can only assume it was a pantry or store-room at one time, which made sense because you could still see where there had been hooks in the ceiling once, no doubt where they had hung meat to cure. Lovely.

Having said all that, the room itself was nice. Cosy. Painted a rosy sort of limewash, it was homely enough but it was ridiculously small. Hardly room to swing a cat. Ha ha.

From the tour of the house I'd seen that the other bedrooms weren't much worse than Henna's. They all had double beds and they were all decorated beautifully with antique furniture. Louisa's room had an enormous oak four-poster bed in the middle and mullioned windows facing out into the valley. She had exposed roof beams and a huge old chandelier in the centre of the room. The walls were painted china blue and there were stylish oil paintings of seascapes dotted on the walls. One door led off to a walk-in wardrobe, the other to her en suite bathroom with amazing power shower, roll-top bath and one of those enormous frosted glass-bowl sinks suspended in a granite surface. In fact her bathroom was bigger than my bedroom down here. Her bath was bigger than my bed.

It was in this tiny annexe that I found myself suddenly wide awake later in the night. It was still pitch black so it must have been fairly early in the morning. Something had woken me up.

I sat up and put the light on. It was four o'clock. I didn't feel too bad considering last night.

There was a noise.

Outside, under my window. Was he back? Was Gwyn outside again?

I sat in bed and listened.

I couldn't hear the sheep, but then my box of a room was on the other side of the house so the chances are I wouldn't hear them if they were bleating at the tops of their sheepy voices.

There it was again, the familiar feeling of terror creeping up on me. Was there a big cat prowling around outside? I could hear something like the snapping of branches.

And then it was gone.

Perhaps it was Gwyn, lurking around the house. Perhaps my worries were real and he wasn't a farmer at all. Perhaps earlier this evening in the cunning disguise of a farmer he had just been carrying out a reconnaissance in preparation for an attack now or another night? Maybe the vet wasn't a vet at all but one of his cutthroat band? OK, he looked pretty vet-like and I could definitely imagine him handling kittens and rabbits, but still — it wasn't a normal evening.

I wished more than anything that I didn't have the downstairs room. In all probability if someone broke in they would explore the downstairs' rooms first and find me lying here with nothing to defend myself with except a hard copy of the latest Freya North novel, which I could hit them over the head with, and a leather bookmark to whip them out of my room. Mind you, it would take a pretty smart person to work out there was a tiny room through a narrow door in the kitchen pantry. Maybe I was safe after all, hidden behind the breakfast cereals. That's if they didn't choose to break into the house via the ancient old window in my room, the one at exactly the right height for someone to get in through.

I shivered.

There was no way I was poking my head out of the curtains and looking outside. I don't think I had the strength to have another shock that night, to see another face at another window. Especially as I was on my own down here. I turned off my light and lay in bed, listening out for any more noise from outside. I listened for a long time, straining to hear the sound of a twig snapping or the rustle in the shrubs outside my window. Or even the sound of an animal being torn in two. But there was nothing more. Eventually it got lighter outside and at five o'clock I finally plucked up the courage to creep out of bed and take a peek, bracing myself in case there were any farmers outside, staring in at me.

Nothing.

I must have imagined the noise outside my window; or it had been in a dream I was having or something. I was obviously too caught up in the big cat mania.

11

Six hours in a cramped bed was no way near sufficient for me, especially when part of those six hours had been spent lying wide awake, clutching the duvet and listening out in terror for hungry wild animals prowling around below my bedroom window. My alarm went off and I was sorely tempted to reset it for half an hour later, pull the covers back over my head and drift off into my dreamless sleep, but visions of Laura barking at me like a purple-faced sergeant-major rapidly changed my mind. I surfaced and threw on my clothes before heading out through the narrow passage into the kitchen, where Cathy was checking the Schedule & Rota.

"You're on breakfast duty then?" I asked, rubbing my eyes and yawning.

"Nope," said Cathy, "Henna is. I'm on washing-up duty." Her phone beeped and gingerly she took it out of her pocket and checked the text. She sighed and put it back.

"Well, I saw Henna just now," said Louisa groggily, helping herself to an orange juice from the hugely impressive fridge, "and no way was she in a condition to prepare food."

"For the love of God…" Laura strode into the kitchen and double-checked her Schedule & Rota (edition 3). Her well-drawn-up plans were going to ruin.

I realised, too late, that Louisa and Cathy were suddenly nowhere to be seen. They had disappeared, leaving just Laura and me in the kitchen. Smart girls! And now there was no way I could sneak off. I was exposed.

"It will just have to be you and me then." Laura sized me up and began to roll up her sleeves. "Let's hope last night's dinner disaster was just a one-off. You get the stuff for the fry up ready and I'll slice the loaf."

"But," I began, ready to have a full-blown whine. It wasn't fair! I had the crappiest room and now I had nearly all the chores to do myself. I was a veritable Cinderella.

"What?" Laura turned squarely to face me. In an instant my courage began to fail me.

"It's just … not fair. That's all," I faltered. "I mean, I ruined dinner last night and now I've got to do breakfast this morning. Just because I didn't get completely arseholed last night doesn't mean I should pick up everyone else's chores." I scowled. I felt about fourteen years old again.

"Look." Laura pulled out a marker pen from her tool belt and went up to the board. "You'll be excused lunch preparation tomorrow and I'll put Henna on in your place. Happy now?"

"Yes," I said sulkily. What else did she have in that tool belt? I craned my neck to look inside as she repositioned the marker pen back where it came from. I saw a small ruler, two pencils, a pad of paper and a torch. She zipped up the belt.

"Good! Now get the eggs, Rachel."

There was something about Laura that didn't cow me like it did Henna. I couldn't really put my finger on it, perhaps it was that if she ever tried nutting me I'd probably retaliate, being at least as tall as she is, probably taller. Maybe it was because I'd seen a vulnerable side to her. I had seen her drunk last night, fawning over Gwyn and trying to seduce him by listing her achievements in field combat. Bless her, it was tragic really.

I was probably safe though, as she didn't seem tempted to nut me. She brought the frying pan over and while we cracked eggs and fried bacon she regaled me with stories from her weekends spent bivouacking on "missions". I quickly realised that the best course of action with Laura would be to follow orders blindly and not question her authority. After all, Louisa had put her in charge and it was Louisa's weekend, so who were we to question anything?

Besides, I think Laura quite liked me for being a dependable sort of girl, and not quite as flaky as some of the others that morning; I hadn't been sick at all. Over the beans she confided in me that I'd "done well" last night, taking charge of the farmer situation, which made me feel all proud, like I'd been congratulated by my boss.

Henna stumbled into the kitchen just as Laura and I were serving up.

"Oh. Oh God." She threw her hand up to her mouth. "Oh, I don't think I can eat anything. Or cook. I feel so sick."

"Well, don't then," Laura spat. "I've changed you to lunch preparation tomorrow – it's all on Edition Four of the Schedule & Rota over there. You'll be sober by then, won't you?"

"Edition four?"

"Yes. I rewrote it while you were throwing up in your en suite bathroom."

Henna's eyes flicked over to me to see if I'd registered the remark about the en suite. I suppressed a smile and stirred the burnt and blackened beans. Shit.

"Did I sign that off?" Henna grumbled argumentatively. "I thought the rule was that we had to sign off each edition. Otherwise how can we keep track of what you're making us do?"

"Next time I'll visit you mid-puke. Any objections to edition four?"

Henna glowered. "No."

She peered again at the Schedule & Rota and sighed. Overnight Henna had morphed from the little lively flirty person of yesterday evening into some sort of walking-dead. The bruise was now a large pinky purple blotch below her hairline which, along with the grey bags under her eyes and the sallow post-party complexion gave her face a sort of horrific rainbow-look. "I am so going for a facial today," she wailed, looking at herself in the hall mirror. "There's no way I can pull any attractive Welsh farmers looking like an extra in a zombie film".

"Excuse me but there's no way you're going to pull an attractive Welsh farmer at all on my hen do," said Louisa, breezing back into the kitchen and dropping off her empty glass in the sink. "Remember?"

"Oh yeah." Henna scratched her head and winced as she caught the bruise.

"You can have the vet if you really want..." Louisa offered.

"Oh cheers for that," Henna said miserably. "Rachel, I can't remember – was the vet good looking?"

"No," I snorted, "he was old and grey and haggard."

"Like really old and grey or just a bit old and grey. Like Richard Gere?"

"Henna, it is a definite no! He was no Richard Gere. How much did you drink?"

"I don't know. Loads. I bet I couldn't even pull an ugly vet looking like this. Look at me! I'm a mess!"

"Good job we're off to the spa day," I said perkily, skimming off the salvaged beans from the surface of the pan under the close supervision of Laura.

"Good woman!" She slapped me on the back.

Henna raised her eyebrows, her lips framing an "oooooh" at me for being in Laura's good books. I winked at her.

Laura strode out to the hallway and, grabbing the beater, she banged on the impressive gong that stood in the corner, summoning us all to the dining room.

Within five minutes everyone had managed to sit down at the table and eat something, although some were a little green around the cheeks. I devoured my fry-up and stared out of the mullioned windows at the sheep in the field below. What did they see last night when they were making that awful noise? Poor things. I craned my neck, trying to spot any blood on the grass but I couldn't quite see that far from where I was sitting. And besides, I didn't really want to see – it would put me right off my bacon.

"You're rather jolly this morning," scowled Louisa, slowly spreading marmalade on her toast, as she had been doing for a good five minutes without getting any nearer to actually eating it. "Are you feeling smug that you didn't drink as much as the rest of us?"

"Oh no," I said, still grinning from ear to ear. "I was just thinking about last night. He was pretty nice looking, wasn't he, that Gwynfor chap?"

"Do you think the farmer knew we were tipsy?" Henna asked, pushing her sausage around her plate. "You were fairly sober at that point, Rachel. We didn't make too much of an arse of ourselves, did we?"

A quick montage of scenes ran through my head from last night: hands wandering and rewandering on Gwyn's thighs. Henna "accidentally" bumping into him in the hallway and even Cathy's pissed application of lipstick to her lips and cheeks, right in front of him.

"I would say," I started slowly, choosing my words carefully not to offend anyone, "that everyone was a little worse for wear last night and it might have been noticed by him…"

"Noooooo." Louisa clapped her hand to her forehead. "What about me? Was I really drunk?"

"Louisa, you put your hand on his thigh –"

"No!"

"Several times actually." I involuntarily grinned, remembering the expression on his face as he removed her hand each time. It had been a mix of half alarm and half amusement.

"I didn't?"

"You did," Henna chimed in, "definitely more than once if I remember correctly. Which I probably don't actually…"

"Oh I can't believe I was so obvious. Did he look like he minded?"

"No," I laughed, "not much. He did look quite glad that the vet arrived though. I think five garrulous girls were a bit too much for one man."

"I think you should stop looking so smug anyway, just because you can hold your drink better than the rest of us. On which note," she said, turning to Laura, "I heard you throwing up in your bathroom this morning."

Henna let out a squeal of delight at Laura's expense before clamping her hand over her mouth.

"Well, if we're going to single people out I heard you throwing up all over your bedroom last night," Laura returned to Louisa, "and Cathy was making a lot of dry heaving noises this morning."

"Could you hear that?" Cathy looked stricken. "Oh, I'm so ashamed. I didn't actually throw up though."

"At least you all got to your bedrooms," Henna said, still pushing her sausage around her plate. "I must have passed out on the landing. I woke up wrapped round the base of a giant vase this morning and my back is killing me. And I look like shit." She looked pointedly at Laura and tentatively touched her bruise. Laura stared blankly at her and carried on chewing her toast.

"I wonder how Gwynfor got on with the vet?" mused Louisa, looking dreamily out of the windows to the sheep field. "Do you think it was a big cat out there last night?"

"I don't know," I said, "but I did hear something outside the house later that night. At about four in the morning." I told them about the snapping of twigs – there had definitely been something out there.

"Could have been a fox," said Laura, "or a badger. They're pretty big."

"Could have been the cat," I said.

"Do you think we should stop by Gwyn's farm this morning and ask him what the vet's verdict was?" Louisa asked lightly.

"No way!" Laura was firm. "We have to be at the

Health Spa in forty minutes and there's still the breakfast things to clear away and everyone has to pack their stuff. In fact," she declared rising up from her chair, "we should be getting ready right now," and with that she bounded up from her chair and took charge of us like unruly squaddies in the field.

12

We set off for the health spa at half past nine with Laura energetically pounding the gong to round us up from our bedrooms and marshalling us through to the hall and out towards the cars.

"Honestly," mumbled Henna threateningly as she was herded out to the driveway, "who does she think she is? Arnold-bloody-Schwarzenegger?"

Cathy and I had been assigned as the drivers so Laura took us aside and with the help of a pre-marked-up ordnance survey map briefed us on the route she had devised.

"Cathy, I'll go in the passenger seat of your car so, Rachel, you can follow us. If you lose us then you should be able to remember the way. But try your best to keep up. OK?"

I nodded, not convinced I'd remember the many detailed and complicated directions she'd just taken me through. I'd been staring at a hill called Lord Hereford's Knob and finding it enormously amusing, rather than paying attention to where I should be going. "I'll just follow you two," I said, hopefully.

"Excellent!" Laura folded up the map expertly. "Come on then, girls, let's go go go!"

"As long as you leave the fucking gong alone," Henna muttered darkly.

I had Louisa and Henna in the car with me, and once Cathy and Laura had driven off we pulled out of the Hen House driveway and followed them up the road as it wound steeply upwards and curved to the left. I cast quick looks to the left and right to see if there were any animals lying torn in two by the wayside, but there didn't appear to be anything more than the usual roadkill. Maybe the attack on Gwyn's sheep last night had just been by a fox or badger?

Turning a corner, I saw the dirt track leading off to Ty Nant farm, just set back off the road. It was an old stone building with a beaten-up Land Rover parked outside. Gwyn's beaten-up Land Rover? From the brief glimpse I had, the house looked very picturesque and well cared for. But it didn't look like there had been a woman's touch on it. No flowers in hanging baskets by the door; no garden to speak of.

"Is that his farm, then?" said Henna from the back of the car, seeing me peering down the track.

"Yes, it must be. I was just wondering what the verdict was on his sheep."

"I bet you were!" giggled Henna, perking up after her two coffees.

The journey was spent talking mainly about big cats and

91

farmers, whether we'd see either of them during the next few days. I didn't join in much, as Cathy was, surprisingly, a pretty speedy driver and I had trouble keeping up with her on the narrow winding lanes. No doubt she had Laura yelling directions in her ear, making sure she knew there were only twenty-five minutes allotted to the journey. Once, when I got close behind Cathy's car, I could see Laura quite clearly barking at Cathy and could imagine it was in some sort of rally-style, "Left! Left! Left! Now right ninety! Hard left! Brake! Brake! Dip ahead..." Poor Cathy.

When I did find a moment to raise my eyes off the road, the scenery was breathtaking. Thick clumps of woodland gave way to enormous vistas of purple-heather hills and rolling pastureland. Every so often there were little whitewashed houses dotted on the roadside, but we didn't pass anything bigger than a hamlet on our entire journey.

Laura had been spotless in her timing – or her management of Cathy. Twenty-five minutes after we'd left the Hen House we arrived at the sweeping driveway of Llangorse Manor Spa and Hotel.

The gravel driveway up to the hotel itself seemed to go on for miles, winding left and right and exposing a golf course on one side, tennis courts on another and then, finally, the house itself, a white stucco Georgian mansion sitting in a dip in the valley and beside an enormous lake.

"Oh my God, look at the cars!" I gasped as I turned into the car park. The place was chock full of very shiny, very new-looking BMWs, Mercedes and Jaguars. I found myself wishing I'd put my car through the car wash before the weekend.

And traded it in for a Porsche.

"Wow, there's a lime green Lamborghini there!" Louisa pointed out.

"And I can see two red Ferraris parked next to each other. Do you think they came together?" Henna added.

"Where shall I park?" I wailed, suddenly despising my once-beloved old VW Golf. Now it looked about as classy as arriving in an ice cream van – I might as well have "Mind that child!" painted in pink on the back window and "Twinkle twinkle little star" blaring out of the stereo. The shame of it.

"Keep driving, keep driving," Louisa said as we inched our way down the rows of immaculate cars, hoping to find something smaller than a BMW 5 series. "Look – park over there! I can see a Vauxhall Corsa! Cathy's parking next to it as well."

I turned around and headed for the Corsa. "It's staff parking!" I wailed. "I can't park there."

"Yes, but there's no way you can park next to these cars here, how shameful would that be? Now come on, let's run for it!" And before I'd even put the handbrake on Louisa and Henna had dashed out of the car. They slowed down once they got to the main car park and sauntered nonchalantly towards the entrance.

"Don't mind me then," I muttered, locking the car up, "I'll just make my own way there."

I waved at Cathy who was parked beside me. Her Vectra estate was a couple of years older than my Golf so the two cars looked right at home in the staff car park, keeping each other company with their mutual shabbiness.

Laura had jogged over to join Louisa and Henna while Cathy locked up, so I waited for her so we could walk in together. She was visibly shaking and very, very pale.

"That was hell." She sounded close to tears and was finding it hard to fit the key into the lock. "You have Laura on the way back. I can't go through that again."

"What was she doing?"

"It was awful. Awful." She finally managed to get the key into the lock and turn it. "She kept shouting at me. She had a stopwatch. Oh God."

I put a hand on her shoulder and she took a deep breath. Together we made our way up to the entrance where Laura was checking her watch and looking over at us anxiously.

Heading into reception didn't improve our feelings of self-confidence much and we huddled together for safety amid all the opulence surrounding us. It was part stately home and part hotel; there were lots of plush-looking sofas and little side tables around, but unlike the National Trust houses there were no po-faced wardens telling us we couldn't touch this or sit on that.

"Oh my God. I wish I'd made an effort when I got dressed this morning," Louisa moaned as we walked up to the impossibly gorgeous receptionist just visible behind an enormous vase of flowers.

"*Bore da*! Welcome to Llangorse Manor Spa Hotel," she beamed at us, "you must be Louisa Peberdy's party of five for the day spa?"

"Absolutely," Louisa piped up.

"Come on through to our spa lounge and I'll run you through your day," she said smoothly, and taking a pile of pre-prepared folders off the counter she walked us through to the spa lounge.

"Rachel," Henna whispered in my ear as we followed the receptionist, ogling her immensely high heels, "what did she say? Borrada?"

"It's Welsh," I hissed back. "*Bore da*. It means 'good morning'."

"Oh, that makes sense." She nodded and we took our seats around a large granite-topped table. There were a few people sitting around in towelling robes so thick they looked like fur coats, sipping noxious-looking smoothies and reading the *FT* and the *Telegraph*.

"No copies of *The Times* I see." Henna looked around dismissively.

I wished just then that I were more like Marvellous Marcia. She would have taken this all in her stride and enjoyed it the more for being so relaxed about the whole thing. I was so in awe of it I felt completely uncomfortable. I felt a bit of a fraud, sitting there with my complimentary cup of herbal tea, trying to hide the mud splash on my tired-looking shoes. I felt, in fact, as if a security guard would rush in on us and say, "Rachel Young! You were brought up in the West Midlands! You have to leave the premises now. This Country Club is only for quality clientele from Gloucestershire and Berkshire – people who were brought up in Walsall are not welcome here. And is that your nine-year-old Golf bringing down the tone of the car park? Remove it immediately or I'll be forced to call the police."

But there were no security guards, just the receptionist who took us through the package that we'd booked months ago. She kept tapping the brochures with her well-manicured fingers. I was going to get me some of that. I didn't know, up until that point, that fingers could look so good. They made Marcia's manicured fingers look like a chimpanzee had attacked her with a bottle of Rimmel Quick Dry.

A whole new world was opening up to me. Maybe this

really would be the beginning of the end of my DLC. I would learn how to do more of this interesting stuff. Learn how to enjoy doing some of this stuff at least. I would go to health spas. I would ride horses. I would hang around country lanes a bit more and meet more dishy farmers...

According to the receptionist with the amazing nails we were entitled to three treatments from a huge list in our files, and we needed to book those in before we left the lounge. We were free to use all the facilities including two swimming pools, one indoors and one outdoors, Jacuzzi, salt-water pool, gymnasium, steam-room, sauna, a place called The Lavender Relaxation Room and the café, lounge and dining-room.

"We encourage you to relax here at the spa," she was saying in her ultra-calm voice, "and a lot of our guests like to spend the day in their robes, so please feel free to keep them on wherever you are. You can pick them up from just over there, along with complimentary slippers that you can take away with you after your day with us."

Complimentary slippers? Freebies! My heart sang with joy.

"When you've submitted your preferred therapies to me I will book them in for you and give you times for your treatments. Then I'll show you where the individual suites are located in the hotel. If you make your way to your suite five minutes before your start time, the beautician will be waiting for you."

She asked us if we had any questions and I bit back the urge to ask if we could keep the towelling robes. Surely she would have said if we could. And if I did ask that then surely a security person would make an appearance.

As it was no one had any questions so she left us to it

and we had the difficult task of trying to puzzle out what the various therapies were.

Looking at the superglossy brochure of treatments I was reminded of those pretentious restaurants that try to demonstrate just how posh they are by describing foods using the most obscure words the chef can come up with. Like using "jus" instead of just plain gravy. Or "a medley of mixed berries" instead of calling it fruit salad. It always got under my skin because it led to the inevitable disappointment. The descriptions made you believe that you had just ordered the most amazing assortment of this and ensemble of that with jus of this and cocotte of that, but what you really got was chicken in white wine sauce and mash, with an ice cream sundae for pudding. So I concentrated hard on my brochure, trying to interpret the purple passages and understand what the treatments really were.

Cathy's phone beeped loudly and made us all jump. We were all edgy after last night, even in the protective lavishness of a luxury health spa. Who knows where big cats might lurk? Cathy frantically texted her fiancé back while an old man with a towelling robe that was slipping horribly open at the front frowned sternly in our direction, letting us know just how cross he was at the disturbance to the peace. I couldn't help staring at the gaping towel at his crotch, mesmerised. I was drawn to it out of sheer horror. Surely he would pull the robe together? Surely he must be feeling a draught downstairs? But no, even my horrified expression, which he must have seen, hadn't convinced him he needed to check himself. He just carried on reading the *FT*. And gaping.

I turned back to the glossy brochure. I'd never been to a health spa before, so while it was great that I was trying something new and being adventurous, it also meant that I had no idea what everything was. Except a manicure.

"Hey guys, have you seen the Rasul Mud Treatment?" Henna was laughing. "I am so going to have this! It says 'three types of mud are applied to body and face. These muds draw toxins from the skin and steam aids the detoxification process and relaxes the body. The ritual ends with a cleansing tropical shower.'"

"Henna, that sounds awful!" I said. "All it will be is a mud bath followed by a hose down. I could have done that for free back at the Hen House."

"Yes but think of the toxins," she said. "That's last night sorted out. I'll be glowing! Bring on the farmers!" she sang.

"Vets," corrected Louisa without looking up from her brochure. "The farmers are all mine."

"Yeah but I thought…"

"Mine!"

"Whatever."

"What about the Shirodhara?" Cathy interrupted. "Apparently it's deeply relaxing because they pour oils onto the forehead which run through the hair for ultimate relaxation." Laura snorted loudly with laughter and then slapped her hand over her mouth as she heard the angry snap and rustle of a newspaper by the loosely-robed *FT* reader behind us.

We were clearly not fitting in to the spa atmosphere. Our guffaws raised the heads of several other spa victims who frowned and then went back to their papers and smoothies. Eventually we knuckled down to business, ticking the boxes of our chosen treatments. I went for a Prescription Facial (including bust) which involved a firming serum which sounded good, then a Toning Streamliner which involved a scary-sounding deep massage which promised the earth – especially good after last night. And then a good old-fashioned manicure, because my hands were horrid and I wanted angel hands like the receptionist. Hands, in fact, that I could display right in front of Marcia's nose as I counted off the list of things I had done this weekend.

Most of the girls chose beautifying treatments that promised they would look and feel like goddesses by the end of the day, presumably in preparation for bumping into a bevy of handsome Welsh farmers in the evening. After all we were due to pay a visit to the local pub that evening for dinner and drinks, and a few of the girls, myself included, were of the opinion that it would be unacceptably rude to walk past Gwyn's farmhouse and not invite him to join us. Even though absolutely no one was going to do anything with him. Never mind that, though, I just hoped he'd see past their temporary facial beauty and notice my stunning manicured hands and fall helplessly in love with me.

Cathy's phone beeped again and she hurriedly checked her text message. The old bloke with the ever more gaping robe snapped his newspaper again in anger. As one we all turned round and smiled sweetly at him.

The phone went off again.

"For the love of God!" Robe-man leapt up, glaring at us.

"Argh!" Henna, Laura and I shielded our eyes from the view. Flinging his paper violently down, he stormed off.

Henna burst out laughing while Laura made retching noises. "That was so disgusting!" She put her head in her hands. "Shouldn't he be wearing pants?"

"Wee Willie Winkie," giggled Henna, holding up her little finger.

Cathy, meanwhile, had dived into her bag again. "It's not my phone," she said meekly.

"Oh! It's mine." Louisa took her phone out and scrolled down the text. "The boys have just started go-carting. Oh my God! Paul has been taken off to the local hospital," she read. "Bloody hell! Apparently he's got a suspected broken leg."

Louisa called up James while we politely listened in. From the conversation we could hear that the boys had already gone paintballing first thing that morning and go-carting was just starting. They must be exhausted.

"So," Laura asked when Louisa finished the call, "what's happening on the stag do?"

"Apparently Paul's not rejoining them. He's going home after the hospital."

"Can he drive?" Laura asked.

"His girlfriend's picking him up. Anyway, the others are going back to the go-carting circuit now and they're off to a local pub this evening for another quiet night."

"It's a bit odd, don't you think?" I said before I'd really thought it through.

"What's a bit odd?" Louisa asked.

"Well, they do all this stuff in the daytime and then just hang around for quiet nights. Seems a bit odd, that's all."

"They're probably tired," Cathy volunteered.

"Really?"

"What are you saying, Rachel?"

"Do you believe him?"

"Of course I believe him! I'm getting married to him. And anyway, what else are they going to get up to in rural Wales? They're only in the next valley and I can't imagine there are any strip joints round there. It's like over here, isn't it? All farms and stuff…"

"Erm, no?"

"What's it like, then?" Louisa suddenly looked concerned.

"Well, you've got Merthyr. And Pontypool."

"Are they bad?"

"Well, they're not rural."

"Yes, but are they bad?"

I looked around for someone else to help me out but everyone was staring hard at their brochures.

"Well…"

"I don't care!" Louisa announced, cutting off what I was going to say. "Whatever they do it's not a problem with me. They can do what they like."

I was glad I hadn't got a significant other at that point. They seemed like a whole lot of hassle to be worrying about. If I were Louisa I would have been worried about my fiancé. However well behaved and responsible James was, his mates were absolutely mental and would no doubt become even more so over the stag weekend. Everyone knew that stag dos were a licence to have one last taste of freedom. Everyone except Louisa, apparently.

13

Therapies booked and robes and complimentary slippers commandeered we headed off to the changing-rooms to start our day. Only Louisa was a spa-expert and knew what the routine was in these places, so the rest of us happily followed her lead. I was glad I wasn't the only one to feel a bit out of place; I was probably more comfortable here than Laura was. She didn't actually want any beauty treatments but had gamely booked three just to show willing.

Within half an hour we were swimming in the glorious August sunshine in the open-air pool. It was raised up so we could enjoy the views of the rolling hills of Monmouthshire, dotted with its whitewashed farmhouses, sweeping fields and pockets of woodland. It was so beautiful, so peaceful and relaxing with just the lapping of water and the cawing of birds overhead. As I splish-splashed my way lazily down the pool I promised myself that I would be back in the countryside as soon as possible after this weekend. I couldn't believe we were only an hour from Cardiff – it seemed like a world away from the busy capital. I could commute from here. Buy a little house in a village somewhere, get membership to the Llangorse Manor and buy a Jaguar to travel down to work in. Well, while I was dreaming, why not make it an Aston Martin and why not move in with Gwynfor the farmer? I could raise hearty farmer-children who played barefoot in the fields and we could live in the Hen House because, really, that was the kind of girl I was at heart. Bohemian. Eclectic. Ethnic but also traditional. I would jack in my project management job and sell my soulless, strip-lit Ikea-clad apartment and come to live here and be a mother and … and a weaver. Yes. That was what I was destined to do.

And I would invite Marcia over and have her stay in the pantry-bedroom and keep her awake at night by standing under her window and snapping twigs.

Ha!

By lunchtime we had swum and sunbathed, been for a sauna, a steam and spent a few minutes in the Lavender Relaxation Room without actually getting what it was supposed to do, except permanently impregnate the smell of lavender on to your skin.

Dressed in our fur-coat-like towelling robes on top of our swimsuits, we went for lunch in the bar beside the pool. It was on a sheltered sun terrace overlooking the golf course and the lake nearby, with palm trees in silver pots.

There were only a few other diners out on the terrace and most of them were talking quietly or reading a newspaper while they ate their lunches. Thankfully Mr Genitals and his ever-rustling *Financial Times* were not on the terrace, enjoying the fresh air. The only sounds were the clinking of cutlery and the polite rumble of conversation from the other guests.

So far all the staff we had seen at the hotel had been immaculately presented and thoroughly professional. The waitresses in the bar seemed to let the side down somewhat. Not that I minded at all – they made me feel all the more classy.

"Do you want any wine, then?" a brassy blonde with ginger roots stared at us, pencil poised in a notepad.

"Ahh, no, not for me," Louisa said. "Just a water."

"And me," I said

"Yeah, me too," Cathy and Laura added in unison.

"Actually, I might have a small glass. Very small," Henna relented. "Hair of the dog…"

"We don't 'ave that one." The waitress flicked through the wine list. "Is there another one you want?"

I laughed. Laura kicked me under the table.

"Oh dear. No hair of the dog?" Henna played along. "Well, in that case it's going to have to be the … er … Shiraz Grenache."

"Small, yeah?"

"Erm, well, why not make it a large."

"Large. Shiraz. Grenache. That it?"

"Yes, I think so."

She slouched off, ripping the paper off her pad and slapping it down on the bar.

"Blimey, she could do with a beauty treatment or two," Louisa whispered when she'd gone.

"Yeah. A pedicure to the face," I added, finishing off my salmon. "Look at her mate, though. She's just as rough."

The peroxide blonde had gravitated to an over-made-up redhead who was busy turning water bottles so that the labels faced the same way. As no one was particularly talkative while we were eating, we could all make out their conversation.

"You missed a bottle there."

"Are you sorting 'em or am I?"

"All right then, you do it. No need to have a strop about it."

"'As he called you back yet?"

"What? The bloke from the club last night? Yeah. He texted me this mornin'. He says, 'Why not bring your mates along too' so I thought you'd like to come. And Bianca's coming an' all."

"Brilliant," the redhead said, "it'll be a right laugh. Didn't you say he was good looking?"

"Yeah. A couple of them are. But the one that invited me, it's his stag do."

We all froze. Knives stopped cutting, mouths stopped chewing. We were all poised, listening in. Louisa looked as though she'd just been shot.

"So where is it?" the redhead was asking, picking at her nail polish while she sorted out the condiments.

"They're in that bed and breakfast up the Merthyr road…"

"I know it. The green one. Where that man hung himself last year."

"That's it. They said we should meet them at the Star and Garter at nine. You don't get many blokes round here like that. I reckon it's gonna be a top night. I'm not inviting Tasha, though, she's a right slag."

"Yeah, fuckin' Tasha…"

Louisa mechanically put her knife and fork down. We

all looked at her. She looked thunderous.

The barman brought over the glasses of water and Henna's wine. The tension was tangible as we all kept a respectful silence until we were on our own again.

"It might not be James," I began the minute the barman had gone, but Henna shushed me as the two local girls had started talking again.

"It's James something-or-other," she was saying, "an' the other one's called Howie or somethin'. You can 'ave 'im!" And the two of them laughed coarsely.

"Bastard," Louisa said through tight lips. "That lying, cheating bastard! Quiet night in, my arse! I knew he was up to something."

"You should definitely shag that farmer then," piped up Henna, going back to her omelette.

"Too bloody right," Louisa snapped, knocking back Henna's wine. "And I'll shag the vet as well."

Cathy, looking shocked and not a little disapproving, set about busying herself with her chips. Laura looked as if she was measuring up the two waitresses in preparation for taking them on. What was she going to do – nut them like she did Henna?

I felt a call of duty to cheer up my pal. I couldn't imagine how she must feel, with James poised to have his wicked way with a couple of valley girls. "You know, it doesn't mean he'll get up to anything, Lou." I put my hand on her trembling hand and gave it a squeeze. "I don't think you should worry about it. Really I don't. Besides, look at them. James wouldn't touch them with a bargepole!"

"But what about his mates? They'll push him to … to…" She looked distraught.

"No they won't," I cut her short. "His mates are up for that sort of thing, maybe, but James certainly isn't. I bet what will happen is the other guys will be chatting up the talent while James occupies himself with the snooker. Or maybe darts…"

"I'm still going to have my share of fun," Louisa said, through gritted teeth, "but thank you, Rach. It's nice of you to be so positive."

"Come on, lets go." Henna downed what was left of her wine in one gulp. "I don't think we want to hear any more from the waitresses."

We went back to our loungers by the poolside for some sunbathing and in-depth discussions on the nature of stag and hen parties and how Louisa now had free licence to go after any attractive man she might meet during the course of the weekend. I couldn't help feeling a pang for Gwynfor the ill-fated farmer. He wouldn't know what had hit him when we came knocking on his door tonight on the way to the pub. Still, Gwynfor was a strong man and could probably take care of himself, if push came to shove came to thrusting him into a bedroom.

Would he accept her advances? Last night he'd been pretty resolute in peeling off her hand every time it strayed back to his thigh. But then he had been on something of a mission with his sheep lying mauled to death in a nearby field. Who could blame him for not being in the mood for love? Perhaps tonight he'd be less quick to remove her hand? Or would he fling her aside and stride over to me, whisking me up and taking me back to his farmhouse, rejecting Louisa's classic beauty and preferring instead my ready wit and sense of humour? Perhaps…

I kept reliving the moment when I opened up the front door and there he was, a roguish smile on his lips, standing in the porch and holding out his proof of ID. Gwynfor Jones. Farmer.

14

$\mathcal{O}ne$ by one we went off for our spa treatments, coming back much the same as before but smelling nicer. My manicure was amazing, however, and I couldn't stop looking at my hands. I went for another swim and every time I pushed my hands out and in front of me at the start of each stroke I gave a little "aah" as I admired the craftsmanship at the end of each finger. The manicurist had buffed and polished the nails, shaping them into smooth almond arcs and then given them three coats of light polish that made them gleam.

But poor old Henna. The girl who had most needed a pick-me-up after last night's drinking. She trotted off happily enough for her mud soak and hose down but an hour later she slunk back to her lounger by the pool, hidden under a towel. Underneath she was bright red and patchy.

"Oh my God. What did they do to you?" Cathy

gasped.

"Yes, OK, thank you," Henna bit back. "You don't have to step back looking quite so horrified, Cathy. I do know how I look. You don't have to make me feel worse than I already do."

"Sorry, I just…"

"Well, apparently," Henna began despairingly, "the redness will go down in an hour. But what they didn't tell me before the treatment is that all these spots that are starting to appear on my face are my toxins coming out. And they're going to be getting worse over the weekend!"

Louisa couldn't disguise the fact that she was just a little bit pleased, probably on account of Henna showing such an interest in Gwyn. Now at least Henna was well out of the race. Pretty, flirty and quick to get rat-arsed she might be, but covered in weeping sores and purple bruises she was no match for Louisa's polished good looks. "Oh dear," Louisa managed, "still, at least you'll be toxin-free by Monday."

"But think of all the alcohol I had last night," Henna wailed. "There's so much toxic crap inside me I'll just be one big gaping sore in a few hours time. I can't believe it! My weekend's ruined – I'll look like a plague victim or something. And my bruise is getting worse…"

Laura looked down at the newspaper in front of her and suddenly became quite interested in changes to hunting laws in Northern Canada.

"My weekend is ruined! No one's going to come near me!"

I looked up from admiring my hands and gave her a sympathetic smile. "We might not see Gwyn again."

"Yeah, right!" Louisa snorted. "Like that's an option."

It seemed like no time at all since we'd arrived but now we were surreptitiously reclaiming our shamefully old cars and driving back to the farmhouse to get ready for an evening at the pub. Laura was sitting in the back of my car, Cathy having argued, whined and pleaded with me not to have the TA terror in her car again.

"Please, please." She clasped her hands together in front of me.

"Fine. Fine. But you can take one of my chores from me for doing it."

"Anything. Of course. Thank you!" She ran off to her car, half-skipping and taking Louisa and Henna with her.

As it turned out Laura was completely relaxed and in a contemplative mood on the journey back. I barely heard a peep out of her; the massage must have done the trick.

"Look at that!" she exclaimed suddenly as we emerged from woodland near the Hen House.

"What?" I peered up to where she was pointing. "Oh!" Overhead two helicopters were circling.

"What do you think they're doing?" she said, winding down her window and sticking her head out for a better look. "Looks like they have their side-doors open and someone hanging out. Oh my God. They've got a gun. I think it's a gun. The one marked as a police helicopter."

"Fucking hell!" I swerved back on to the road, having momentarily veered off a little in all the excitement. Perhaps I'd better concentrate a bit more on my driving. And perhaps I'd better stop taking my eyes off the road every few seconds to admire the sheer brilliance of my beautiful nails on the steering wheel.

There was a noticeable chill in the car as Laura and I started to consider the same thing. Surely the helicopters overhead were connected to that big cat sighting? They must be. So perhaps a big cat had attacked Gwynfor's sheep? Outside our house last night. Suppose we were actually in mortal danger?

"Do you think we'll have to go home early," I asked, "you know, if the police come and have a word with us or something?"

"Do you know how hard I've worked arranging all this?" Laura slammed her hands down on the seat. "Do you think we'll give up just because there might or might not be a cat out there? No. We're perfectly safe."

"OK," I agreed, nodding. I wasn't going to argue with Laura. I didn't want her to lean over and nut me while I was driving and then make out that we just happened to collide when we went round a corner...

It still gave me the creeps to imagine that there could be a dangerous animal lurking out there, watching us, but we couldn't see it. Anything that merited policemen with guns hanging out of helicopters had to be a fairly substantial threat. Or maybe they were training their guns on Laura? Maybe she was AWOL from the army, escaped in a frenzy of madness...

"I wonder if there are any big cats over in the valley that the boys are having their stag weekend in?" she interrupted my thoughts.

"Well, the danger of a big cat is nothing to James in comparison with what Louisa is going to be dishing out when he gets back to their flat," I said. "Anyway, the boys will be fine," I added, "they've got paintball guns to shoot it and go-carts to escape from it. And isn't big game hunting one of their activities?"

"If it wasn't before then it could be now," Laura said, deep in thought.

15

Laura was pacing up and down the sitting-room, the gong beater twirling from one hand to the other, looking like a majorette in a military band. The usual plain combats had been ditched for combats (shock!) but with an embroidered hem. She'd also chosen a close-fitting white T-shirt that beautifully accentuated her six pack.

"Four minutes to go." She glanced at her watch for the twentieth time. "Do you think one of us should go and check on Cathy?"

"Give her time," Henna sighed, raising her eyes skywards. "God, I should think that she knows what time she's due down. You told us often enough."

"I told everyone to be down here five minutes before we were due to leave."

"Yeah well, last time I saw her she was texting her fiancé but she was all dressed up and ready to go," Louisa said, picking at the sequins on her sparkly strapless top.

"Stop fretting, Laura," Henna moaned.

Laura spun the beater angrily, bringing it to a halt, pointing it at Henna. "I think you'll find that I am not fretting."

I'd had enough bickering with Marcia to last me a lifetime. I got up and strode out of the sitting-room. "I'll go check on her."

"Good woman!" Laura nodded her approval to me and I shot Henna a mock-superior look. I was definitely in Laura's good books. Henna stuck two fingers up but hid them the minute Laura turned round to see what I was smiling at.

Upstairs I knocked on Cathy's door. "Come in." Her voice was small and tight.

She was sprawled across her vast double bed, staring up at the beams in the ceiling, her mobile phone flung on the pillow.

I perched beside her and put the phone on the table. "Trouble?"

She sighed. "I don't know. Maybe. What do you think of this?" She sat up and grabbed her phone, flicking through the messages. She handed it to me and I read the message. *That's it. Enough!*

"Hmm." I put the phone down again. "That's not great, is it?"

"What do you think he means?" she asked

I shrugged. "You know better than me. What do you think?"

"I don't know! Should I go back home? Louisa must be really pissed of with me as it is. I've been absolutely rotten this weekend. I'd probably be doing everyone a favour if I went home, wouldn't I? Are they talking about me downstairs?"

"Laura's a bit concerned that we're not strictly adhering to the Schedule and Rota."

Cathy grabbed her watch. "Oh crap. I should have been down five minutes ago!"

"Don't worry about it. The crosser she gets with you the more sympathy everyone else has with you."

"True. So what do you think I should do?"

"Ditch the phone and come out with us. Whatever it is between you and Heath it can wait another day or so. Leave the phone on the table and come out and enjoy yourself."

She nodded. "Very good advice."

I beamed. I was recommending spontaneity and a little recklessness. Hardly a DLC thing to do.

"Is that what everyone's wearing?" She pointed to my black t-shirt, jeans and kitten heels. Pretty understated compared to Louisa's strapless sequinned ensemble but then at least I wasn't going to be overly conscious about what I was wearing.

"Louisa's got a strapless sequinned top on, Henna's got a gold halterneck and mini-skirt combo and Laura's got combats on. Again."

"So Henna and Louisa have really dressed up then?"

"Yeah, well to be honest with you," I leant in and whispered, "Henna's face is looking pretty bad, even under all her make-up, so it's probably a good move to draw attention everywhere else."

"Do you think my dress is too showy? I wasn't sure about red."

"It's great! Really. You look fab, now let's go. No, leave the phone there. Come on, Laura will go mental if you stay up here any longer."

Cathy actually laughed. "Yeah. I heard she actually nutted Henna the day they arrived."

When we got downstairs it was clear that something had happened between Laura and Henna. Henna was sulking in her chair, curled up and picking at the wounds on her face while Laura was pacing up and down in front of the fire. Louisa was staying well out of it, applying more lipstick and then hoisting up her spangly top, which was falling down on her recently-trimmed pre-wedding figure. I looked at her from the corner of my eye, taking in her appearance from her pointy sandals to her daring cleavage and ruby red lipstick. All dressed up in sequins. She really was taking the seducing Gwyn plan seriously. She naturally looked stunning, being so thin and blonde and Scandinavian-looking. Dressed up in a sequinned top and gold stiletto sandals, how could anyone fail to notice her? Especially when she was on display in a rural pub tucked into the Welsh hills. And yet ... and yet was it really so bad? At the end of the night she might well get her man because, it had to be said, she looked just fabulous and you couldn't take your eyes off her. How could any man fail to notice her great figure and her pretty face? It was there, right in front of them. Where as I? I wanted the same thing as she did, if I had to be honest with myself. I hadn't been able to stop thinking about the Welshman since I'd met him last night, and while Louisa was going out there and trying her hardest to make it happen, what was I doing? Wearing jeans and a black T-shirt, and tying my hair up? Did I want to bag a man out of sympathy? Did I hope that my manicure alone would be enough to entice him to me? Even Laura had made an effort with her embroidered combats.

What would Marcia do?

"Back in a minute!" I dashed out of the living-room, into the kitchen and ducked into my room, hearing the exasperated shouts of Laura in the hallway.

I pulled the brush through my hair and let it fall loose over my shoulders, whipped out my concealer, mascara, liquid rouge and then a bold red lipstick. I checked the tiny mirror. Better.

Laura was in the doorway. "Rach, what the…"

"Ready. Sorry!" I turned out the light and followed her back into the hallway, having slipped several notches down in Laura's estimation.

Laura stood in front of the gong, still twirling the beater. "Now we're all finally ready, shall we walk up to the pub?"

Cathy looked troubled, "Walk? What about the cat?"

Ah yes, the cat. Somewhere along the way we'd managed to temporarily forget about the big cat threat.

"It's not that far to the pub," Louisa whined, "and we need to call on Gwyn anyway. Come on."

"Don't you think we could get attacked?" Cathy insisted, adopting a serious expression that said, "I'm a doctor, listen to me." "It's a dark road and there's no one about until we get to the village. Anything could happen. Besides, I'm wearing red, it'll go for me first."

"Actually, that's bulls that go for red. And we've got torches," Laura argued. "Don't worry. Off we go then!" She swung the beater in the air but Henna deftly grabbed it mid-swing before it hit the gong. "Don't," she said. "Just fucking don't."

It was still light when we walked up the road to the pub, but that didn't stop it being a mind-bendingly terrifying experience. While no one went as far as to talk about the possibility of being torn in two by a big cat it was obvious that we were all thinking about it. We huddled together in the middle of the track, speed walking as fast as our completely inappropriate footwear would allow us, heading uphill and shooting nervous glances into the thick black woodland on either side. What had seemed like a two minute trip between the Hen House and the pub actually turned out to be a twenty minute walk of sheer terror. Several times one of us would drop behind as our kitten heels slipped off in the rush or we wobbled into potholes. Then there would be a cry of "Hold on!" and we'd have to wait while shoes were hastily slipped on again and we could continue. The rutted farm track was not the easiest surface to negotiate in our best footwear. Still, at least our killer heels could be used in self-defence if needs be. But could any of us high kick? My jeans were so tight I could probably only manage a high kick to just above my ankle level. Would that be sufficient to ward off a cat attack? Maybe I could spear its paw with my heel? I bet Laura could high kick, and with her loose-fitting combats she'd be perfectly dressed to deliver a knock-out blow to any feline attacker.

Midway up the hill we came to Gwyn's farmhouse.

"I'll go and knock," Louisa selflessly volunteered. The rest of us stood in a group and watched her dash across the front yard as best she could in her four-inch heeled gold sandals, which was a feat in itself. With the dexterity of a woman on a mission, she dodged the ruts and dung piles in the path and knocked at the door. She stood in the porch, stamping her feet to keep warm – the evening was rather chilly, especially as she was wearing about as much material as went to make the handkerchief sensibly stowed away in my handbag. My God, I was turning into my parents…

Louisa knocked again.

Nothing.

I, like most of the girls, was spending my time peering nervously into the surrounding trees, hoping not to see a pair of eyes watching us. The smallest sound of a bird on a branch or a rabbit on the ground and I got palpitations. I really hoped Louisa would give up; he wasn't there and I didn't want to be standing out here any more than I had to. There was a worrying amount of rustling and snapping coming from the woodland that bordered the farmyard. The whole woodland was alive.

"There's no light on," Henna shouted over to Louisa. "He's not there! I think we should press on."

Louisa looked crestfallen. "Does anyone have a pen and paper on them? We could write him a letter so if he gets back in time…" But no one had. Not even Laura who might have been expected to carry that sort of thing. She'd left her trusty tool belt back at the Hen House. I know because I'd seen it abandoned on a chair in the kitchen and was about to take a sneaky peek into it when Louisa had appeared and ruined my chance of discovering just what a TA girl carries in her workman's handbag.

Louisa click-clacked back to us and we hastily continued walking up the hill.

We reached the pub and practically clambered over one another in the rush to get through the narrow doorway and into the warm smoky safety of the bar. All pretence at politeness and "you first" was abandoned as we pushed and shoved our way to safety.

Once inside, with the solid old wooden door closed firmly behind us, we began to relax and look a bit sheepish at the various pushings and shovings that had gone on. I could feel my shoulders begin to unknot and I saw Henna arching her back while Laura was doing some sort of breathing exercise. Had they all been as scared as I had? Shit! I'd only been managing to hold it together thinking that the others were feeling more confident than I was. Walking home would be fun then. Perhaps I should drink myself into a stupor and then any cats that come prowling round would be put off by the alcohol fumes.

16

We made our way through the crowded room over to the bar, suddenly able to talk now and there was plenty of "you should have seen your face" and "I thought you were going to wet yourself when that bird flew out of the tree" while we got the drinks in. The female equivalent of backslapping, but it needed to be done.

While we were at the bar I looked around and took in our surroundings properly. It was an amazing old place with most of the stone walls exposed and only the enormous chimney, which ran up one side of the room, painted a chalky-white. There was the usual mix of maroon pub carpet, dark wood tables and chairs, and dried hops hanging from the rafters.

"There must be a hotel around here," Henna said quietly, "there's a whole coach load of Germans down near the front of the room."

"Really?" I asked. "What on earth are they doing in

deepest Wales?" I peered over to where she had indicated, trying to catch a glimpse of the checked-trousered, wire-frame-bespectacled tourists.

Cathy looked amused. "Why do you think they're Germans, Henna?"

"They're talking in German," Henna answered, with a "duh!" look at Cathy.

"That's not German, it's Welsh," Cathy said, more amused than ever. We braced ourselves for a linguistic lecture. It didn't come. Cathy just stood there with her arms crossed looking very superior with an "ask me! ask me!" look on her face. But no one asked her. We all strained to listen and sure enough, I could make out that they were speaking Welsh.

"That is just so weird," Louisa said loudly. "Now I really feel like I'm on holiday, hearing a foreign language. Do they really speak like that here? I thought it was one of those dead languages, you know, like Belgian."

"Belgian?"

"Well, I don't know what you're laughing about, Rachel. It happens to be true. No one speaks Belgian any more."

"Oh, OK."

"As a matter of fact Louisa's right," Cathy said to me, looking utterly serious, "no one speaks Belgian."

"See? The linguist agrees with me. You lot are constantly laughing at me on my hen weekend and it's just not fair." Louisa gave a haughty look and turned back to the bar to get served.

"So do you speak Welsh then?" Henna asked, starting to pick at one of her spots. "Living in Cardiff, I suppose you must do."

"Should you really be doing that? Anyway, no, I don't

speak Welsh. I might try to learn though. You know, it would be a bit weird to be married to Gwyn and not be able to talk to him in his own language."

"I heard that," Louisa said without looking round from the bar.

Henna and I exchanged glances.

I was rather sick of wine so I ordered a pint of some Welsh beer and walked over to the table Laura had commandeered near the entrance, beside the non-German Welsh-speakers.

"So, Rachel, you're the tallest here, can you see the fit farmer?"

"No," I said mournfully. "I looked the minute we got in but he's not here. To be honest, I'm a bit disappointed, I had hoped he was representative of the male population in rural Wales, but it doesn't seem to be the case."

"You can say that again," said Henna, swigging her pint. "We must be the youngest in here by about two hundred years. Maybe in their heyday they were something to look at but bloody hell, there are some real munters here."

"Shush!" Laura hissed. "Some of the munters probably understand English."

"I bet the barwoman was a looker," whispered Cathy and we all turned en masse to have a look at the woman who had just wiped our table down. She caught us in the act.

"Everything all right?"

"Oh. Yes. Fine," we mumbled. Honestly, talk about pack mentality.

"I think you're right," I said quietly, still hot with shame, fiddling with my beer mat. "I mean, she must be about sixty but she's got a nice face. Good bone structure and all that. I bet she used to look a bit like Mae West in her younger days."

"That old farmer bloke over there thinks she's still got it." Laura nodded in the direction of the bar and we turned again en masse to look. An old red-faced man was sitting nursing a pint in the corner of the bar, huddled up in his waxed jacket and wearing a knackered old cap.

"He looks familiar," I said. "Where have I seen him before?"

"Down in the city maybe," Louisa giggled, "at one of your nightclubs on a night out with his mates?"

"You're right though." Henna was studying him. "He is watching the barwoman, isn't he? Do you think that's her husband?"

"No way," I said, examining him for a moment, watching the furtive little looks he kept giving the woman behind the bar, in between staring into space and taking the occasional sip from his pint. I had the best seat from which to examine him and the old man certainly didn't have that everything-you-say-bores-the-arse-off-me look that a lot of people of that age tend to have when they look at their spouses. I was pretty sure he wasn't her husband.

"Lovers, then?" asked Laura.

Henna snorted and then started picking at the skin around her toxin-spots. "He is staring at her, though," she said, "that would really freak me out if that was me."

"Well, it's not you," said Louisa, "and sorry to break it to you honey, but he seems to prefer looking at the old bar woman than looking at you."

"Now that's sad," Laura said and Henna had to agree.

While this conversation was taking place, Cathy had gone to the loo but now she returned with an odd look on her face. She wordlessly dropped a pile of leaflets on the table in front of us.

"Look guys. These were by the front door – we must have missed them in the rush to get in. It must be serious…"

We scrabbled for the rough photocopied sheets and read. My hands went clammy as I got down the page.

CIRCULATED BY SOUTH WALES POLICE –
AUGUST 2007
What happens if you see a big cat? Dr Richard
Maiden of London Zoo recommends:
The danger to countryside users from the species
of cats thought to be present in Britain is small.
However, there is a significant risk that a cat
may attack a human if it is cornered, if its young
are threatened or if the person encountering it
otherwise aggravates the cat. If you encounter an
exotic cat…

"Fucking hell! Have you got to the bit about shooting them?" Henna slapped her copy down on the table and stared at us wide-eyed.

"No," we all chimed in. Being a journalist Henna had powers of speed-reading well beyond us mortals.

"Sorry." She hung her head and we carried on.

If you encounter an exotic cat you should carry out
the following procedures:
a)   Walk away, without turning away from the cat,
slowly and deliberately. DO NOT RUN.
b)   Do not make full eye contact with the cat or
try to stare at the cat's eyes, as this is considered
threatening behaviour and may instigate territorial
behaviours from the cat.

c) Hold out your arms and try to make yourself look
big. Shout and jump up and down if appropriate.
d) Act human; talk and make noise as you walk.
Do not walk away quietly.
e) Allow the cat to move away at its own pace
and in its own direction. DO NOT ATTEMPT TO
FOLLOW THE CAT.
f) DO NOT ATTEMPT TO SHOOT THE CAT.
Not only is this a safety issue, since an injured cat
may represent a significant danger to humans, but
there may also be serious legal issues involved.
In most cases the cat will take off, fairly quickly.
Most cat species are very shy and contact with
humans is rare.
If you think you have seen a big cat call your local
police on the numbers below.

One by one we finished reading our leaflets and put them back on the table, expressionless. Laura was just about to say something when the barwoman came over and began to serve dinner.

Suddenly walking up the hill in inappropriate shoes seemed like a really stupid idea.

"It's all a hoax," the barwoman said, seeing the leaflets and our pale faces as she dealt out the plates. "Scampi? That yours, love? Yes, we've had big cat scares before and we'll have them again. No doubt about it. I wouldn't worry about it, to be honest. It's young lads having a laugh."

"Rachel here met a farmer, didn't you Rachel. He didn't think it was a hoax." Louisa verbally pushed me forward.

"That'll be Tomos or Gwynfor, then," she said,

smoothing down her apron and looking at me questioningly.

"Gwynfor," I said and I blushed when I saw the nod she gave me. She managed to convey an awful lot in that one small tilt of her head; a sort of 'and-I-bet-you-liked-what-you-saw-eh?' nod.

"Well, anyway," I continued, trying to act all cool about it, "he said one of his sheep was attacked last night. And he didn't think it was attacked by a dog."

"It's true," came a deep voice behind me. I looked round. It was him – all dark eyes and thick black hair – standing there in a T-shirt and cords that I couldn't help noticing were rather stretched over his thighs.

How long had he been standing there?

I caught fire, burnt up and crumbled into ash on the carpet below my chair. Oh, the shame. Most of the girls round the table were staring up at him semi-open-mouthed. At least they weren't looking at me, writhing in my own private little hell in front of a plate of scampi.

"Hi," he said, looking down at me burning away.

"Hello," I managed, "how's the sheep?"

"Still dead."

"I meant, what's the verdict on the sheep?" I asked, trying to recover a smidgeon of my composure and making room for him as he was pulling up a chair next to me.

"Don't mind if I join you?" he asked, sitting astride the chair like it was the tiniest of footstools. Five open mouths surrounded the table, with five plates of untouched food on the table. How good did he look in those cords?

"The vet said he just couldn't tell what predator got the animal, so it's gone on to higher powers. He did say, though, that it showed signs of being a big cat kill because a dog would have attacked the other sheep in the group.

But he couldn't be sure from the tissue damage. Anyway, I should know more tomorrow."

"Great," I said, again without thinking. Why had my brain suddenly decided to leave me alone at this point? What was "great" about it? That his animal had died? That it could be a big cat killing? Doh!

The barwoman brought over a pint of something dark for Gwyn, and the two of them exchanged a few more words in Welsh. I shot a glance around the table and saw that most of the girls had regained their composure, closed their mouths and were tentatively picking up knives and forks. Louisa was running her hands through her hair, smoothing it down, and, when she thought no one was looking, she glanced down at her cleavage, considered it for a second and yanked her strapless top down a couple more centimetres. My DLC self was mortified. I was sure I could see nipple.

I picked up my cutlery and forced myself to eat. The scampi was good, which was fortunate as I didn't seem to have much of an appetite and could easily have left the plate untouched. Why is it that finding yourself next to a devilishly handsome man completely takes away your appetite? What good does that do anyone? It means that Romeo and Juliet must have been absolutely famished – I couldn't imagine Romeo squeezing a wedge of lemon over his scampi and chips after he'd spent an evening under the balcony with Juliet. Infatuation should come with a health warning.

"So who's the hen then?" Gwyn looked round the group of us, measuring us up before tentatively pointing to Louisa.

"Yes!" she said, absolutely delighted to be singled out, "how on earth did you guess?"

"You have a badge on." He pointed to her chest.

"Oh that!" she laughed and fiddled with the "Chief Hen" pin that Laura had given her.

Gwyn started making polite conversation about her wedding plans and so on, so I ate my scampi in silence trying not to be super-conscious of the man sitting centimetres away from me, his enormous muscular thigh almost touching mine. He wasn't talking to me anyway, he was preoccupied with talking to the others about the plans for the weekend. Laura told him about the incident at the spa with the two waitresses and the subject of the stag do was brought up. Louisa jumped into action.

"Why don't I call James?" she said suddenly, when Laura had finished explaining to Gwyn about the overheard conversation.

"Why?" I asked, with a mouthful of chips. "What good would that do you?"

"Well," she considered for a moment, "it would put my mind at ease if he still said he was staying in tonight."

"And you'd believe him if he told you he was staying in?" I asked.

"Maybe not."

"And what if he says he's going out," asked Henna, "would that make you feel any better?"

"He could be honest about it, couldn't he? He might say that the lads were up for a night out so he's going along although he really doesn't want to…"

"Really doesn't want to go out for a night on the town on his stag weekend?" Laura said, pointedly.

"Well—" Louisa searched her thoughts for the most positive outcome. "He might just want to play darts or snooker or something."

"I think," said Cathy with a mouthful of lasagne, "that

you should call him. Otherwise you'll just be worrying about it all night."

We all stared at Cathy for a moment. Was she actually advocating that Louisa phone her fiancé? This advice from the girl who wouldn't phone her fiancé and suffered endless texts all weekend.

Henna, who was managing to rub off most of the concealer on her toxin-spots, thought for a second before saying, "I agree with Cathy. You should phone him and get it out into the open. You'll just dwell on it otherwise."

"Does everyone think that?" Louisa asked.

"No, I don't," I said eventually.

"Why not?"

"Well, I think it's probably best if you don't know and just expect the best of him. If the lads aren't meeting up with the girls at the pub then everything is rosy, but if they are – well, James will either lie to you and you'll hate him for it, or he'll tell you the truth and you'll hate him for it. And if the lads aren't meeting up with the girls and James tells you that they aren't, you won't believe him anyway. So he can't win. I say you should definitely not phone him. Just have a good time tonight." I tried to say the last bit without looking directly at Gwyn.

"And I agree with Rachel," Gwyn added, looking at me impressed, "I think she's got all the angles covered."

Louisa thought about it deeply for a moment. I, on the other hand, thought about nothing deeper than just how lovely it was to hear Gwyn say my name in his lovely Welsh accent. All basey with sing-song lilting vowels.

"OK," Louisa said slowly, "I've made my decision. I'm going to call James. Just to ask how things are going. Nothing heavy. I won't ask anything specific. And then I can gauge things from there. That's a good plan, isn't it, a compromise between the two? Not come out and question him about the girls?"

I wasn't so sure that there could be a compromise, but I nodded anyway. Louisa remained seated at the table while she made the call. She stuck to her plan of not directly coming out with any accusations but just gauging how things were from what James was saying. She was looking pretty positive about whatever James was saying so all of us girls around the table were giving her the thumbs up.

"Oh right," she was saying, "oh right … and did he get his vision back? … Oh that's good … Yes we're having a great time. Great … No we were at the health spa … No that's tomorrow … Yes …"

Henna and I gave her a big thumbs up. She was definitely playing it cool.

"The health spa was interesting actually," Louisa continued.

The thumbs froze.

Laura held her hands out in a "don't do it!" motion. We all looked tensely at Louisa who looked down and was tracing the pattern of the wood on the tabletop and ignoring us.

"So are you fucking around with valley girls then tonight or what?"

None of us put our thumbs up after that.

Gwyn leant to me and whispered, "She doesn't work in PR by any chance?"

"Estate agent," I whispered back.

"Oh, right then." He nodded.

"Well, it's no fucking good telling me that, you naive fucking bastard!" Louisa shouted at the phone, spit flying everywhere. "I overheard some rough Welsh TARTS talking about your plans today. And I know what your mates are like for egging you on so don't think I'm fucking stupid!"

I looked around at the faces of our fellow diners turned towards our table. I smiled tightly and hoped that Welsh was their only language and they hadn't got round to learning English yet. It was a long shot and judging by the expressions of some of the women at least it was a pretty sure bet that they spoke English and not just the polite bits.

Gwyn kept himself busy by eating my dinner, stealing chips and scampi off my plate when he thought I wasn't looking. I shot him a mock-disgruntled look and he shrugged innocently. Louisa watched us both with beady eyes before eventually snapping her phone closed.

"Well, girls, and Gwyn," she said in a brittle way, getting up, "I'm going to the bar to get a very large drink. Very large. Everyone OK for drinks?"

When she was safely at the bar and out of earshot Henna whispered, "Sounded to me that James told her nothing was going on this evening. Big mistake! You were right, Rachel, I don't reckon she should have called."

"We should rally round her in her hour of need," piped up Cathy in her matter-of-fact way. "We have a job to do on this hen weekend and that's to make sure Louisa has a great time. And gets over this evening."

"And you're responsible too." Henna pointed one of her chips at Gwyn.

"Me?" he said innocently.

"Oh yes," Henna laughed. "You've got to help her in her hour of need!"

"And how do you propose I do that then?" he said good-naturedly, playing along with them. The great thing about him was that he was so unaffected by it all.

He wasn't playing any kind of game or flirting, he was just being himself – well, I was pretty sure he was being himself. Not that I knew him at all well having only met him yesterday. But he seemed a really genuine person and I can't say I'd met many people like him.

"Oooh, I have just no idea how you could cheer Louisa up!" Henna burst into giggles and Gwyn almost looked like he was blushing.

"I think you have to turn on the Welsh charm," I said to him.

"It's on already!" he said in despair, making us laugh.

"Glad to see you're all having fun without me," the hen returned, mournfully, bearing a double gin and tonic. "Can you believe that they don't have Bacardi Breezers here?"

"Well, yes," I said, failing to picture the local farmers coming in after a hard day spent mucking out the cow sheds and ploughing the fields and then cracking open pineapple alcopops.

Louisa perched herself down on a footstool near to Gwyn and asked the magic question, "So, Gwyn, are you married then?"

Clearly the phone call had sharpened her tactics – she was going in for the kill.

Five pairs of eyes fixed on him. Gwyn smiled and contemplated how to handle the question. However he did it, I knew he wouldn't answer like the greasy City boys with "So what if I am darlin'" or "Would it matter if I was?"

"No," he said, after what seemed like an eon and a half, "no I'm not."

"Oh." Five heads nodded. Five heads started to be filled with all sorts of saucy ideas if the faraway expressions on our faces were anything to go by. Actually, five except Cathy, who looked as though she were straining to listen in to the conversations around her going on in Welsh, no doubt getting her linguistic kicks from that.

"I expect it must be quite lonely tucked away in your farm on the mountains," Henna said after a moment of day-dreaming. "Are there many women round here?"

Now that, I knew, was a stupid question. Thank God it wasn't me that came up with that one. Still, you had to wonder if there was an element of truth in it. How many people lived round here anyway? Slim pickings...

"There are women." Gwyn hid a smile by taking another swig of his pint. "There's a woman over the valley in Brecon. And I believe there are a couple up in Builth Wells, well, so I've heard anyway."

"Oh, you have such a wicked sense of humour," Louisa gushed, tapping him on the arm playfully. "Honestly, Henna, what a silly question to ask."

Louisa was flirting like her very life depended on it and it was painful to watch. It was as if she had wiped from her memory the fact that a) she had a fiancé and b) she'd just turned purple shouting obscenities at him in front of Gwyn and her mates. Here she was acting as though nothing had happened and she was this fun-loving flirty girl. It was all a bit weird to me. Added to this her left nipple was now completely exposed, her top having ridden down over the last few minutes. I was in a real dilemma whether, as a friend, I would do better to tell her about it, or whether to not tell her and hope she just tugs her top up unconsciously and never realises what a tit (ha ha) she's made of herself. Total quandary.

I sat back and picked up my pint. It was half-gone. I looked at Gwyn who looked mock-surprised and then turned back to Louisa again, concentrating hard. A group had just left the pub and I now had a clear view of the old farmer sitting at the bar, still casting furtive little looks at the barwoman pulling the pints, hastily concentrating on his pint the moment it appeared she might look his way.

I think he probably did love her. The way he was gazing over at her was so expressive. Sad almost. In my mind he was a would-be lover of this woman. He probably came in to the pub just to be near her and I wondered whether in all the hustle and bustle of running the place she ever really noticed him looking at her. He was quite subtle in his looks, just casting a quick glance in her direction every now and then. She worked hard – she hadn't stopped since we'd got there, serving drinks and food, taking orders and cleaning tables. But surely, surely she must be aware of him? And how many months or years had he been coming to the pub, sitting there with his pint, content just to watch her flit about him?

He was finishing his pint now and pushing it across the bar when he must have caught the glass with his sleeve. It began to fall to the floor and quick as lightning his other hand shot out from beneath his coat and caught it.

I took a quick intake of breath.

His hand! It was cut and bloodied. There was dried blood in great gashes running along the top of his hand and up his forearm. The wounds were still a livid red so they must have been fairly new.

He looked round to see if anyone had noticed so I feigned interest in the remains of my scampi until he resumed his position, left hand tucked into his jacket pocket protectively, right hand now cradling the empty glass.

"What is it?" Gwyn brought me back down to earth.

The girls were talking amongst themselves and only he had noticed my reaction.

"The man at the bar..."

"What, Tomos?" he asked, pointing subtly in the old farmer's direction with one of my chips.

"Yes, him. He looks familiar. Why?"

"He was on that picture I showed you last night. You know, the one with the renovation works. He was looking miserable. He does that."

Ahh yes. The rafter photo.

"So do you know him, then?" I quickly pushed all stripped-to-the-waist images to the back of my mind; after all Louisa wasn't going to let anything come between her and her farmer quarry so why bother letting myself get too carried away with the whole thing? Very sensible of me.

"It's more like I know of him. Nobody really knows him." Gwyn leant in towards me and I caught a whiff of his aftershave or deodorant. Something good smelling. In that moment I became super-aware of just how close he was sitting next to me, and although Louisa had positioned herself next to him, his body was more aligned to where I was sitting than to where she was sitting. My heart beat that little bit faster. It was very hard not to get too carried away.

"The man keeps himself to himself," Gwyn was saying, munching the chip and going to get another from my plate. "Always has. Nice enough chap, bit morose I suppose. Why?"

"He's not a friend of yours?" I said, wanting to clarify his relationship with the man before I went and talked about him. I'd been caught out by that before – talking about someone behind their back only to find out I was talking to that person's best friend. Not good. Still, a valuable lesson for the future – if that's not too much of a DLC thing to say.

"No, he's not a friend of mine," Gwyn confirmed, "just another farmer who keeps to his own company. Why do you ask?"

"Well, the thing is," I began quietly, looking around in case any of the other girls were listening in, which they weren't as they were all trying to console a tearful Louisa who had finally cracked and started to talk about James. "The thing is I've been watching that old farmer for a while this evening, and just now I thought I saw a glimpse of his left hand, the one that he keeps hidden, can you see? It looked like it was all cut up. I was just a bit shocked to see it like that..." I petered out. Now I'd said it, I felt a bit silly having mentioned it at all. It was probably nothing, just some regular sort of farming accident. And accidents must happen all the time in farming, mustn't they? It wasn't as if he spent his days in an office filing sheets of paper and operating fax machines. The man did real work which involved sharp blades and machines that had rusty edges and jagged bits. He must get scratched up all the time. Mind you, office work can be pretty dangerous; I once shot an enormous staple through my thumb when I was binding the colossal end-of-year reports in the office. I passed out with the pain and bled over six sets of appendices. After I'd been bandaged up in the first aid room, I had one hell of a job organising the printing up of unbloodied replacement sheets. But that was just me. Most people don't maim themselves in the workplace.

Gwyn was peering over at Tomos now, hoping to see for himself a glimpse of the wounded hand. The old farmer was busy emptying his pocket no doubt looking for change for another drink. He was clearly trying very hard to keep his injured hand hidden beneath his coat. But it couldn't be done – he couldn't get to the change and keep his hand hidden at the same time. In a flash, he exposed the wounds again, emptied his pocket and buried the offending limb back in his coat, looking round to see if anyone had noticed, but thankfully not looking in our direction.

"Christ, you're right." Gwyn let out a low whistle. "That's a bad injury, that is. Wonder what did it? Looks like it goes all up his arm as well. Did you see that?"

"No. I just saw the top of his hand up to just above the wrist. The cuts look pretty deep, don't they?"

"A cat attack?" Gwyn looked at me and raised his eyebrows.

"You think so?"

He nodded, slowly. "There's got to be something out there."

I shivered. "Have you read the flyers?" I pointed to the leaflets on the table.

"Yes. And I saw that news report where the reporter was attacked. They re-showed it on the news this morning. Apparently there are police helicopters coming over."

"I know. I saw them this afternoon."

"There you go then."

"Gwyn." I leant over to him, conscious that Louisa was starting to watch me with hawk eyes. "Why would Tomos have been attacked by a big cat and be keeping it a secret? Wouldn't you be boasting about it if it was you? Or at least sharing it with someone?"

"It might not be a cat attack…"

"I know." I rethought for a moment. "Does he have a dog?"

"Yes, but I can guarantee that those injuries didn't come from his dog."

"How do you know?"

"Old Shep lost all his teeth years ago. The animal never leaves the farmhouse these days, he's so decrepit."

"But –"

"Gwynfor, we have a theory," Louisa cut in, all thrust bosoms and dazzling smile. "Does that old farmer have a thing for the barmaid over there? He's been staring at her all evening."

"Well, that's very perceptive of you." Gwyn instantly snapped out of his reverie and, finishing his pint, he put it squarely on the beer mat in front of him. "It's no secret that many many years back he did have a thing for Angharad there. I mean, we're going back some time now, over thirty years."

"Oh, how charming. A tragic love story," Louisa sighed.

"Something like that." Gwyn looked amused. "The pair had eventually got together and were all set for marrying one another when along comes this chap Elijah from mid Wales and settles in the farm at the top of the valley. This Elijah was something of a handsome man in his youth and Angharad was smitten from the moment she set eyes on him. The wedding between Tomos and Angharad was called off, families were set against each other and within a year Angharad had married Elijah and a son was on the way."

"Thwarted love!" exclaimed Cathy, usually so quiet but now animated. "How romantic."

"Not for old Tomos it bloody wasn't," Gwyn said. "He's still pretty bitter about the whole thing and won't talk about it. Not that he talks about much, but still…"

"So sad," I said, pushing what few chips Gwyn had left me around my plate. My perfectly manicured fingernails glinted in the lamp on the table. They really were beautiful. I spread them on the table top in front of me, just in case Gwyn looked down and paid attention to something other than what was on my dinner plate.

The evening wore on, and in proper hen weekend style we managed to keep Louisa out of the black mood that was on the horizon. Many gin and tonics later she was back to her normal vivacious self. And it hadn't taken long before she'd toned down the manic flirting with Gwyn as she realised she wasn't getting anywhere with him. He remained as friendly as ever but didn't actually go so far as to flirt back at her, or indeed with anyone else, so it looked as though she had resigned herself to a good night out with mates rather than going on a mission to bed the farmer. For tonight at least. I was relieved she'd stopped her manhunt for the time being, not just because I would have been not a little jealous, but also because it would have put a real damper on the evening. She was the glue that bound us; an evening without her would seem very odd – just a collection of people thrown together for no particular reason. It was all very well knowing Laura already but I wouldn't choose to hang out with her. And Henna was good fun but watching her pick her face all night was definitely one of the contributing factors to me not eating much of my dinner. And Cathy – it was obviously a bad weekend for Cathy. Perhaps ordinarily she would be quite a laugh but right now she seemed rather wet. We were an odd bunch really. Louisa certainly didn't pick her friends according to a strict set of criteria.

As the gin and tonics flowed Louisa became quite the entertainer, regaling us with tales from the Absorb-

O department where apparently James had turned round the fortune of the brand by applying the same marketing device that cosmetics companies were using. He was single-handedly responsible for the limited edition Absorb-O prints. They were so well received that an artist had even made a roll into a piece of artwork that had been installed in the Tate Modern for a season.

"So, like, what sort of prints are they?" Henna asked, dabbing a weeping spot with a napkin.

"At Christmas he did a cracker-joke roll with jokes printed on it. And there was even a Hitler roll with his face printed on every sheet. That was enormously controversial, but it sold like you would not believe."

"Oh my God, I heard about that. It was all over the news," I said.

Louisa nodded, smiling. "Actually I think that was going a bit too far, but that's just me. His latest one is a Valentine's Day print that's being sold through those high-street sex shops."

Cathy's eyes were as wide as saucers.

"Do they have hearts printed on them or something?" Laura asked, lining up her empty Guinness pints on the table.

"Not exactly." Louisa looked uncomfortable but knew she wasn't going to get away with not saying any more. "Remember those *Joy of Sex* books?"

"With the bearded man?"

She nodded. "He got access to the pictures."

"Oh that's just brilliant!" Henna clapped her hands together. "Inspired!"

"God help us if he gets promoted to the toothpaste division," I said. "What's he going to do to them? *Joy of Sex* toothpaste?"

I'd gone too far. The others groaned and Gwyn looked at me half-shocked. I could feel myself turning bright red. Damn Welsh beer, it was strong stuff.

Fortunately Angharad shouted in Welsh from the bar, adding "Drinking up time!" for the benefit of the English speakers.

"Come on then, girls." Gwyn rose to his feet. We'd all finished our drinks a while ago and no one had bothered to go to the bar to get more. "I'll walk you home. Don't want you mauled to death by a kitten or anything."

"That's not funny actually," Cathy said quietly. "You said yourself you think there's a big cat out there."

"Ah, don't worry. Think about it, why would it want to attack a group of people? No point. But I'll walk you home all the same."

"And who will walk you home afterwards?" Louisa grinned and linked her arm in his. "You'll have to stay the night."

Gwyn laughed and patted her hand.

In a flurry of commotion we piled out of the pub and reassembled on the road outside. I drew my arms around me; it was surprisingly chilly and the wind had picked up, whistling down the road and shaking the trees. And it was super-dark again. I peered into the black woods straight ahead, imagining eyes staring out at me. What if it was just there, watching us?

"Rach?" Laura slapped my shoulder.

"Fucking hell, Laura!"

"OK, OK! Calm down. Come on, let's go."

We made slow progress down the black lane to the Hen House. Mostly because Gwyn was impeded having Louisa clinging on one side, Henna on the other and

Louisa employing various tactics to peel Henna off and have him all to herself. Laura, Cathy and I brought up the rear, concentrating hard on Gwyn's rear rather than looking about us and shining our torches into the dense blackness that loomed on either side. We preferred not to know what was there.

Nobody said much. Every so often Louisa would shout, "Henna!" when Henna tried to get Gwyn all to herself and Henna would say, "What?" but apart from that everyone listened to the creaks and cracks and flutters from the black woods. It was hard to navigate the pot holes in the road and as before every few steps one of us would wobble into one in our inappropriate footwear and be tugged back by the others.

Finally we were back at the Hen House. The lights were on downstairs just as we'd left them, making it look even more inviting; a sanctuary away from the danger outside.

"There you go then, girls." Gwyn stood back as we walked inside, glad to be out of the escalating gale that was whipping round us.

"You are coming in, aren't you?" Louisa looked mortified, smoothing her hair down as best she could and yanking her top up unceremoniously.

"I don't think so, sorry. I'll be up at five and need to get some sleep."

"Yes but…"

"It was nice to see you all again." He nodded at us and made to walk away.

"Wait!" I ran into the hallway and grabbed the poker. "Take this. Just in case." I ran out onto the driveway and put it in his hand. He took it and briefly he put his hand on my arm.

"Thanks. I'll bring it back."

"OK." I stood rooted to the spot. He touched my arm!

"Well, you ought to go in…" He smiled.

"Oh yes. Of course." I bounded in to the hallway where all the girls were watching. "Night, then."

He waved and walked into the night again.

"You were a bit forward there, Rach," Louisa muttered. Laura wagged a mock-accusing finger at me behind Louisa's back.

17

$\mathcal{A}$ gale was blowing. The wind had been picking up when we came back from the pub but an hour or so later when we headed off to bed it worsened, howling round the house and crashing into the woods making one hell of a din.

Was this normal? For the second time that weekend I lay in bed clutching the duvet, terrified. I had half a mind to go run upstairs and ask Laura whether it often gets this windy out in the middle of nowhere or whether this was really serious weather. But then she'd just think I was a pathetic townie and really, what good would it do me to know whether this was normal or not? It wouldn't make the slightest difference.

On its own the gale wouldn't have worried me, but combined with the possibility of a big cat stalking around outside it terrified me. Now the howling gusts and violent cracking of branches, along with the creaks and groans of the old house, took on a more ominous tone. Maybe that howl wasn't the wind at all but a baying big cat? Maybe that rattle of the door was someone trying to get in? Maybe that crunching of gravel was the cat prowling around outside?

My heart stopped.

Crunching of gravel?

I listened, every muscle tense.

Crunch, crunch, crunch. Outside my window, by the front door.

The wind wouldn't do that! The wind couldn't crunch gravel, could it? No! It might blow it along a bit but not make it crunch in the measured steps I could hear. Oh my God. The cat was outside the house.

Outside my window!

That Discomania! man had caused my impending death. Thanks to him I was the last to arrive at the house and now I had this poky room right by the front door where the cat was prowling and no doubt preparing to hurl itself at the window to get in. Could an old leaded window sustain a body blow from a blood-hungry big cat?

As I lay there in the dark I could picture a pack of slavering leopards hurtling through the woods towards the house, fangs bared and claws at the ready. Pounding towards me...

And there it was again, crunching on the gravel. Without a doubt something was prowling outside between the front door and my room.

ACT LIKE A HUMAN! I scrambled up in bed and whacked on the table light scattering everything on the floor.

I froze, listening. Surely it can't be Gwyn wandering outside again?

There was a scratching sound at the window.

I screamed. Fighting with the bed sheet, I fell on to the floor, picked myself up and pelted out of the room. I tore through the pantry, sending boxes of cereal flying. I pushed past the narrow shelves and emerged into the kitchen running to the hallway. When I got there I saw Laura, Henna and Cathy hurtling down the stairs looking equally frenzied.

"Did you hear it too?" I shrieked, coming to a halt on the stairs.

"We're going to die," squealed Henna. "Tonight. That's it. We're doomed!"

"It's outside," I wailed. "It was right by my window. Right there. Oh my God. Do you think it can smell us?" I saw a movement in the corner of my eye and turning my head I looked up the staircase. My mouth opened involuntarily. "Oh … my … God …"

Everyone stared at me and then, fearing the worst, slowly turned to follow my line of sight. En masse we saw Louisa slowly descending step by step. Hair curled and set, full make-up on she sauntered down towards us, dressed in a tiny black negligee, tinier black pants and a pair of feather trimmed kitten heel slippers.

"Do you think its Gwyn outside?" she asked, wide eyed with an innocent expression as though she really had been fast asleep looking like that.

"Oh thank God, it's Gwyn!" Laura's expression, that had up to that point been somewhere between petrified and more petrified, relaxed. "I knew he'd be back." She put her hand on her chest and breathed deeply.

"It's not Gwyn," I said slowly. "It's definitely not Gwyn out there."

"Is it just the wind?" Henna volunteered with a shaky

voice, holding on to the banisters for support.

"Well, there's that as well but – listen!" Cathy stuck her hand up for silence and we all froze, ears straining to hear the noise again.

It was distorted by the gale but it was there, right outside where we were standing. Something was scratching at the front door.

And then there was a howl.

Henna was visibly shaking.

Louisa was frowning. "It sounds like Caaa-eee," she said. "Do big cats make that noise? Is that a call? Laura, you must know. Is it a cat? Are we going to die?"

"How do I know?" Laura flung her hands up. "Shit, no one has ever prepared me for a cat attack. We don't do that in the army. I don't know what to do! I don't have anything on me! Shit!" She looked around for a weapon.

Henna held her hands up to her face and wailed, "Oh my God, we're going to die. We're going to die. WE ARE GOING TO DIE!"

"Shut up Henna!" Louisa shook her but Henna wouldn't be stopped. "Should we call the police? Should we do something? Are the doors all locked? Did anyone check the cellar door? Is the cellar door locked?"

There was an ominous silence. The wind howled round the house and there was another "Caaa-eee" wail. We stood motionless on the staircase. No one breathed.

"What cellar door?" said Cathy slowly.

My heart, which up to this point had been pounding away in my chest, now leapt into my throat. Was there a cellar door?

"The cellar door," Henna said hoarsely, "at the back of the house!"

Everyone was looking blankly at one another all

thinking the same thing: *We have a cellar door?*

"I didn't know there was a cellar door!" wailed Louisa in a small voice.

The noise came again. Closer. Nobody moved. I felt tears prickle behind my eyes I was so scared. This was it. There was a cellar door and it was open. We were going to be torn in two. Every one of us five girls, torn in two where we stood huddled against the banisters in our night wear. Ten bloody pieces of girl and a pair of black kitten heels – that's all they'd find when the police came round in the morning. I haven't even made my will. Who would get my Ikea furniture?

Henna had started to cry. "You gave Gwyn the poker," she sobbed, pointing an accusing finger at me. "That's all we had to defend ourselves with and you gave it away!"

"We should call the vet!" I said. "I could press redial on the phone and get Gwyn's vet from last night. He'd know what to do."

"Oh!" Cathy exclaimed. She'd been standing at the top of the staircase up to this point, but now she suddenly threw herself down the stairs, two at a time, heading straight for the front door.

"Cathy!"

She ran across the hallway. She was at the front door.

"What?" Laura made a move to stop her, but it was too late.

"Cathy, NO!" Henna screamed.

Already the bolts were being driven back and the huge iron key inserted in the lock.

Surely she wasn't going to open the front door?

She opened the front door.

"NO!" we all screamed, scrambling up the stairs.

Cathy ran out into the night.

The wind rushed in and up the stairs. Louisa's negligee flew upwards. She gripped it down around her thighs. "Jesus Christ! Someone shut the fucking door."

It was banging on its hinges in the gale, groaning.

I looked at Henna. Laura looked at Louisa. Henna looked at me.

Laura was the first to move, her TA training finally kicking in. Leaping down the stairs she ran out into the night after Cathy.

"Laura! Oh Fuck!" Louisa sank onto the stairs, her head in her hands.

Henna and I looked at each other, wondering whether we ought to go out after Laura. But then neither of us was that stupid. We wouldn't willingly let ourselves be the equivalent of a walking can of Whiskas.

The three of us that remained stayed where we were, not uttering a word between us, staring at the black night through the wide-open doorway below.

It seemed like an eternity, but suddenly Laura emerged from the gloom, clinging on to the doorframe, red-faced and panting.

"It's OK," she managed, gasping for breath, "it's OK."

"Oh thank God." I managed to let go of the banister. My fingers ached with the force of gripping the handrail.

"What...?" Louisa began.

"It's not a cat," Laura panted.

"Oh thank God." Henna slumped onto the stairs and started crying again. "I thought we were going to get eaten. I really thought that was it."

"What is it then?" I came down into the hallway now that the coast was clear.

"It turns," Laura gasped, "it turns out ... its Cathy's

fiancé. He's come to see her."

Oh.

I sat down on the stair.

Oh.

It all made sense now.

The crunching of gravel, the scratches at the front door. And of course! The howling. It was her fiancé! "Caa-eeeee" was "Cathy".

Henna was still sitting on the top stair crying, but now out of relief. Laura climbed the staircase and came to a stop at Henna's step. She sank down and put her arm round her. "Come on." She pulled her to her. "You're safe, you know."

"I know." Henna's voice was small and wobbly. "It's still fucking scary though."

"Hi guys!" We all looked down to the front door. Cathy was standing in the doorway, a-glow with an enormous Cheshire-cat smile on her face.

No one said anything.

"I guess I owe everyone an apology," she beamed.

"No, let me!" A short blonde man strode in from behind her. He was prematurely balding with small mole-like eyes and ruddy jowls. He had the look of a man that rarely turned down the offer of a pudding. Cathy was engaged to him?

He stepped forward and holding Cathy's hand in his own announced, "Laura has just been telling me what's going on with this wild cat thing and I just can't tell you how sorry I am that I might have scared you all."

"Fucking try, arsehole," Henna muttered, blowing her nose into Laura's handkerchief before handing it back to her. Laura tried not to look too disgusted.

"Heath and I ... well, we've been through a rough

patch." Cathy was still standing in the doorway, looking at her jowly fiancé lovingly.

Heath put his hands on her shoulders. "And I decided to come up and see her. I didn't know what to do when I got here though. Her phone was off and, well, it was dark and I wasn't completely sure I'd got the right place. So I was trying to tap at the door quietly." He looked at us all, unashamedly amused at his having scared the shit out of us. His appearance changed, ever so briefly, as his eyes rested on Louisa and her windswept negligee, but then he politely turned his eyes away, only glancing in her direction a few times more.

"So you tapped on the window quietly so that you wouldn't disturb anyone?" I asked.

"I'm sorry. I, well, I didn't know about this wild cat rumour."

"Big cat," Laura cut in.

Cathy seemed oblivious to the mood of the house. Still smiling and fawning over her porky fiancé, she nudged him forward, whispering in his ear.

Turning back to us she announced, "I'm sorry guys, but I've made the decision that I'm going to go home with Heath. Is that OK?"

"Fine by me," Louisa said.

The rest of us nodded, mutely.

"Good luck with the rest of the weekend," she said, arms around Heath. "And I hope that cat thing works out OK. Come on, Heath, help me pack my stuff."

And with that they walked upstairs, Heath slowing to ogle Louisa who was now trying desperately to hide her breasts.

"Do you think there are any other men out there?" I stood up, still shaky, "because I don't think I can take another night of terror."

"I don't know." Louisa rose up. "It's OK when they turn out to be fit farmers, but overweight jilted lovers? No thank you. Anyway, I'm going to get a dressing gown."

"Whiskey!" Henna emerged from her hunched position. "We need whiskey. Now."

Laura and I followed Henna into the lounge. I was angry and tired and spent. I needed a drink like Marcia needed an audience. Louisa came down, wrapped up and make-up free and together we sat and stared into the fireless grate and drank our whiskeys in virtual silence.

Half an hour after they'd gone upstairs, Cathy and Heath wandered in to the lounge red-faced and tousle-haired.

"I think we've packed everything," Cathy said sheepishly to us, "so we'll be off."

"Yeah, bye then," said Louisa, not taking her eyes off the empty fireplace. "You take care now."

"I'm really sorry…"

"Sure. Just go."

"OK. And bye Laura, Rach, Henna. It's been nice to meet you. See you at the wedding."

Within a few moments we could just make out the noise of a car starting up and we heard it drive off into the windy night.

"I don't care what just happened upstairs in her bedroom," I declared. "I am definitely having that room. There is no way I am spending another night sleeping downstairs on my own. I don't care if George Clooney comes knocking later on, I'm going upstairs." And with that I walked back into my old room, threw my belongings into my bags, hoisted all six of them up onto my shoulders and staggered up the staircase to Cathy's old room. I unpacked in the comfort and space of a proper bedroom. A bedroom with a double bed, a wardrobe, a chest of drawers and a chair. With space in between to walk. Luxury. I threw on new sheets I found in a cupboard and collapsed into bed. No hungry cats, no dishy farmers and definitely no heartbroken fiancés were going to keep me awake another hour.

18

It would be fair to say that, come breakfast the next morning, I was feeling pretty jittery. I was feeling as though I had actually come face to face with a big cat. The terror of the midnight prowlers and the drama of the TV reports combined with the cold facts from the big cat leaflets had merged in my mind to become one. I felt as though there really was a big cat out there, and I had actually seen it.

In fact all that had happened, as I tried to force myself to remember, was that we had seen someone who had been told by someone that one of his animals may have been attacked by a big cat. And that we'd read the leaflets in the pub that neither confirmed nor denied that there could be big cats out there. And we'd seen the TV report which may or may not have featured a big cat. So really, no one even knew if there was actually one out there. I tried to take my mind off it by focusing on Gwyn, stripped to the waist, hoisting rafters in the hot summer sun. But it was no good. I couldn't shake the feeling that I'd seen a big cat and the three other remaining hen weekenders, it turned out, felt much the same way. We were well and truly spooked.

In this spirit Laura called the stables to ask whether our planned day of horse riding should be cancelled for fear of us being mauled to death on a bridle path. While she went off and made the phone call Louisa, Henna and I sat round the table eating our breakfast in silence broken only by, "Can you pass the butter?" or "More tea?" Our interrupted nights were getting the better of us. I was rather enjoying it though; it was a good alternative to my usual routine. Being so sensible and Dull Life Crisisy, I tended to go to bed at a reasonable time, especially if it was a work night. But I don't think I'd ever felt quite so alive as I was feeling this morning. I was completely alert and awake – perhaps I'd been getting too much sleep before and I was permanently stupefied with rest? Or maybe this new feeling of being super-alert and alive was just the result of breaking out of my weekly grind of work work work work work shop shop.

Perhaps I wasn't entering my "pipe and slippers" years quite yet.

"Pass the marmalade," Henna asked me. "Cheers." She spread a thick layer on her toast and took a bite. "Hey, I don't suppose either of you have ever read that Agatha Christie novel *And Then There Were None*?"

"No."

"I don't think so."

"Well, there's this group of tourists who are stranded in a remote hotel and end up getting picked off one by one. And here we are with Cathy gone – who's going to be next?"

"Louisa," I said, lining my crusts up on the plate.

"Thanks for that, Rach!"

"I mean you'll be camped out at Gwyn's."

"Oh. Right. I thought you meant…"

"It's still on!" Laura strode in from the hallway. "The owner of the stables says there's no danger whatsoever. Same as at the pub, the word is the big cat scare is a hoax and they've had it loads of times before. And anyway, a cat isn't going to attack a group of horses out on a trek. Everyone OK with that?"

She had a brittle way about her this morning, the sort of brittleness that comes with farmers and jilted lovers and exotic animals threatening to ruin your hard-worked plans. She stood, legs astride, arms crossed. Like a terminator, she slowly looked at us each in turn, waiting for one of us to crack. She was, at least at that moment, scarier than the prospect of actually being ragged by a big cat. So one by one we all nodded and went on chewing our toast, caught up in our own reveries.

My thoughts now wandered away from the subject of Gwyn and his lovely broad shoulders and on to the much less pleasant subject of horse riding. In all the noise and activity of the last couple of days, I'd almost managed to forget the fact that I would be going horse riding, but now it was looming all the old fears came flooding back to me.

Basically, I couldn't ride.

Well, that wasn't actually true because I didn't know that I couldn't ride on account of never actually having ridden a horse before, but there was every chance that I would be entirely crap at horse riding.

I was not an animal lover, and having grown up in a

city and considered suburbia to be "the great outdoors", I hadn't been one of those country-raised horsey-girls like Laura that has rosettes pinned to walls and pictures of themselves hard-hatted cradling the head of some enormous stallion they'd just jumped over random fences with. The only times I had ever been near a horse was at the Notting Hill Carnival three years ago when the police were manipulating enormous beasts through the crowds. I was standing near to one when it decided to have a wee – and my God they can clear a space when they need to go.

Horses terrified me. They were so big. They could wee for Britain. Their muscles showed through their skin. They could kill me with a light flick of a hoof. Or I could fall off it and be killed, or trampled underfoot and killed, thrown from it, bitten by it, crushed by it. There were, now I came to think about it as I sat and chewed my toast, whole ranges of diverse and remarkable ways my life could be ended when I came in contact with a horse. That meant that they were, therefore, more of a threat to my personal safety than the big cat and even more of a threat than Laura.

Still, I didn't say anything to the others because:

a)   Laura had resumed her seat opposite me and was very close to the bread knife. There was no doubt in my mind that she would kill me for jeopardising her plans if I tried to get out of riding.

b)   I would look like a complete loser in front of everyone. All the others had ridden before and were talking horse-talk now around the table.

c)   I might well surprise myself and actually be very good. I mean, I had ridden a donkey once on a beach in Wales. Apparently it was a long ride and I had been right at home on the back of the animal, although I was five and my mother had held my hand pretty much constantly. Still – I might be a natural.

    d)   It wasn't as if we were going show jumping over white fences and prancing sideways around arenas. We were going trekking in the countryside. That implied slowness and safety. It would be fine. ...

    e)   I would be able to look Marcia in the eye and say, for once, YES! Yes Marcia! I, Rachel Young, have ridden a horse. I have done that life-threatening activity. Yes, I have been at one with nature, or whatever bollocks she was spouting about horse riding. I would be able to tick one experience off my list. Providing I still had full use of my hands, that is...

We got to the stables and I don't think I remember ever having sweated so much in my very precious and soon-to-be-ended life. I could feel the sweat running down my back, down my chest, down my stomach and even behind my knees. How could a person sweat so much? Was it dangerous?

    We headed for the stable buildings and when I peered inside my heart actually stopped beating.

    The horses were huge!

    Was this right? Had they bred freak giant-horses for the Welsh hills? Five big hot whinnying beasts were thumping their hooves on the ground and snorting. The other three seemed oblivious to the peril they were in and milled around the front end of the animals, patting noses and stroking necks while I stood back, into a lump of horse shit. Laura was in her element, examining all the horses and clambering up on them almost straight away, patting and stroking them.

Within a very, very short space of time the girls had begun to choose their horses and mount them, while I remained where I was standing, watching in horror. And horse shit. I desperately tried to look on the bright side. It didn't look too hard. You just fling a leg over and pull the reigns a bit. Easy.

They trotted off getting used to the steering and there was just me left. Me and an enormous brown animal called Beelzebub or something. I didn't quite catch the name as the sweat had pooled in my ears and made me temporarily deaf.

"I can't ride," I squeaked in a very tiny voice to the owner of the stables who was so horsey she looked and smelt like one. Even her frizzy hair resembled a mane.

"Pardon?" she bellowed at me. She was waiting for me to climb on board but now looked at me like I was mad.

"I can't ride."

She stared at me with the same expression of surprise that she would have shown if I was a parsnip that had just started a song and dance routine on her kitchen table.

"Have you ever ridden before?"

"Well, no." More sweating. I would slip off a horse if this carried on.

"Come on Rach," Laura shouted from outside, perched on some gigantic white snorty thing that she'd just taken round the yard, "we should have started five minutes ago!" More watch-tapping. If there was one thing I would remember about this weekend it was the sight of Laura tapping her watch at me, hurrying me up. Well, that and Gwyn. Gwyn…

I snapped back to the present. What should I do?

Stop sweating would be a really good start.

I shot Laura a nervous smile and looked imploringly at

the horsey-woman. 'Please have mercy on me,' I projected at her. 'Please spare me the shame of being so scared.'

Beelzebub snorted and pawed the ground, no doubt calling for its demonic master below.

"You could have Old Ned I suppose," horsey-woman said finally, patting Beelzebub like he was a kitten.

Old? That sounded good. "Is he a horse?" I asked, dry-mouthed. Maybe he was just a large dog that I could ride.

"Yes of course he's a horse," she barked, "but he's a Shire horse breed. Slow as you like."

"Oh that sounds good," I gushed.

"How tall are you?"

"Five eleven."

"Well, you're tall enough. Syllabub here would have been a better fit for you but he'd be no good if you can't ride".

Syllabub! Now that wasn't quite so bad. He didn't seem so demonic now, but still – he looked like a flighty sort of beast, Syllabub or not.

"What's up Rach?" Louisa had steered her horse over to where we were talking. Once again I mentally implored the horsey-woman to spare my shame and she must have caught the vibes I was shooting in her direction and felt pity on me.

"She's too tall for this horse. I'll have to bring another one out. Won't be a minute."

She headed off, but not before she shot me a look that said "you'd better tip me well, young lady" and I was already mentally rifling through the notes in my wallet preparing to gladly hand over every precious one of them to her.

Louisa went to join the others and explain what was

happening and I, buoyed up with my lucky break, looked over at them and gave an exaggerated shrug as much to say "Honestly, I wish we could just get on the road and go."

Within a couple of minutes horsey-woman had returned with Old Ned. He certainly looked like a quieter and slower animal than Syllabub, but oh my goodness me he was a whole lot larger.

"He's bigger!" I yelped but horsey-woman clearly wasn't having any more of me and grabbing my arm in a pincer-like grip, she frogmarched me over to steps along a wall to mount the beast.

"He's a bigger breed, but he's slow and steady. You're perfectly safe on him. Now get on!"

Biting my tongue so I couldn't argue that he might be slower but there was now much further to fall, I trembled my way up the steps to prepare to mount him.

I kicked him several times getting on and he didn't flinch, bless him. He just stood there staring into space. He certainly didn't look fast or flighty.

Once I was safely on with my feet in the metal hoop things, horsey-woman patted Old Ned's bottom and he headed out into the bright sunshine, following the others who were starting to make their way out of the stable yard. We were on our way!

After about ten minutes of reign-gripping, teeth-clenching sweating, I began to relax a bit. I loosened my grip on the reigns and gradually the blood came back to my hands. I dropped my tense shoulders and relaxed my jaw, sitting back a little in the saddle now I was more confident that I'd actually stay on the animal and not slide off when he cornered. I took a deep breath. Then another. I could do this. I could enjoy it, savour it. Horse riding was fun, it was freedom, it was all about being totally at one with nature. Isn't that what Marcia had gone on about? Here I was, me and nature, as close as bosom pals, on top of Old Ned who plodded steadily along the muddy bridle path ascending the valley and up into the beautiful August sunshine. I could get used to this, I reflected, ducking too late and suffering a low hanging branch slap me across the face. I sat upright again and fixed a smile on my face. I would enjoy horse riding. Even if it was retrospectively, some years from now and from the comfort of a deep armchair. It was possible. Although how the bloody hell Angela and Marcia could make a week long holiday of it I don't know. Didn't they get bored? My heart sank a little as I thought of my friend holidaying with Marcia. Was all lost? Would I ever have the courage to face Marcia again and put her in her rightful place? Could I possibly out-manicure her with these nails?

Old Ned seemed a very nice sort of horse and was quite content to follow the others without any involvement on my part, although he couldn't keep up and we soon lagged behind. It wasn't too much of a problem, however, because Henna's horse, who I was following, kept crapping every few steps and I didn't want to get too close a view of its rear end in action. Nevertheless, I did start to get a bit concerned that it would just be me and Old Ned lost in the wilderness, as the others were now getting really quite far ahead. But Old Ned seemed to know where he was going, and it wasn't like there was much choice of direction – the path was bordered on both sides by thick hedge. Anyway, it was nice to have a bit of space away from the others and I even became bold enough to tentatively stroke Old Ned's neck and whisper nice things to him about carrots and grass.

We climbed up and up onto the heather-covered hills, leaving the woodland behind us in the valley floor. Big brown birds were circling above and every so often a rabbit would scurry into the undergrowth. I was at one with nature! We'd just passed a stream and Old Ned had paused for a drink when I heard a loud bang come from down in the valley. The birds swooped and vanished into the distance, but fortunately Old Ned carried on, plodding ever onwards, unflinchingly. What was it? Did farmers carry guns these days? Were there poachers about? Whatever it was it was miles away; the noise had been a tiny pop really. Maybe it was a kid with an air rifle shooting cans off a log or something wholesome like that.

Half an hour after we started I was completely on my own but almost happily so, pottering along and thinking about Gwyn and his Welsh loveliness. I heard a thundering noise and looking up saw horsey-woman pelting back to where Old Ned and I were moseying along, admiring the view. She deftly pulled up and turned the horse, all in one smooth action. "The others are champing at the bit. They want to pick up the pace. Ned's not up to it so if you don't mind we'll take off and you can catch us up at the lunch stop." She then pointed out the route, explained that Old Ned would follow it anyway as he had been doing for nearly two decades, and gave me some tips on steering. If either of us got into trouble, "Which Will Not Happen," she said sternly, catching me looking terrified, I should stay by the horse and she'd come back for me.

And then she was gone. I tried to relax again and really embrace the experience, but I couldn't say that it came at all easy to me. The whole horse riding thing seemed completely forced and unnatural. After all, Old Ned would much rather be eating grass in a field somewhere, and I would much rather be walking on my own and the others would much rather I wasn't there. Really, no one was happy. My plan to disguise my horse-riding-less past had somewhat fallen flat, but at least they could go at their own pace now without going slow for me.

Old Ned and I had reached the head of the valley now and as horsey-woman had predicted Old Ned was on auto-pilot, taking the broad track that descended into the woodland. I looked back at the valley and all of a sudden I saw something out of the corner of my eye. It was over by the edge of the wood. I pulled the reigns and said, "Whooah," like I'd seen Laura do to her horse earlier but Old Ned carried on regardless. "Whoaah there." Still nothing. "WOAH UP A BIT NED!" I yelled and tugged hard at the reigns. He walked on. We passed a dense group of trees that blocked my view of the edge of the wood. "NED WILL YOU FUCKING STOP FUCKING WALKING FOR ONE GODDAMN MINUTE?"

Picking up his pace for the first time, Old Ned trotted on and the edge of the wood came back into view. I gripped his neck in a bid to stay on him now that he was bouncing so much. I had a chance to see the valley again. Holding his mane, I craned my neck to see something moving over in the near distance. It was the old farmer, Tomos, who I'd seen in the pub the night before. The man with the suspiciously wounded hand and arm. From this far away and bouncing violently up and down, it was hard to see him clearly, but it looked like he had a large bag slung across his chest. A large bag with bright red blood across it and across the front of his coat.

Thankfully he hadn't seen us as Ned and I had been pretty much camouflaged in the sparse woodland. Why was the old farmer sneaking around the valley covered in blood? Was it connected to the sound like a gunshot I'd heard?

"Hello there!"

HOLY FUCK.

I leaped off my seat and almost fell off Old Ned, who carried plodding on anyway. I looked down. It was Gwyn, standing on the path beside me, grinning.

"Hi," I managed, heart pounding from the shock and then pounding doubly for seeing the dishy farmer resplendent in faded old blue t-shirt and very short shorts. Those legs!

Now the pressure was really on to look like an accomplished horse-woman. I surreptitiously loosened my grip on Old Ned's neck and picked up the reigns again. He'd slowed right down again to a plod so I could at least try to get some of my composure back. I certainly think I looked the part, although as Gwyn was standing still and Old Ned was still walking on, I had to crane my neck further and further just to keep Gwyn in sight. I could hear his muffled laugh. "I'm sorry Gwyn, I just can't stop the thing," I yelled as Old Ned turned a corner into a dense bit of woodland and I was completely out of sight of Gwyn.

The farmer casually strolled over to us and laid a hand on Old Ned's neck. He stopped. Was that all it took?

"Out riding on your own?" he asked, smiling cheekily at me. Knowing full well that a pack of girls had just adeptly thundered through the valley before me.

"Well, I've never done it before," I said, giving him the honest answer and hoping for the sympathy vote.

"Really? You surprise me."

"Oh ha ha. Anyway, forget that – have you seen Tomos down at the edge of the wood?"

"Tomos? What, this wood?"

"Yes. He's just come out of it near the river. He had blood all over his coat and a big bloodied bag slung over his shoulder."

"Get down." He stretched his arms up to me and lifted me off the horse. For one wonderful moment I was in his big muscly arms and everything else dissolved into nothing. He put me down in front of him and we both looked at each other. I thought I saw in his face a look that mirrored how I felt, but it was quickly gone and taking the reigns he tethered Old Ned to a tree by some nice grass, which he dutifully began to eat.

"Where did you see Tomos, then?" Gwyn came back over to me.

I led him through the woodland to the edge, back the way I'd come. And sure enough, there was Tomos, much further away from us now, making his way along a thin track on the valley floor back in the direction of the village.

"Where do you think he's been?" I whispered as we crouched, wonderfully close to one another, watching the old farmer retreat. I glanced down at Gwyn's legs. They were tanned and solid-looking. So close…

"Goodness only knows," Gwyn interrupted me, his lovely lilting accent bringing me back to the present, "but there's only Elijah's farm nearby and Tomos wouldn't be paying a visit to his place, that's for sure."

"Elijah is the bloke who stole his fiancé Angharad all those years ago?"

"That's the one. So you were listening last night, then?"

"Of course! Why would Tomos be out here? Does he own land round here?"

"Just a strip or two. He owns the woodland here and up

the valley. But nothing that should give him any reason to be around these parts."

"I wonder why he's covered in blood?"

"It's trouble all right." Gwyn sank back on his heels and contemplated me for a moment. I felt myself blush. The temptation to lean across and kiss him was almost too much. Honestly – I was more brazen than Louisa.

"I want to see where Tomos has been," he mused, oblivious, thank God, to my staring lustily at him, "but there's no way of knowing. And even if we try to follow him along the open valley floor, which is nigh on impossible as it's so exposed, he'll probably just be returning home now."

"Maybe you should follow him another day," I said, feeling rather sad all of a sudden that I wouldn't be here "another day." I would be leaving tomorrow. The weekend had shot by so quickly and even if I was scared to bits I still wanted to know if there really were any big cats out there. And why the old farmer had a freshly scarred hand last night and was covered in blood this morning.

Christ, what was the time? I checked my watch. It was almost midday! I should be at the lunch stop by now. Laura would kill me.

"I'd better get going," I said, standing up reluctantly from my crouching position blissfully close to him. "The others will be expecting me and I'll just piss them off more if I hold them up any longer."

"Where are you meeting them?"

"Near the river. They're having a picnic at a place called Peddler's Well? Something like that."

"I know the spot. Shall I walk with you?"

"If you can keep up," I laughed, and he helped me up onto Old Ned. I desperately tried to be as light and agile as I could, and not push my arse in his face, but it was all pretty clumsy and awkward. I wished I'd written to *Jim'll Fix It* all those years ago and asked for horse riding lessons.

Taking the reigns in one hand he walked beside me through the woodland, talking about big cats and farms and pubs. Every so often I'd sneak a glance at him and once or twice I caught him doing the same to me. I'd forgotten how it felt to be head over heels about someone, which was a shame because it felt so very good.

19

The expressions on the girls' faces were absolutely priceless. When Old Ned and I emerged from the woodland with Gwyn at the reigns I wished I'd got my camera with me to capture the looks. I felt like a queen with her entourage – the only thing missing was the trumpet fanfare.

We descended from the woods and wound our way downwards towards the field where the girls had already set up picnic blankets and were tucking in to the food. I almost lost my cool and shouted out, "Look what I found in the woods!" but didn't – principally for fear of falling off Old Ned rather than not wanting to gloat that I'd picked up Gwyn. In the hare and the tortoise race, it certainly was the tortoise who won in the end.

We pulled up where the other horses were tethered and Gwyn chivalrously helped me down once more, and again there was a spark of something as my body slid against his.

I smiled bashfully and he did the same, busying himself with tying Old Ned up to a post. I bounded over to the picnickers, beaming.

Louisa, Henna and Laura were delighted to see Gwyn. The minute he came over to join us Louisa fussed around him, making sure he sat down to join in the picnic. Would he like a blini? Would he like some hummus? She managed to be all smiles and laughter to Gwyn, but shot me a dark look that said, "Back off – he's mine this weekend," which I chose to ignore by examining which sandwich I would start off with. Salmon, probably. There was no way I was going to stand my ground with Louisa over something that, sadly, I didn't think was going to happen to either of us. I could dream though, which is what I did during most of the picnic, glancing over at Gwyn from time to time as he lay on his side and accepted whatever delicate morsel Louisa offered him. At one point she turned her back to get the lemonade and he looked over at me, shot me a cheeky wink and then went back to "mmm-ing" and "ahh-ing" in agreement at her account of how difficult life was for a London estate agent operating at the high end of the market.

After that I couldn't stop grinning and once again my appetite completely failed me. At this rate I'd reach my ideal weight with no problem whatsoever. I'd lust my way to skinniness.

So avoiding the sandwiches and salads I lay back, propped on my elbows and gazed over at the fields to where a rather loud river rippled and splashed its way along the valley floor. We had been so lucky with the weather. It was wonderfully hot, with a fine heat haze rippling the grass ahead of us. Last night's gales had blown themselves out and a peaceful summer's day had been left in its wake.

The sound of droning insects buzzing around us made me think of my childhood – the odd day spent on a visit to the countryside with my parents, eating sticky ice creams and playing football. Was it really that long ago since I properly spent some time outside a city? Why hadn't I done this sooner? It was wonderful. I lay back on the soft grass and closed my eyes, content to sunbathe and listen in to the conversations that were going on around me. As much as I wanted to talk to Gwyn, there was no point even trying to distract his attention from Louisa. It would be suicide and besides, what I really wanted to talk to him about – Tomos and the bloodied bag – was between Gwyn and me and I didn't want to share it with the others. It was our secret.

A phone started ringing, cutting in to the steady drone of our picnic. It wouldn't be Cathy's this time.

"Those bloody things should be turned off!" barked the horsey-woman, who had been flicking through a newspaper, sitting on the edge of our group and minding her own business up to that point.

"It's James." Louisa hit call accept. "James! Well?" She walked away towards the river and out of earshot. The three of us girls watched her intently while Gwyn nonchalantly helped himself to a handful of sandwiches.

"First time she's spoken to him since last night?" he asked. I propped myself up on my elbows again to join in the conversation.

"Yup." Laura looked on as Louisa, arms now waving wildly in the air, shouted what was in all likelihood a stream of abuse down the phone.

"What do you think she's saying?" Henna squinted in concentration, trying to make out what Louisa was yelling.

"Well, I definitely heard the word 'arsehole' just now," I said, taking the last fondant fancy before Gwyn could have it. He frowned and went for the last cherry bakewell.

"Yeah. I heard that." Henna was still watching our friend. "And something about loose stags?"

"It was slags, loose slags."

"Oh yeah, right. That would make sense…"

"Shhh!" Laura put a finger to her lips. "She's coming back."

Sure enough Louisa, red faced and wild-haired, was walking over to us, mobile phone held in a white-knuckled grip at her side.

"Well?" Laura prompted when Louisa huffed down on the picnic rug.

"Well, he's lying." She lay down on the picnic rug and closed her eyes.

"Come on then." Henna was bobbing up and down. "What happened? Spill the beans."

Louisa sighed. "He says that they did go out last night, that they went to a local pub, the name of which he can't remember…"

"Ooooh, suspicious!" Henna burst in.

"And he says there were women there but they didn't have anything to do with them." She opened her eyes and propping herself up looked over at us. "And that's it."

"And you don't believe him?" Gwyn asked.

"No. No I bloody don't." She sank back on the picnic rug and closed her eyes. "I know that he will have been egged on by all his stupid mates to do something that he wouldn't usually do. I know James, obviously I do, and he would never be unfaithful to me. But some of his mates are real arseholes and I bet they were egging him on, and they'd be drinking and…"

She looked close to tears now and I shuffled over and threw an arm around her and gave her a hug. "Don't worry about it. Nothing will have happened, you'll see. Anyway, what are they up to today?"

"Hiking," she said, still miserable. "And I hope they bloody hike into a sodding ravine or get clawed to death by a pack of leopards or pumas or lions or whatever is supposed to be out there."

"Out here," I added, suddenly remembering.

"Or set upon by mad old farmers," joined in Gwyn with the briefest of glances at me.

"Or fall into a disused mine shaft," Laura offered.

"Or shot by anti-English farmers."

"Or stampeded by cows…" And so it went on, and the more horrific the hiking disaster the more Louisa perked up, convinced that there would be some sort of karma-like event looming for her fiancé. If he had got up to anything unsavoury last night, then some balancing peril was sure to befall him today.

Gwyn had tied some grasses together in the shape of a star and presented them to Louisa, which soon brought back the smiles, and before long she was back to her old self, talking to Gwyn and every so often touching his knee and giggling.

It was after nearly an hour of eating, drinking and sunbathing that horsey-woman folded up her paper and announced that we needed to head back on the last leg of our journey. I half expected Laura to whip out a pocket-sized gong and start hammering away to signal the start of the next phase of our schedule. I was already getting conditioned by her this weekend like Pavlov's Dogs, but instead of salivating I jumped to attention at the sound of a gong.

Louisa pleaded with Gwyn to join the group but he chivalrously declined – he had business up at the top of the valley so had to make a move. Before he left he came over to me and helped me fold the picnic blanket up, which was causing me enormous problems.

"You grab this corner and I'll take that," he directed, smiling as he effortlessly sorted it out for me. "How on earth do you cope on your own?"

"I don't," I admitted, my head suddenly filled with a montage of images of me stumbling round the bedroom inside a duvet cover, tangled up in sheets, tripping on pillow cases like a comedy ghost in a pantomime.

"What's up with your friend?" he said in a quiet voice as the others milled around nearby.

"Which one?" I asked. They all had their issues.

"The one with the blotchy face."

"Oh, Henna! It's her toxins. Apparently they're coming out."

"Oh, OK." He grimaced and went back to folding the rug while I marvelled at the muscles in his arms.

"So," I pulled myself together again, "what are you going to do about Tomos then? Have you reached a final decision?"

"Yep. I've decided that I am going to have to follow him. There's nothing for it. I want to know what the blood is all about."

"Goddamn it! I wish I was staying longer," I sighed. "I'd much rather be out here stalking the neighbours than going back to my sensible old office job. This is much more exciting."

"Need a bit of excitement, do you?" he said in his

174

lovely lilting accent, laughing as he fitted the blanket into a pack that Henna's horse was carrying.

"Something like that. Life's a bit, well, pedestrian I suppose."

"In what way?" He turned to look at me and I momentarily forgot what I was talking about, staring at his dark eyes under those thick brows…

"In what way?" he repeated.

"Oh. Well, you know, go to work and write some reports, come home and microwave a meal, go to the bar, go to the supermarket, hire out a film…"

"No boyfriend?"

"No boyfriend."

"That's a shame," he said, smiling again. I couldn't help but smile back and was about to attempt to say something witty when Laura sauntered over with the white snorty horse and told me to "saddle up" because we'd all be riding together over the rest of the path back to the stables. Laura tapped her watch and raised her eyebrows at me and it took all the self-restraint I could muster not to leap up and grab the watch off her wrist and throw it into the river.

"See you around then," I said to Gwyn as I inexpertly clambered up onto Old Ned again.

"I guess so," he said.

I fought the urge to grab him by his T-shirt and blurt out, "But when will I see you again? Are you going to the pub tonight? What are you doing tomorrow? You're so lovely!"

The ride back was nowhere near as peaceful and, well, enjoyable, as I realised my solitary ride there had been. This was due entirely to the fact that Laura, schedule timings at the forefront of her military mind, had taken it upon herself to ride behind me in the hope that by yelling out instructions every five minutes she could teach me to ride Old Ned like he was some steroid-crazed young racehorse.

"Kick his sides! Like this! Look!" She barked at me and demonstrated on her horse which lurched forward and was stopped only by Old Ned's enormous horsey arse blocking the path. I had a go at copying her but only managed a sort of body-wiggle that had no effect whatsoever on Old Ned and nearly unseated me.

"Look, Laura, I don't think my horse is programmed to do anything else except what he's doing." I craned my head back to look at her.

"Well, do this then." She did something with the reins and again her horse advanced. I tried on Old Ned and still no effect. On he plodded.

And then it happened.

Up ahead Louisa was leading the group.

She screamed.

It was a warbling, animal-like scream and everyone stopped – a few of the horses clearly startled. Old Ned, however, plodded on regardless and horsey-woman stuck out her hand to check his progress.

A man burst out from the heather to the right of us. He was dressed in camouflage gear and had a large matt-black gun held out in front of him. I felt my hands turn clammy, grasping the reigns tightly. Had we ridden so far we had reached the Middle East?

"It's OK." He dropped his weapon when he saw our startled faces. "PC Daniel Robinson, Rhondda Cynon Taff police. I'm a marksman." He came over to where we had stopped.

We stared at him dumbfounded. Laura looked

impressed.

What was a police marksman doing in the undergrowth? There was a second of silence before Henna's journalistic instinct started working and made the connection.

"Is it about the sightings of the big cat?" she piped up.

PC Daniel Robinson, marksman with Rhondda Cynon Taff police, nodded smartly. "Yes, miss. We're following up reported sightings," he said, choosing his words carefully. "Actually there are a few of us marksmen in the valley today, but I doubt whether you'll come across any of my colleagues, they're further down the valley floor."

"That's a pity," purred Louisa, smouldering on her horse and treating the policeman to a thousand-watt smile.

"Who's in charge here?" he asked, after being momentarily beguiled by my friend's flirting.

"I am," horsey-woman dextrously weaved her animal through the girls to the front.

"Well, I would get back to base and stay there. We've had further reports of sheep attacked by an animal and a horse was set upon earlier today," the policeman said.

Oh my God. The net was closing fast. I could feel the pant of the big cat behind me. Its eyes watching me from its lair in the undergrowth...

And then I remembered. The old farmer. The blood!

"Er, where was the horse attacked?" I called from the back.

"Over at the head of the valley." The policeman pointed in the direction of where Tomos had come from. "But you don't have to be unduly concerned. There's safety in numbers and you're not far from the village here." He paused for effect. "However, I would advise you to stay to main roads for the next few days and take extra precautions."

I wondered, should I mention the old farmer? After all, it was looking pretty damning that he was covered in blood and seen to be walking away from the scene of the crime at around the right time. But then, considering the build and age of the farmer, would he have the strength to attack a horse? And why? Why on earth would some doddery old farmer do such a thing? He wasn't mad. You couldn't be mad and run a farm. Could you? Maybe you could.

But then who was I to go blackening someone's character? I knew nothing. I'd only seen something I thought was a bit fishy, and besides, Gwyn was going to be following it up. Quite literally. For all I knew there was a perfectly reasonable explanation behind the old farmer's cuts on his arm and the fresh blood on his clothing this morning, and if there wasn't, well then Gwyn would get to the bottom of it. I'd drop in to his farm when I left tomorrow and let him know what the marksman had told us. Maybe I could leave him my number, purely so he could give me a call and tell me what he found out when he trailed Tomos on one of his outings.

Tomorrow. I was going home tomorrow.

Again there was that sinking feeling in the pit of my stomach. My one truly exciting weekend was coming to an end. And still there had been no sighting of the big cat. Never mind, sighting or no sighting, my weekend would beat hands-down whatever Marvellous Marcia would be doing with herself. She could be skydiving naked from a burning plane while juggling snakes and I'd still have had the most interesting weekend. But urgh, the prospect of plodding back in to work on Tuesday and normality closing in around me just like before filled me with a kind of cold horror.

Death by boredom.

"I'll accompany you back to the stables," the marksman was saying to the group when I emerged from my black thoughts, "if you don't mind. Better to be safe than sorry."

"It's OK." Louisa shot me a look. "We were only making slow progress anyway, so I doubt whether you walking with us is going to slow us down any more".

What was it with her? Did she still hold a grudge because I'd bumped into Gwyn in the woods? I shrugged it off – it was probably more to do with the fact that her fiancé might have been having it away with a rough valleys girl and she was just in a snappy mood. I hoped so anyway. I didn't fancy the prospect of losing another friend like I might be with Angela. Perhaps I ought to forget Gwyn altogether. Not even talk to him if we saw him again. Let Louisa work her charm on him…

We plodded on the same as before, with the policeman ahead of us and Louisa walking her horse alongside him whenever the path allowed it. The rest of us trailed behind slowly, Old Ned plodding along as fast as a snail on caffeine.

I kept shooting nervous looks into the undergrowth, convinced I'd see a big cat ready to lunge at me. The other girls must have had much the same thoughts as I had because when I looked at them I could see them looking around with renewed vigour. Were we really in that much danger?

By the time we'd arrived back at the stables it was early evening and we were all tired. Heads were hung low, shoulders were hunched and every so often one of us would let out a yawn that would set the rest of us off. The last hour had really dragged with everyone, myself included, wanting to go faster to get back to the Hen House and crash. There was nothing much to see on this side of the valley and most of it was in the shadow of the western hills so it was much cooler, especially as the afternoon gave way to early evening.

Louisa jumped off her horse, helped down by the police marksman who waved as he walked off back to the valley, his gun now raised ahead of him and ready for action. God forbid that any small domestic cat should shoot out in front of him now.

"Well," Louisa said, ruffling her hair after taking her helmet off, "we've got ourselves a party tonight!"

"What?" Laura looked momentarily horrified. Edition five of the rota clearly showed tonight was the Formal Dinner prepared by Henna and Laura, followed by the Women's Evening Hen Extravaganza, for which we'd all had to bring something. I'd done pass the parcel with an enormous vibrator-shaped chocolate wrapped up in layers of *Vogue* magazine. Both classy and tacky – the perfect hen night game.

"I was talking to Dan and he comes off work in a couple of hours. He was saying that the valley is full of single young policemen like him. They're coming round at eight. Woo-hoo!" She danced round her horse in delight. "Party, party, party!"

20

"**It's** fine Laura," Henna said, studying edition six of the Schedule & Rota, now barely more than a graffitied scrap of paper showing "PARTY!" as the activity for this evening.

We all stood round, drinking our vast goblets of wine.

"Maybe it is just a bit messy," I conceded.

Louisa nodded. "Yes, but it still does the job. Well done you!" She patted a sceptical Laura on the back. "I'll keep it forever. It will remind me how crazy this weekend was. Really, it's great."

"Hmm." Laura took a swig of wine and put the pen back in her tool belt.

"So how many policemen did you actually invite?" I asked Louisa.

"God knows. Enough for us all. Anyway, seeing as you're so pally pally with Gwyn, I task you with inviting him round tonight to my party."

"I'm not pally pally with him," I said, delighted that she thought so but not wanting to show it.

"Whatever, but remember that he's mine tonight. What time is it? Shit!" She bounded upstairs and Laura headed into the kitchen.

Henna watched them disappear and then putting her wine glass down whispered, "Help me with this, will you?" and grabbed the gong. Together we walked it to a hidden cupboard under a turn in the staircase. "I never want to hear this bloody gong again," she said as we heaved it into its hiding place.

"If she finds it she'll know it's you that hid it," I whispered.

"Yeah, well. No one will notice another bruise if she nuts me again, will they?"

She wandered off and I headed into the lounge on my own.

So: good news about me having the opportunity to invite Gwyn to the party. But how? There was no way I was going to drive now I'd had half a goblet of wine. And there was no way I was prepared to pay him a house-call and walk up the road on my own in the early evening. Not when police marksmen had been out and about hunting big game in the undergrowth.

All that was left was to phone him.

Presuming that he had a phone of course. Of course he did! He had a mobile because the first time I met him he told me he'd gone out without his mobile, and that was why he wanted to use our phone. But how would I get hold of his mobile number? Impossible. Surely it was easier to get his landline number? If he had one.

Was the village even on the national phone network?

And was there even one of those?

After digging around in an enormous old walnut bureau in the sitting room, I found a battered telephone directory – or *Y Llyfry Ffon* as it was in Welsh – and at that point I realised that I didn't know his surname. Had he told me that night at the Hen House? I think he had – it was Thomas or Jones or something. But I couldn't be sure. Stumped, I leafed through the directory.

HOW many Joneses? There were seven pages of them and it was no better with Thomases – six pages. And that wasn't including Tomoses and Tomases.

I would never find him.

I put *Y Llyfry Ffon* back in the cabinet and sat down on the sofa to think it through.

Ha! I could probably get his number from the local pub. Digging out the book again I managed to locate the Crossed Keys, Tretower, and feeling nervous for no good reason I dialled the number.

"Crossed Keys."

"Oh hi. Yes. Hi. It's Rachel here."

"Rachel?"

"Yes. From the Hen House. I mean *Ty Mawr*. Just down the road from the pub. You know…"

"I know." I could hear the smile as she spoke to me. It was Angharad, the barwoman, I recognised her voice.

There was a pause and I knew that it was now that I should ask her for Gwyn's number, but I was too embarrassed to do it. I sank back into the huge soft sofa and pulled my feet up. I felt like I was at school again and a page in my exercise book scrawled with "I love Matt Dickinson" had just been discovered by Matt Dickinson. This was ridiculous. Taking a deep breath, I tried to sound as matter of fact about the whole thing as I could. After all, I was thirty and had a career and an apartment and a car. I wasn't fifteen any more. I could do this. I would try to sound, in fact, as though I needed to get in touch with Gwyn on some very important farming issues and not because I fancied the arse off him and wanted to invite him to a party tonight.

"Yes, I was actually after Gwynfor's phone number."

"Oh were you now?" she laughed.

"Mmm, yes," I managed. Oh come on! I could do better than this. I knew all sorts of secrets about her, there was no reason why I should feel at all embarrassed about what I was asking. I knew all about Tomos and Elijah and broken engagements and family feuds. Why should I feel ashamed of her thinking I fancied a handsome farmer?

"You like him, then?"

"Pardon?"

"Gwynfor. Nice looking, isn't he?"

"Well, I suppose so. If you like that sort of thing. Anyway, I was just after his number because … because I think another one of his sheep beside the house might be wounded."

Ha ha! With lightening mental ability I had put myself on the moral high ground.

"I thought he'd moved all his sheep up by Tenter Field this morning?"

Shit.

"Well anyway, my love, I've got his number here if you want it. Do you have a pen?"

I grabbed a pencil and wrote down the number.

"Will we see you up at the Crossed Keys again before you all go home?"

"I'm not sure what we're doing." I idly scribbled hearts around Gwyn's number.

"Careful as you go. I'm not so sure that cat thing is a

hoax after all. I'd keep inside tonight if you can."

The tip of my pencil broke against the paper.

"Right. Well. Thanks for that."

As soon as she'd rung off, I punched in Gwyn's number. I was already wracked with shame so why wait until I calmed down? Better to immerse myself in it now and get it over and done with. Then I could look forward to seeing him tonight, perhaps with loose jeans on and a white shirt thrown over his rugged, sun-tanned, farmer's body…

There was no answer. Damn. And after hanging on for a good minute or two it appeared that there was no way to leave a message either. Hadn't he heard of answering machines? I put the phone down, images of the handsome farmer receding fast. I went up to her bedroom and broke the news to Louisa.

Hair in rollers and face-pack on, she was propped up on her vast bed flicking through a magazine. "Oh bloody hell, Rachel, how am I going to shag him if he isn't here?"

"Yes, I see your problem."

"Did you leave a message?"

"I couldn't."

"How many times have you tried?"

"Five." What a natural liar.

"Well, keep trying. He really is the absolute icing on the cake, you know."

"I know."

She looked up from her magazine briefly. "You're not carrying a torch for him?"

"Oh crikey no," I said, all wide-eyed surprise.

"Listen." She put her magazine down and shuffled across the bed towards me. It took a while as the bed was so incredibly large. "There are going to be lots of single young marksmen coming round tonight."

"With guns?"

"Probably without their guns. And you can have your pick, can't you? I mean, Henna's … well, she's got toxin issues. And Laura's an absolute love but she's not a patch on you. You'll be the belle of the ball. After me, that is. But of course, I'll be with Gwyn…"

"Really? I'll be the belle of the ball?"

"Of course you will!" She gave me a hug and a shoulder of clay face mask. "Ooh sorry hon, you've got some face mask on your shoulder now. Anyway, you should really have a bit more confidence in yourself you know. Go out there and get 'em."

I laughed. "Yes, but what if they're all complete muppets?"

"So?" She shrugged. "It's a hen do! Go for it!"

"I thought you were going to be focusing on your last weekend with girlfriends? I thought it was all about friendship and so on?" I smiled.

"It is! It's all about friendship. And sleeping with Gwyn. Hey, you haven't got any condoms on you, have you?"

"Lou!"

"OK, don't get all prudish. I'll ask Henna, she'll have some. Right, go and try Gwyn again. I have to peel this mask off. Jesus, I hope I don't end up as mutilated as Henna."

21

Even though none of us had an appetite, we all dutifully sat down and went through the motions of eating. Half way through, forcing ourselves to eat the pudding, Louisa's phone went. She checked the display. "It's James again," she said. The tension in the room was palpable. Which way would this phone call go? "Hi hon!" The breezy voice was switched on. "How are you doing? How was hiking?"

There was a period of "ooh yes" and "ooh right" while James must have rattled on about what they had been up to that day. Louisa was drumming her fingers on the table, waiting for the opportune moment.

"So what are you doing this evening?" She asked the question lightly enough, but all of us around the table tensed up immediately. Spoons were clutched that bit tighter. This was it – make or break. She would either come away from the phone call safe and secure in the knowledge that her husband-to-be was a thoroughly decent chap who didn't dabble in any nonsense with local girls. Or, she'd realise she had some catching up to do and there were a group of policemen on their way to the party tonight with absolutely no idea of what they were letting themselves in for.

What would James say – that they were taking another trip to the local pub? Going on to a club? Louisa carried on drumming her fingers on the table while she listened to him.

"Oh, you're staying in the bed and breakfast tonight?" She looked round the table at us and we all did a tentative thumbs up. "Yes, I suppose you must be tired. What are you going to do then? Oh yes? And the owner is OK with you bringing drinks in then, is he? Well, that's good, I suppose. Are there any other people joining you? No? Just the other stag weekenders. OK. Are there other people staying in the bed and breakfast while you're there? That's fortunate! Us? Oh we're just having a do here at the house. No, nothing fancy. Bit of a party, you know, get some music on, have a dance … No! No absolutely not!" She slapped her hand down on the table and Henna and I jumped. Was this the point that it all started to go wrong again? Was this when the shouting started?

'What?' mouthed Laura to Louisa, shrugging her shoulders. Louisa covered the mouthpiece and hissed, "James just suggested the boys come over tonight for the party!"

There was much frantic head-shaking around the table and horrified faces. No one wanted the boys over here. After what Louisa had told us about them and from the one or two that I'd met when I'd lived in London, they were a dodgy group of lads at the best of times – not helped by the fact that some of them went by the names of Dingo, Jerky, Spanner, Howie and Radder. I mean, what kind of idiots go by those nicknames after the age of twelve? Except gangster pop stars but even then...

Louisa was putting forward a very convincing argument on the phone, determined to have her evening free to bag a policeman or farmer. A fiancé turning up at the door would definitely scupper those plans. Egged on by Laura, who similarly wasn't overly keen on seeing any of the layabout lads take over her weekend, she started by telling James that we were going to be watching *Pretty Woman*, then play some CDs with titles like *All Woman* and *Classic Love Anthems* while we conducted a beauty session to swap make-up tips.

It worked. And to be honest, it would have worked on me too had I been told that was the evening's activities. I've never been one of those "I'll crimp your hair if you crimp mine" girls.

It was clear by Louisa's tone of voice that James had been convinced he shouldn't come and within a minute or so she gave us the thumbs-up and we were relieved that the party was still very much our party and the lads would not be coming over here and taking it over as lads are wont to do – commandeering the stereo and the drinks table – the very heart and soul of a good bash. Much better to have the women in charge and the men as "polite guests". Policemen would be much better behaved than the stag boys. Would they be in uniform?

"So the stag boys are staying in the bed and breakfast tonight then?" asked Henna when Louisa came off the phone.

"Yup. So they say, anyway," she added, warily.

"Do you think they've got other plans?" I asked,

spooning in great mouthfuls of gateau.

"No. I don't think so. Well, they might have but I believe James. Apparently there's a resident's lounge so they're going to sit in that, watch videos and drink. There aren't any other guests staying so they're not going to disturb anyone." She picked at her pudding, moving it around the bowl with her spoon without the least interest in eating it.

Laura watched her closely. "Louisa, you don't feel bad, do you?"

"Why should I feel bad?"

"For not inviting the boys over here for a party?"

Louisa sighed. "I guess so," she said eventually, "I don't know. You know? Maybe James didn't get up to anything last night, and maybe it was really terrible of me to think that he did. After all we are getting married in a few weeks and it's not as if he's that kind of a man. Maybe it's a bad idea inviting all those policemen over..."

Henna coughed pointedly. "Excuse me," she said, "but if you don't want them then there are plenty who do," and I seconded her by raising my spoon in solidarity.

"Honestly," said Laura, appalled, "it's like we've gone back to the Stone Age!"

"So some handsome policeman starts talking to you and you won't be at all interested?" Henna asked her.

"How do you know they're handsome?" Laura asked back.

"Urgh!" Louisa threw down her spoon. "Come on, girls. Let's stop talking and get ready."

"Except for Henna who is on washing-up duty," interrupted Laura briskly.

"I am what?"

"You can see the rota, can't you?"

"Yes, I can see your bloody rota. But surely you're not going to get me to do the washing-up right now?"

"I'm not going to get you to do anything. Hopefully you'll just do it."

"But there'll be lots of mess from the party. Why bother about a bit of washing-up now. We can do the lot tomorrow. Think of all the glasses…"

"Actually," added Louisa, "I don't think I want plates of old chicken in the kitchen at the party. It's a bit shoddy".

"It's so unfair," wailed Henna, getting up from the table and stacking the empty bowls noisily, "I need more time to get ready than any of you. Look at my toxins! They're disgusting. I need hours in front of a mirror to cover this lot up." Louisa just raised her eyebrows, unimpressed, and took the cutlery out to the kitchen.

I offered to help Henna with the washing because, really, she was quite right, the girl needed the most time to get herself ready. The spots had become even more horrific – more like weeping sores than regular red blemishes. The bruise from Laura had spread down to near her eyebrows and she really was looking quite awful. Poor Henna.

I did come to regret offering to help, though. Laura had decided to "busy herself" with something that involved being in the kitchen at the same time as Henna and I, and the two of them bickered like an old married couple.

"It's just completely un-bloody-fair," moaned Henna through gritted teeth as Laura walked out of the kitchen for a second. "No one is going to worry about dirty plates in the kitchen when there's a party. It's bloody stupid!"

"It won't take long." I took another plate from her and dried it up.

Henna scooped up a mass of cutlery and pushed them

into the sink. "Fuck!" she said as a knife fell on the floor blade first.

"More haste less speed." Laura reappeared and put some papers in a drawer and took some other papers out. "Henna, that plate you gave Rachel is still dirty."

"So what, Laura? We won't use it again so it's someone else's problem. Put it at the back of the cupboard, Rachel. No, not in the bowl, Laura – no I'm not bloody washing it up again. Laura! Come on! I want to have a shower and we've still got all that to do over there…"

"Whinging isn't going to get it done quicker, Henna."

"You just don't understand! Your face is smooth! Sod that stupid bloody mud treatment. I'm going to sue."

"Whatever you decide to do, Henna, that bowl still isn't clean."

"Oh for fuck's sake, give it here then!"

"Come on you two," I said, standing in between them in case crockery started to fly. "Laura, Henna really needs to have time to get ready. Can you clear away the table for us – that would save time? Come on, we've all got to pull together now Cathy's gone. Please?"

"It's not what it says on the rota," muttered Laura, crossing her arms, "but I suppose I can spare a minute from my filing."

Filing what??

Laura walked out of the kitchen, mumbling.

Henna gave me a soap-suddy high-five and attacked the plates with renewed vigour. "Thanks, Rach, you're a real pal. I think you'd make a much better organiser than Lieutenant Killjoy over there. And anyway, you're practically in charge of the weekend, aren't you?"

"Am I?"

"Yes! You sorted out the farmer for us, and you

kept your head better than any of us when Heath came calling."

"Thanks, Henna," I said, delighted to be praised, but a bit sad all the same, "but does it mean that I'm just a boring person who doesn't get hammered on a hen weekend?"

"No!" She slapped me on the back with a soapy hand. "Anyway, you got hammered as I remember. It was just earlier than the rest of us when you were 'cooking'."

"I guess so."

Laura came back in, frowning. "Henna, Rachel, have either of you seen the gong? I can't find it anywhere."

22

I started to get myself ready, washing my hair before setting it in the giant rollers I'd snaffled from Louisa's room. I'd never used rollers before so it was a bit of a gamble, but when I loosened them free and combed my hair, it shone and curled down over my shoulders and made me feel, in that remote Welsh valley for one night only, a little bit like a film star. I would definitely be picking up rollers when I got back to town tomorrow.

Tomorrow! In twenty-four hours I would be back in my brightly-lit box of a flat and all this would be over. I'd be at work on Tuesday. Urgh.

I pulled on my dressing gown and padded down to the phone in the hallway. From the kitchen I could hear Henna still clanging and banging the pots, stashing them away quickly in the backs of cupboards.

I tried Gwyn's number again. It rang and rang and Gwyn didn't pick it up.

Downhearted but not done yet, I headed back to my room to get dressed.

I knew exactly what I was going to wear. I'd packed my absolutely favourite dress that I now carefully took out of my suitcase and put on. I examined myself in the mirror and knew that I looked pretty good. Really good, if I had to be honest with myself. I sincerely hoped Gwyn would answer that goddamn phone and be at the party tonight to see me.

The dress should, by rights, be hideous. It was made of gold and brown velour, which is a gruesome material at the best of times and was made especially worse as it was in really dodgy colours; but somehow it looked good. It clung to all the right places and disguised all the bad places and had a plunging neckline and skinny braid belt. I'd found it in a chichi boutique near Bond Street when I was going sale shopping with my sister a couple of years ago. She was busy trying on nice looking things and I picked this hideous-looking dress off the rail and went to while away the hours waiting for her by having a laugh. But for some reason it looked completely fabulous on and I ended up buying it. Despite it setting me back over two hundred pounds. In a sale.

The cost didn't matter though, according to the various magazines I get. Apparently the important thing is cost per wear and in that case it was an absolute snip!

The curtains were drawn, the lights were dimmed and music was stacked up next to the stereo with someone's indie pop compilation currently playing. I checked with Organiser Laura to see if it was "optimum fire lighting time" and found out that it was.

"Just something ornamental, though," she added, seeing me start to pile on an entire tree-worth of logs, "it is still August."

I struck the match well away from my beloved velour and set it to the kindling, watching out that my oh-so-flammable dress wasn't anywhere near – the Tarzan-and-Jane half singed and torn look was so last season. Within a few minutes the fire had caught and I stood back proudly admiring my work. I was really getting the hang of this countryside lark – sunbathing on picnic rugs, building fires and horse riding. I was nearly as countrified as Laura and soon I'd be twirling a strand of hay in my mouth, one mud-encrusted kitten-heeled foot resting on a five-bar farm gate, watching the world go by while cows frolicked in the fields below.

The lighting was kept dim, which suited the room and also suited Henna. The standard lamps cast a soft yellow light but the corners of the room were still in gloom – blurred and indistinct; I could barely see up to the roof beams. The furniture was all arranged on one side, away from the dance floor area that Henna had designed and was now demonstrating how to use while Laura looked on, appalled. There was no way a representative of Her Majesty's Armed Forces was going to embarrass herself on a dance floor she told me as I stood and admired Henna strutting her stuff.

There was a more than plentiful supply of alcohol arranged by Laura on the nearby sideboard. Gin, whisky, vodka, many, many beers along with two litre-sized bottles of lemonade.

All that was missing were five policemen and one farmer. I tried Gwyn again.

Still no answer.

Louisa was sitting on the sofa drinking gin and tonics, leafing through a five-year-old copy of *Country Life* that featured the house we were staying in. It turned out my guess about the people who lived in the house hadn't been too wide of the mark. The couple who lived here (unmarried) were both painters (I knew it) and had two children who were called Araminta and Jocasta, who sat in stylised poses in a number of the photos draped over chairs or idling on mossy stone benches, looking like the models they so clearly wanted to be. So not far wrong at all.

There was nothing to do now until the boys arrived. I milled around the drinks table for a minute, trying all the different crisps, before sneaking into the bay window as I'd done a couple of nights ago, hidden by the thick curtains. I don't know what I was expecting to hear – the strangled cries of ravaged farmers or wails of heartbroken lovers – but there was no way I would hear anything over Madonna, who was pounding out of the stereo. And although a big blue-white moon was out over the valley, I still couldn't see more than a few yards from the window. And in those few visible yards there were no farmers staring up at the window now. Or jilted lovers either. Or big cats, for that matter. Nothing. I wondered whether anyone or anything could see me though, lit up in the house. Because I had the eeriest feeling that I was being watched. At one point I could have sworn I saw movement right at the edge of my circle of vision, shifting quickly on the edge of the light out towards the woodland in the empty sheep field.

It was nothing. I had an overactive imagination, that was all. I shivered slightly and went back into the room, helping myself to another goblet of wine and settling in to an armchair next to Henna.

All the girls were wearing their party gear. Henna had

emptied what must have been an entire bottle of concealer on her face to cover the emerging toxins, and looked a bit like Mr Potato Head. She'd sensibly gone down the TITS! route and refocused attention on to her not inconsiderable chest. Louisa was half-wearing a blouse, practically unbuttoned to her knees, tight jeans and stiletto boots. Laura had put aside the combat trousers in favour of plain brown trousers and T-shirt combo, so instead of looking like a Territorial Army girl in the field she looked like a Territorial Army girl off-duty at a party.

"Did you see anything out there?" Louisa asked.

"No. No farmers. No lovers." I didn't mention the fact that I'd seen something shifting and moving in the gloom. After all it could have been a sheep. Or any manner of completely harmless animals. Why worry anyone?

"No big cats out there then?"

"A ha ha ha."

"Hey, Henna, how's your article going for the newspaper? When will they publish it?" Louisa asked.

"It'll be in next week's supplement," Henna said proudly, sipping her wine with gusto, "that's unless there's a more pressing story to be had, in which case it goes back a week."

"Are we going to be in it?" Laura asked.

"Oh yes."

"Well, it's all good I hope."

Henna snorted loudly and took another gulp of wine.

"I wonder if we'll actually see a big cat if there's one out there," I mused.

"Perhaps tomorrow on our hike," Laura said. Louisa, Henna and I kept our heads down, none of us wanting to be the one to tell her there was no way we were going on a hike tomorrow when there were police helicopters, marksmen, news reports and leaflets from people in authority all suggesting, quite strongly, that there might be something out there. Besides, were we really going to be in top form tomorrow morning for a hike? Better to slog on over to the Crossed Keys and have lunch there. At least that way we might get a chance to see Gwyn again.

"Well, I've got my camera to hand so if a big cat comes along..." Henna did a mock "click" of a camera. Heartwarming. I'm sure my parents would enjoy opening up the Sunday papers to see a close-up picture of their daughter's severed and mangled legs with the caption "Rachel Young: Tragic Cat Attack Victim".

We sat in silence again, watching a log catch fire and shift and settle in the grate. Should I tell them about Tomos and the bloodstained clothes? Mention the deep gashes on his arm and the fact that he was seen coming from the direction of the latest attack? Perhaps I should.

There was a rapping at the door. We all leapt.

"Christ!" Henna clutched her chest. "What's that?"

"It's the policemen," sang Louisa, dancing over to the door.

"Are they using their truncheons or something?"

"They're probably just used to knocking loudly on doors, being policemen," Laura said matter-of-factly.

"Wait!" I stopped the hen in her tracks. "Are you sure it's the policemen?"

"Of course it is!" Louisa looked incredulous.

"It might not be you know. It could be anyone. Don't you think we ought to arm ourselves?" But she had raced out of the sitting room and was opening the front door.

"Hello! Come in, come in! Oh!"

23

It was the policemen. We all got up off the sofas and started to mill around looking party-like and relaxed. Which we stood a much better chance of doing when we were sitting on the sofas – but such is the way of things.

Louisa led the way back into the sitting room and shot us an odd sort of a look, like "Look at this!" When she stepped aside we saw why.

Five well-built policemen had turned up.

Plus one.

From the minute he stepped over the threshold of the Hen House, all of us girls were made very aware that the extra man, Josh Mitchell, was solely the property of Louisa and no one was allowed to talk to him. Or look at him. Or even stand near him.

He was a marked man.

He strode confidently into the room, shook a few hands and said a few hellos before Louisa whisked him off to the drinks table and opened up a beer for him.

"Oh my God," Henna whispered to me, "he is gorgeous"

"Not my taste," I whispered back honestly. He looked a bit too self-confident for me – too much floppy blonde hair and manly-swagger for my liking. He was good looking, but he knew it. He was also incredibly tanned, which I doubted came naturally from days spent outside roaming in the Welsh countryside. How could anyone legitimately get that brown in the UK except in a tanning salon?

But the answer was he wasn't native. Within minutes of the men arriving, we found out that Josh Mitchell was nothing less than a big game hunter with the Kenyan Wildlife Association. Open mouthed, we learnt that the local police force were under so much pressure to capture the animal causing the recent killings that they had drafted him in as a specialist to deal with the potential big cat problem. He'd be around for the next couple of weeks, and so far they'd been "on safari" in the Welsh valley without a sighting of the animal.

"Fuck me, so there really is a big cat problem then," Henna put it succinctly while we opened up a bottle of wine. "There's no way the Welsh police are going to fork out on a South African hunter for a figment of the public's imagination."

While the policemen were sorting out their drinks, Laura, Henna and I huddled together on the opposite side of the room and were toasting our good fortune. Louisa abandoned the hunter for a minute and tottered over to us.

"This is the best hen do ever." She hugged Laura who beamed back. "You are a genius! Policemen, hunters, farmers – what more could a girl ask for?"

"Male models? Actors?" I said. Really, the list was endless.

"Pah!" Louisa laughed. "No way. These are real men not some poncy actor types. They have guns, for God's sake. Oh, just look at Josh's forearms. He's amazing, isn't he? Apparently he's from Milton Keynes but that doesn't really count because his parents moved over to Kenya to farm when he was four. He loves it over there – says he hates the British weather…" and she floated back to her hunter, passing him a bowl of cheesy puffs.

At ten I tried Gwyn's number for what must have been the twentieth time that night but, as before, it just rang without being picked up. I wondered where he was. Surely farmers didn't work this late into the evening? Did they?

Maybe he was hurt? Maybe that mad farmer, Tomos, had called round to Gwyn's house earlier in the day with an old sharpened bread knife, concealed it behind his back, asked to come in, and when Gwyn's back was turned…

Perhaps I should mention something to the policemen? Perhaps I really should tell someone. Tomos could have found Gwyn snooping into his business and now maybe Gwyn was in real trouble? No, Gwyn would be just fine. Tomos wouldn't have stabbed him with a bread knife. Gwyn was probably in the pub, an outbuilding or anywhere for that matter. What was so odd about him not being at home? I was just being melodramatic. Besides, when I looked round the room I didn't fancy passing on my concerns to the others and necessitating any action which would involve prising drinks out of hands or indeed prising the men out of the clutches of the women. Everyone was far too absorbed in getting to know one another. I could hear snatches of the conversations within the babble, all of which centred on big cats and the hunting of them.

Henna had practically got her notepad out, she looked like she was taking on board everything that she heard, ready to write her column in the morning. Laura was looking more animated than she had done all weekend, discussing weaponry with a scary-looking policeman who was staring at her chest, while Louisa was laughing and flirting with the hunter, laying her hand on his shoulder and trying to look coy. I poured myself another drink and went to join a couple of policemen by the crisps.

There was a certain inevitability that a gorgeous blonde Kenyan hunter would not be left to one girl for long, and by around half past ten the inevitable had indeed happened and a group had gathered round Josh and Louisa, listening agog at what he had to tell us about Big Game hunting in Africa.

"So have you actually seen the wild cat here in Wales yet?" Henna asked, breathily.

"Well, ma'am, strictly speaking it's not a wild cat. There haven't been wild cats living in this part of the UK for years."

"He's right," one of the policemen added. "Last one was killed right outside my house nearly three hundred years ago."

"We're not looking for your native cat," Josh continued, in his odd, twangy accent. "What you probably have here is an escapee from a zoo. Or maybe the offspring of an escapee. Judging by the attacks on the animals and from the tracks I've seen."

"You've seen tracks?" I squeaked, hand suddenly clammy on my wine glass. Tracks were very real. Sightings could be disputed, attacks to animals didn't seem to be conclusively made by a big cat, but tracks? They couldn't very well be disguised. Tracks were tracks.

"Oh yes. I'd say you've got yourself a puma. Full-grown by the looks of things."

"A puma!" There was a hush over the room as everyone had now gathered round to listen to the hunter.

There was a puma in the countryside.

Outside.

Outside here.

Tearing things in two.

I turned the music down. It wasn't entirely appropriate for Kylie to be singing "I should be so lucky" while this conversation was going on.

"So, what actually is a puma?" Louisa asked the question we all wanted to ask but didn't want to appear stupid for asking it.

"Well, technically speaking it's not even a big cat…"

"What?" More disappointed faces.

"The puma is the largest of the small cats, but don't get me wrong, it's a vicious beast. It can stand about a metre high, one and a half metres in length…"

"And that's not a big cat?" I asked, returning to the group. In my eyes it seemed pretty huge. I couldn't imagine the size of the ball of wool needed to occupy that cat's attention.

"Is it black?" Henna asked.

"Can be, but this one's tawny coloured, brown and orangey. Well disguised in the heath scrub you have round here, which is probably why it's managed to evade us so well. These cats have every chance of survival once they're let into the open. There's abundant food for them and no natural predators. I wouldn't be surprised if there were more than one to be found round here."

"How do you know what colour it is?" I asked.

"I found hairs on a bramble." Josh crumpled his can

and tossed it into the bin.

"Oh my God," we all said in unison.

"Have you caught any cats in the UK before?" Henna gushed.

"Two. A puma in Greenwich, London…"

"In London?"

"Yup. The other was a Eurasian lynx which we found in Somerset."

"Did you kill them?" Louisa asked in a small voice.

"No, ma'am. The puma we shot with a sedative and it went to London Zoo, but the lynx was in a poor way when we found it and it died once we'd got it back to the veterinary practice."

"So you aren't going to kill our puma here?" Henna asked. Did he know she was a journalist?

"We're going to try our best not to kill the animal. We'll use sedative darts again, but if something goes wrong…"

"Something goes wrong?"

"Like we miss it or the dart doesn't connect properly, then we may have a wounded animal on our hands and that's when it becomes a serious problem. That's when we'd kill it."

Louisa had had enough of sharing him with us. Wrapping an arm around his waist, she escorted him over to the drinks table.

I stayed where I was, sipping my wine and staring at the ornamental fire. Their plans for the puma sounded awful. Now I began to feel rather sorry for the little big cat. After all it was only trying to make a living for itself out here.

Gwyn! I'd completely forgotten him in the excitement about the hunter. I ducked out of the lounge and picked up the phone again and dialled his number. Still no answer.

Perhaps he was at the pub? Perhaps he lay dying…

Stop it.

I poured myself another glass of wine (my fourth?) and flopped down next to a rosy-cheeked policeman called Joe.

I must have been rather drunk by this point as I remember him asking me what I did for a living and me launching into a long dialogue about my career progression in business management and where I could take it in the future. I was drunk enough to think that it might be interesting for someone to hear about modern business management theories, but I was sober enough to recognise that within a couple of minutes his eyes were glassing over and he was starting to look for an excuse to leave the sofa. I changed the subject back on to more familiar territory, feeling guilty at so obviously having bored the pants off him.

"So, Joe, tell me – how many sightings have you had reported then?"

Joe snapped out of his daze and leant forward to me. "We've had nine in this immediate area in the past two weeks. Mostly they have taken place around early evening, which is when the animal will hunt. Josh gave us all a briefing on the puma when he arrived here, so we're all up to speed on what we're looking for. Did you know that the puma gets to within a few metres of its prey and then they pounce? A single jump can span twelve metres! Isn't that incredible? Twelve metres!"

"Great!" I nodded, seeing a picture all too clearly in my mind. Torn in two.

"And then they leap on the back of their prey and break its neck with a single bite. I mean, I saw pictures of pumas and thought they looked quite domesticated. Not now though. Bloody fierce things. Zoos are the best thing for them, in my opinion. Put it in a cage and throw away the key."

"Oh quite," I said, when there was nothing "Oh quite" about it. Miserable bastard, wanting to get rid of a cat. Even in my red-wine-fuzzy head, though, I knew that it would be the wrong thing to argue animal rights in a room full of police marksmen and one big game hunter.

"So, Joe, aren't you scared being out there looking for the puma? If what you say is true, then it can jump you before you even see it."

If there was such a thing as a seated-swagger then Joe did it. "Ha! I'm not scared. We work in pairs and I work with Josh." He swelled out his chest in pride. "I'm not really concerned. Besides, it's more likely that the puma would be scared of us, so why would it attack us?"

"Why would it attack a horse?"

"A horse is food, isn't it? A horse stands around and doesn't do much, so it doesn't present much of a threat to the cat. But humans are constantly moving around and making a noise so it isn't too sure about us. Plus we have the guns which make a hell of a noise."

"Yes, I thought I heard one go off this afternoon," I said, suddenly remembering a noise when Old Ned and I were taking the air.

"That was me." He pointed to his chest proudly. "There was an animal right in front of me and I aimed and shot it. Killed it first shot. Only it was a squirrel. But you can't be too careful…"

I concealed a smile by taking another sip of my drink.

Joe looked at his drink for a moment, running his fingers along the rim of the glass and looking as if he was debating in his head whether or not to tell me something.

"What is it?" I asked quietly. I was intrigued by his silence – was there something about the puma he wasn't supposed to say?

He leant towards me and looking around him whispered, "Josh thinks someone's manipulating it."

I stared at him blankly for a moment. Someone was controlling the puma? "Really?"

"Think about it." The policeman put down his drink to concentrate on what he was saying, glancing over at Josh to make sure he wasn't listening in. But Josh was far from caring what was being talked about over the other side of the room. Louisa had him cornered and was tossing her hair and laughing and smiling and giving it everything she'd got. Far from encouraging him, from what I could see Josh had the look of a hunted animal, caged in and not a little bit frightened. Ha! The hunter becomes the hunted.

"You have to ask yourself, where did the animal come from," Joe was saying, "and it's more than likely that it was released into the wild when the change to animal licences was brought in. Do you know that it wasn't even illegal to let a puma loose in the countryside?"

"No way," I said, horrified, my attention well and truly grabbed by Joe now.

"Seriously, Josh told me that – now what was it – the Countryside and Wildlife Act, something like that, a few years ago there was this act passed that made it illegal to release animals that weren't native to this country into the wild. Scary stuff, huh? Makes you wonder what went on before that!"

"You could legitimately release a lion or something into the wild before the new law?"

"Apparently so, but I'm not dead sure of the details.

Anyway, Josh was saying that things are much more tightly controlled now than they used to be. The chances are this thing has been around for a few years and not released recently. We checked with zoos and circuses and so on – no one has reported a missing puma. So in all probability what we're dealing with here in the Beacons is either an ex-circus animal or even the offspring of an animal that was released a few years ago."

"But surely if it's been out and about in the wild for few years then you would have had sightings reported all the time," I argued. "You would have known about it before now?"

"We did know about it."

I gaped at him. That wasn't good. "You mean to say that you've had people in this area report sightings of a puma before now?"

"Of course. All the time. It's just now it's making the headlines because all of a sudden it's attacking livestock. Horses, sheep, a dog…"

"A dog?"

"There's an old farmer over the way called Tomos –"

"I know him!"

"Oh. Well, it was Tomos' dog that was attacked." Joe was silent for a minute. "The strange thing was that the cat didn't injure the old hound too badly. Apparently Old Shep is nearly blind and can hardly walk, so how it defended itself against the puma I don't know. But Josh said the markings were unmistakable. It was definitely the puma that attacked Old Shep."

My heart was racing and there was a thought in the back of my mind that I just couldn't grasp but I knew it was important. Something he was saying was very important. There was some clue that my Merlot befuddled head just couldn't process.

"Anyway, it's all turned nasty these past two weeks now that personal property is at stake," Joe was saying. "Suddenly everyone's more interested in capturing the thing when they've got something to lose. When there were just reported sightings of a big cat, or when there were dead wild animals like birds and rabbits, we used to go about having a token look for the animal and to be honest with you it was a bit of fun for me and the lads. And we never saw anything to make us think there was actually a big cat living round here. Looking back though," he laughed, "we probably made so much noise and commotion that the cat would have known we were coming while we were still putting our uniforms on at home in the morning. That's what's so great about having Josh – he's a professional and he tells us just how we should go about capturing the thing. Now we've got a full-scale investigation into it. Budget allocated, plans drawn up and people like Josh here are brought over to help out. We've got no option but to throw all we've got at it. The national media are on our case and it's our necks on the line if we don't do something about it."

An apt choice of words.

I wondered whether or not to tell him that the media were right here in this room, currently dipping their hands in the roast beef flavour crisps. But then that wouldn't be very fair on Henna if she "interviewed" him and he was already prepared for it. Let him find out in his own time.

"So why is the cat attacking livestock now?" I asked, still not getting why things should be different now.

Joe dropped his voice again into just above a whisper. I leant closer to him in a bid to hear over the noise of the party, in particular Louisa screaming with laughter at something one of the policemen had said. "That's why Josh thinks that someone is manipulating it. Not letting it go about its usual routine satisfying itself with killing rabbits and birds. Maybe they're starving it somehow and …"

"Excuse me!" Henna tripped over, wobbly and drunk. She looked straight at Joe and said, "Your mate over there said you went to Sheffield Uni ten years ago. You didn't study Geography, did you?"

"Yes." Joe looked nonplussed for a minute

"I thought so! It's Joe Williams, isn't it? It's Henna! Henna Smithson!"

Joe shot up from the sofa with an, "Oh my God, Henna!" and the two of them exploded into conversation leaving me open-mouthed on the sofa.

Josh believed someone was manipulating the puma. Tomos! It had to be Tomos the old farmer.

I sat for a few moments staring into the fire and trying desperately to clear my head and put everything I knew into place. There were loads of things that pointed to the old man being associated with a big cat! For a start there was the bloodstained jacket I saw the other day, and the torn hand and arm. Maybe the cat had turned on him? If Joe had said the cat was likely to be a circus animal then it wouldn't be afraid of humans per se, but it would defend itself and if Tomos was forcing it to do something it didn't want to do, like preventing it from going out on its regular hunts in the countryside…

And then there was Old Shep, Tomos' dog. I realised now what had been bugging me about what Joe had said. The dog was ancient and almost blind. It was absolutely unable to defend itself but when the cat had attacked it, the old dog hadn't been killed. Because Tomos had been there to protect his dog from the animal. That had to be the case!

Now it all fitted in to place.

Because the most important fact was that it was Elijah's animals that had been attacked – the animals of a man that Tomos had a particular reason to despise and wish ill.

Tomos had the puma!

By now my heart was pumping in my chest.

I had to see Gwyn. This was too much of a coincidence. I had to tell him. I'd worked the mystery out. Now Gwyn would know that, if he did trail Tomos another day on one of his walks, it would be likely to lead him to wherever the farmer was keeping the big cat!

"Hello there, you're staring quite intently in the fire." One of the police marksmen stood in front of me, holding out a plate of hummus and dips. "Mind if I join you? I'm Peter."

"Oh. Right. Back in a minute."

I made my way over to the door, checking to see if any one else had noticed that I was leaving the party. Laura was occupied talking to two scary-looking marksmen about her job: "They're just animals. That's what they are. All children under five are no more advanced than a dog; they eat, they sleep, they crap. You treat them like you'd treat an animal and they give you respect."

Henna was busy interviewing another overwhelmed-looking policeman, "So how do you know where it lives? What would you do if it attacked one of your policemen? How do you know if there's just one of them?"

And Louisa was pinning Josh to the wall and using her breasts as a lion tamer uses a chair to keep an animal where they want it.

So far so good; no one had seen me get up and leave.

I slid out of the room and bounded upstairs to my bedroom.

24

Even though I'd drunk the best part of a bottle of wine I still knew that it was a brainless idea to go out in the night to see Gwyn.

Of course I knew it was.

Every ounce of my sensible self was appalled at my half-formed plan. But my sensible self was put in check by my new bottle-of-wine self. Stuff sitting around on a squashy sofa. Stuff talking to over-confident policemen about how exciting their jobs were. Why not grab this one opportunity to embrace a bit of a risk? Why should I bring my Dull Life Crisis here to the Hen House? This weekend was all about being a different me, living here in this amazing place, secretly flirting with handsome farmers and uncovering all the local secrets. This weekend was my manicured two-fingers up at Marcia.

I was due back in the city tomorrow, back in work on Tuesday and then I would be back to a life of making calls, going to meetings, writing reports and buying the same old sandwiches from the same sandwich man who visited our offices every lunchtime. All my days were spent being sensible and normal – why not take a risk and go and see Gwyn tonight? The party wasn't such fun that I wanted to stay. Louisa had grabbed the most interesting bloke, the other policemen had more than enough on their plates with the other girls and really, I was more of a spare part here. The music wasn't great and all the decent wine had been drunk. Only the £2.99 bottles of Chateau de Tesco were left and I certainly had more common sense than to start drinking those.

The rational course of action – that my rational self would have taken – would have been to go back downstairs and speak to Josh about the possible connection between old Tomos and the big cat. It would have been a matter of moments to prise Louisa away from her quarry and have a word with him. Or even approach one of the policemen first, for that matter. Then they could be the ones to go and do the prising, which would be far more sensible from a personal safety point of view.

But then what? I would tell them about my suspicions and they might nod and say, "Yes, let's think about that," and have another drink, thereby leaving me back where I started, a spare part at a party, but this time without the reason to go and see Gwyn. Or alternatively they might say, "Of course! The missing link!" and dash off in their riot van into the night and I'd be left with a room full of very angry girls looking at me. And cheap wine.

But this way, going out right now to find Gwyn, ensured that I didn't disrupt the party. It also meant that I didn't unnecessarily blacken a man's reputation because, after all, what did I know about Tomos? I still only knew what

I'd been told about him from other people. And there might be all sorts of explanations as to why he had been so badly cut, why there was blood on his coat and why his dog, against all the odds, had survived a cat attack. Mind you, I couldn't think of one. Still, the idea of an old Welsh farmer manipulating a ferocious puma could be wide of the mark and I'd look pretty stupid blurting it all out only to be proved wrong.

In addition to all this, I reasoned, by talking to Gwyn I would be passing the responsibility on to him and he could follow it up when I'd gone. It also meant that the party could continue with the full complement of policemen and hunters and there would be more supermarket wine to go round.

And it meant I'd get a breath of fresh air to clear my head.

Oh, and it meant that I got to spend just a bit more time with Gwyn.

That small point.

Provided that he was home by now.

Should I try to call again? No, probably not. No doubt someone would see me coated-up in the hallway and ask where I was going, and then I'd have to explain and then the policemen would be getting back into the riot van and driving off... There was that image of a hallway full of angry girls looking at me again. I should definitely just sneak out quietly. Quickly.

I crept down the stairs and pulled out my coat from the alcove underneath the staircase. Then I stole into the kitchen for a weapon of some sort. After all, there was a puma on the loose and although the walk up to Gwyn's was a matter of ten minutes, there was still a chance I could meet it. And having drunk so much wine I could hardly drive up to his farm, not with half a dozen policemen in the vicinity.

Spatulas and the potato masher didn't really look like proper weapons, and I couldn't really imagine fending off a foaming-mouthed puma with a Philippe Starck orange squeezer, however much a design classic it might be. Checking behind me to make sure no one was standing in the doorway watching what I was doing, I pulled open the knife drawer, ogled at the array of weapons for a moment and then closed it again, horrified. There was no way I would be going up to Gwyn's brandishing a knife. I'd probably stab myself by accident and if I did get attacked by the puma, there was no way I would be able to knife the poor animal. I needed a weapon of defence, not slaughter.

A fork might do the trick! I picked one up and contemplated it for a second. I could jab at the animal. I jabbed the air experimentally. But then it would have to get pretty close to be jabbed and I could easily drop the fork and then where would I be?

And so it was that, a few minutes later, I walked out of the front door, closing it quietly behind me with a very large wooden rolling-pin in one hand and an impressive looking torch in the other.

I sobered up the minute I stepped outside. The noise and heat and beery-smell of the party disappeared and it was just me out in the cool night air. I flicked on the PowerBeam Mega Three. Instantly there was a blinding ray of light up the gravel driveway. Christ, it was bright. It was also eerily silent except for a soft rustling of leaves in the woodland beside the track. With my back pressed hard against the knobbly ancient front door, I swept the beam across the driveway, watching for pumas in the thin band of light, clutching the rolling-pin tightly. The woods on either side of the steep road looked black and ominous – only the very tops of the trees visible in the moonlight, shifting and rustling in the breeze. The lane, lit up by the thin white light of the moon, snaked its way up towards the village. If I was going to do this I should do it now.

I took a deep breath, which sounded juddery as my heart was pounding away in my chest.

I set off. Dull Life Crisis be damned.

I walked past the cars and out of the safety of the fenced driveway and into the lane. Flicking the beam of light left and right, I scrunched my way up the stony track in my ridiculously inappropriate kitten-heeled shoes desperately trying to think through the plan in my head.

The beam flickered. I stopped and shook the torch. It seemed fine again.

I started walking.

It cut out.

"Fuck!" I shook it again. Nothing.

I bit my lip. What should I do? Turn round and go back? I looked behind me. The orange lights of the Hen House were just visible down the road. But I was only a few minutes from Gwyn's farm.

What if Gwyn wasn't at home by now? Then I'd have to go on to the pub looking for him. He was bound to be at the pub and if he wasn't, well, I suppose I'd go back to the Hen House and I'd have put myself through sheer terror for no reason. But at least I would have tried – if I hadn't tried then no doubt I would be still sitting there on the sofa, bursting with the revelation about old Tomos with no one to tell. A sudden gust of wind howled down the valley and rushed into the woods around me, creating a din of rattling branches and swishing leaves. I crouched down and put the dead torch on the side of the road. It was too heavy to be carrying for no reason. I could collect it on my way back. I gripped the rolling-pin tighter and started to walk towards Gwyn's farm. The track went quite steeply uphill now and I was panting as I walked, trying to avoid the potholes without much success as the moonlight was hazy. My shoes kept slipping off and I had to backtrack every so often to put them on again. I was a quarter of the way there. I looked behind me and saw the warm orange lights of the house disappear as I turned the corner. My last glimpse of safety…

I heard something. Quickening my pace, I shot nervous glances into the impenetrably dark woodland on either side. Only the tips of the branches were visible in the moonlight, reaching out into the lane.

A new sound came from the woodland a bit further up from where I was, on my right. A snap. A twig. Something…

I kept walking. I could feel tears prickling behind my eyes and I felt horribly sick. I carried on, not daring to stop or turn back.

Again. The same noise. Snapping of twigs.

I lifted my eyes from the track and looked into the murky woodland. I could just make out the nearest tree branches and the grassy verge before it all blended into blackness.

And there it was.

The puma.

Up ahead at the edge of the wood. Two big eyes, a white face. It was huge. It was looking at me.

I could hear nothing except the blood pounding in my ears. I was still trying to walk and I stumbled into a pothole and reeled, desperate to stay upright.

I was crying now. It was here. It killed by pouncing.

What should I do? My mind went blank as I tried to recall the list of things to do from the pub leaflet. What was it? What was it? I knew that stopping would be suicidal. I had to keep going.

Torn in two!

I was nearly level with the cat now – I could just make out its form through the blur of tears that were streaking down my face. It hadn't moved and stood surveying me from the tall grass verge at the side of the track. Shit. Shit shit shit shit shit shit shit. I kept walking.

Talk loudly. That was it! Talk loudly and act human. Hold my arms out and look as big as possible. Don't run. Keep walking.

Keep walking.

Again my mind went blank.

What could I talk about?

I was really near now. Just a few metres. What did that policeman say? Twelve metre pounce? Shit shit.

I slowly raised my shaking arms and held them out at shoulder height. All I could think of were wildlife programmes about big cats and birds and fungi and deer and Bill Oddie in bird-watching gear presenting those endless rounds of nature programmes…

"BILL ODDIE," I said loudly in a wobbly voice, "er … IT'S … IT'S REALLYANNOYINGTHEWAYTHAT HE'SALWAYSONTHETVALLTHETIME." I drew a big shaky breath and carried on, "HE'SPRESENTINGNATU REPROGRAMMESABOUTBIRDSANDTHEONSETO FSPRINGANDIREALLYDON'TCAREABOUTTHESE THINGSIMEANWHOCARESWHENTHEFIRSTBUM BLEBEEISSEENINBRITAINAND…ANDIHATETHE WAYTHATHELAUGHSTHATSTUPIDLAUGHWHEN

HESEESABIRDDOSOMETHINGHETHINKSISFUNN
YBECAUSEIT'SNOTFUNNY…AND…ANYWAY…H
EWASN'TTHEFUNNIESTONEINTHEGOODIESITHI
NKTIMBROOKE-TAYLORWASTHEBESTONE …"

I drew a breath and carried on. I'd now passed where the puma was standing and was walking away from it. It was behind me. I didn't look back to check. I didn't dare. I was super-aware that the back of my neck was exposed when the breeze caught my hair. Waiting for the teeth to sink into it … Twelve metre pounce…

"I'MSUREHE'SAVERYNICEGUYANDALLTHATB
UTHE'SSOOVEREXPOSEDTHATYOUJUSTCAN'TH
ELPGETTINGFEDUPWITHHIM…ER…ITHINKHES
HOULDGIVEOTHERPEOPLEAGOATPRESENTING
WILDLIFEPROGRAMMESITHINKSTEPHENFRYW
OULDBEAGOODPRESENTERORJEREMYCLARKS
ONORMAYBEBOTHTOGETHERTHENI'DFINDTHE
MINTERESTINGANDWANTTOHEARWHATTHEYS
AYABOUTBUMBLEBEES…"

I wobbled on. No teeth in my neck yet...

Tears were still coursing down my face and through my watery eyes I could just make out the turning to Gwyn's farm on the right. I could see the light of a building through the trees. Was he home? My nose was running. I didn't dare drop my arms and wipe my face. I was panting, sobbing, but still managed to carry on talking about Bill Oddie, arms outstretched brandishing my rolling-pin.

I turned into the track towards Gwyn's farm, which meant more exposure to the woodland where the cat was standing. But there was no way I would be able to walk another ten minutes to the pub – I had to get to safety right now. I didn't know how my legs were able to keep moving but somehow it was happening.

My arms ached.

"ITHINKTHERESHOULDBEMORENATUREPRO
GRAMMESABOUTTHEDANGERSOFNATUREANY
WAYLIKEPUMASANDSTUFFANDHOWTOSURVIV
EANDSTUFF. GWYN!"

I'd reached the front door and pounded on it with the rolling-pin.

"GWYN!!!" I screamed.

Nothing. I turned round, flattening my back to the door and holding the rolling-pin out in front of me like Luke Skywalker with his light sabre. I couldn't see the puma, but I knew it was still there, in the woodland, watching me. I don't know why, but I knew it could still see me. The moon had gone behind a wisp of cloud and I could now only make out the surface of the yard a few metres from the lit window.

"GWYNFOR!!" I screamed again, pounding the door.

The door opened.

"Oh thank God!" I tumbled in.

25

I must have momentarily passed out and fallen to the ground because the next thing I was aware of was Gwyn leaning over me, lifting my head off the flagstone floor. Raising myself up, I managed to thrust out a leg to slam the front door shut behind me before giving way and sinking to the floor again in a jumble of filthy boots.

"Rachel, what's wrong?" He knelt down beside me.

I started sobbing and shaking again, desperately trying to wipe away the snot and tears with my sleeve. My ringleted hair was all over my shoulders and my gold dress was half way up my legs but I didn't have the energy to move. I was completely exhausted.

He put a warm hand on my head and looked into my eyes. "What's up, Rachel?"

"The cat," I snivelled, trying to draw breath, "it's outside."

"Outside here?"

"Yes!" I burst into tears again, out of relief. I was so grateful to be safely inside. In one piece. And not two.

Gwyn was silent for a moment. "Stay there." He left me on the floor and went into the room next to me and I heard a window closing. I hastily wiped my face with my sleeve and ran a hand through my hair, not that it would make me look remotely better. I must have looked shockingly bad. He came back and put his arms around me, hoisting me up like a bridegroom carrying his bride over the threshold. I winced, waiting for him to turn purple and stagger forward under my weight, but he walked down the hallway saying, "Come on, come and sit in the kitchen." Maybe, just maybe, I was lighter than one of those rafters he'd been hauling in the Hen House photographs.

I put my head against his shoulder as he carried me through the narrow dark passage to the kitchen. Was this moment worth the terror I'd just gone through outside? Probably.

"You need a drink." He gently put me down in an old rocking chair and turning to an ancient cupboard he pulled out a bottle of brandy.

"Wait there. I'll go and find some clean glasses."

He walked off and I looked around for the first time, taking in my surroundings now that I was calming down. Gwyn's kitchen could not have been more different to the kitchen I was used to. For a start, my kitchen was small; ergonomically designed to fit only what was necessary and no more. This kitchen sprawled and turned and seemed to go on forever. I was used to a strip-lit spotlessly modern room with shiny plastic surfaces and gleaming metal appliances. Gwyn's kitchen was dim and poky with a dark stone floor, dim red-painted walls and the most enormous redbrick fireplace complete with a spit along an entire wall. There was no fitted kitchen or melamine worktop in here, just dusty old kitchen drawers, the tops of which had doubled up as chopping boards for what must have been many generations. A huge Belfast sink was positioned by the window with a makeshift drainer next to it loaded with chipped crockery. There were still meat hooks in the ceiling beams, turned from black to grey by the accumulation of years of dust, with wispy cobwebs floating from them, moving in an invisible breeze. The paint was bubbling and peeling from the walls, the stone floor was gritty underfoot and the wooden cupboards and drawers were stained and grubby. But despite all this, the overall impression as I sat in the lamplight, huddled into the creaking chair, was of a very beautiful room. Somewhere with character and integrity. And somewhere in need of a woman's touch.

A loaf stood half-carved on the worktop with a wedge of cheese and a pack of butter beside it. Was that dinner?

"Sorry. I didn't know I'd be having a guest…" He came in with the glasses and poured us both a drink. "That's twice I've been caught off guard by you hen weekenders. I'll dress in my suit tomorrow, just in case I bump into any of you again."

I accepted the glass of brandy and took a big gulp, feeling it burn its way down. And then I had a coughing fit. I gripped the glass tightly and tried to force a smile, hoping against hope that he didn't think I was wholly dreadful. Because just maybe this was the kind of look he liked in a woman?

"I'm so sorry," I began when I got my voice back again, "I can't imagine what you must be thinking. I had to come up and tell you something I worked out. I had to tell you straight away. It couldn't wait until tomorrow."

"Obviously," he laughed, looking at the state I was in.

"Top up?" He filled up my glass before I could answer. "So what couldn't wait until tomorrow?" He was sitting opposite me on a rickety stool, his face lit by the soft light of the lamp on the mantelpiece. He looked so breathtakingly handsome just then that I almost forgot why I was there. Almost. His dark appearance was all the more rugged for being lit at an angle which threw his features into shadow. His eyes, shaded by his strong brow, and the curls of his black hair that fell forward as he leant towards me. And his old white shirt was part unbuttoned, the sleeves rolled up and covered in scuffs and marks. Man's work…

I took a deep breath. "I think I've discovered a connection between Tomos and the puma."

"Puma?"

"That's what they think it is." I paused. "And having seen it on your doorstep, that's what I think it is too. I mean, it's definitely not a lion. And it's definitely not a regular cat. I would say it's something in between."

"Who are the 'they' who think it's a puma?"

"OK, hold on, let me get my story straight…" I knocked back the second brandy, coughed and launched into what I knew. I told him about the party at the Hen House and about the policemen and Josh the big game hunter. He listened, frowning with concentration while I related what the policeman had said about it being a puma: the tracks, the style of attacks, the fur caught on a bramble. Then I told him about Josh's theory that the cat was being manipulated by someone and had probably been living in the wild for years without anyone being affected.

"So," I said, sitting back in the chair, "I reckon Tomos has captured the puma and is starving him and then by some means dropping the animal in the middle of Elijah's farmland around dinner time."

Gwyn nodded slowly, taking it all in. "That would certainly explain the fact that it's mostly Elijah's animals being attacked," he said eventually, "but I heard in the pub this evening that Tomos' dog has been attacked. I know he loves that animal and there's no way on earth that he would let it be attacked by this puma as a way of covering up what was really happening."

"I was thinking about that." I leaned forward. "And I reckon Tomos hasn't got as much of a hold on the puma as he thinks he has. I mean, presuming this animal is an escapee from a circus or something, then it's going to be pretty tame. But a few years in the wild will have sharpened it up a bit. So perhaps the cat turned on Old Shep and Tomos had to wrestle it off him? After all, an old half-crippled dog isn't going to be able to defend itself against a puma, is it? Tomos probably separated them and in the process he got the cuts to his hand and arm that we saw in the pub the other night."

Gwyn was staring into the fireless grate, deep in thought, saying after a moment, "You know, Rachel, I think you could be right."

"It makes sense, doesn't it? It explains Tomos' injuries, and why his old dog was attacked and survived and why only Elijah's animals have suffered." I paused for breath. "What do you think we should do now?"

Gwyn was silent for a minute, twirling a curl of his thick black hair in his hands. "We should go and talk to Tomos."

"Really?"

"Yes, really. I've known Tomos all my life, and while he's no close pal of mine –" he paused "– of anyone's really, I don't think it's out of order for me to say something to him."

"You don't think we should go down to the Hen House and tell Josh my theory instead? I didn't want to say anything to him in case it was all rubbish and I got Tomos into trouble unnecessarily. But if you think it's really something…"

"We can go and talk to Tomos about the cat and if he admits something we can always go to that Josh chap afterwards. Out of interest, just what did your man Josh say he would do with the cat once he'd found it?"

"Sedate it and send it to a zoo. But if the sedative doesn't work then he might have to kill it."

Gwyn looked unimpressed. "I can't pretend that I like the sound of that. I don't much care for zoos. And as for the sedative plan, how capable a marksman is he or any of those policemen at shooting animals in our countryside?"

"One of the marksmen shot a squirrel this afternoon."

"Oh, great. So their aim is good but their sight is bad. Maybe we should be concerned that they'll shoot at us?"

"Not tonight they won't."

"True – and that's why we should go and see Tomos tonight, when they're out of action and out of our way. If we have to, we can think about involving this Josh afterwards."

"Go and see Tomos right now?" I asked, quite happy to be safely inside and not careering round the cat-infested countryside.

"Yes. I was up at the pub earlier this evening…"

"Oh, I wondered where you were," I said, without stopping to think. I bit my tongue to stop saying any more. I sounded embarrassingly over-keen.

"Why?" he asked, half smiling.

"Well…" I tried to look more detached than I really

felt. "You know. I called you to invite you to the party at the Hen House. Actually I called the pub beforehand to get your number. Didn't Angharad tell you that I called?"

"No. But I didn't see much of her, she was working in the bar and I was out back helping shift barrels. Sounds like you had enough policemen and hunters to keep you occupied though, surely I would have been an unnecessary addition?"

He was playing with me now so I ignored him, feigning disinterest and staring over towards the window.

"I wonder if anyone at the party has noticed that I've gone?" I mused.

"Do you want to call up? They might be worried."

I laughed.

"Seriously," he said, "if there's a puma on the loose and someone's gone missing in the night, well, the policemen are going to be interested even if your friends aren't, which I don't think would be the case. If you don't want to break the party up, maybe you ought to call and tell them what you've done? Otherwise they might come looking for you."

"No. Don't worry about it. I don't think anyone will miss me this evening. Besides, we can go and talk to Tomos now and maybe when we're done you can come back to the party with me. That's if you want to?"

He shrugged his shoulders in a maybe, maybe not sort of way.

"We can go in your vehicle, can't we? We're not walking anywhere?"

"Of course," he said, "so there'll be no need for you to take that rolling-pin with you."

"Oh. I'd forgotten about this." I sheepishly put it on the table.

26

I stayed in the comfy old chair while Gwyn went round the house turning on all the lights in a bid to deter the cat if it was lurking directly outside the building waiting for its moment with me. Then he opened the front door, rapidly closed it behind him and headed over to the barn next door to get his vehicle. I sat there for what seemed like half an hour, although it was only a fraction of that. I couldn't hear a thing from outside. My imagination started to get the better of me again and I had visions of Gwyn's beautiful body lying mutilated, torn in two on the yard outside. But all was OK; I heard an engine starting up and then he was back at the door.

"Come on then," he said, "there's no puma outside now, I had a good look."

I walked up to the front door, heart racing. He'd parked his Land Rover tight against the front door and it was the work of a second to jump from the doorway and into the passenger seat. Gwyn shut the door behind me and I was safe again. Trembly, hot and sweaty, but safe all the same.

Unless the cat was in the back of the vehicle!

In horror I jerked round to look. There was nothing there.

Gwyn climbed into the driver's side and shot me an amused look. "Any cats in the back?"

"Ah no," I said lightly, trying not to be embarrassed about it. After all, it was only sensible to check. I pushed the lock down on my door.

"Why," he asked as he manoeuvred the vehicle out of the yard, "did you just lock your door?"

"Well," I said, trying to hang on to my composure, "the puma might be able to open a car door, mightn't it?"

"How?" He was laughing now.

"Think about it. It's an escapee from a circus or something. So it probably had a trick or two that it performed. What if one of those tricks was to open car doors?"

"Are you serious?" He looked at me and brought the Land Rover to a halt. "You are, aren't you?" He laughed out loud. "Oh you're so…"

I looked at him. He stopped and pursed his lips together.

"I'm so what?"

He shook his head.

"Urgh!" I said in mock indignation, but secretly overjoyed and wondering what his word would have been. What was I? So lovely? So sweet? So damn quirky? Or was it mad, bizarre, deranged…

I chose to think that it was probably one of the former. Did he like me? Did he look at me the same way that I

231

looked at him? I shot him a sideways glance as he drove up the track, admiring his strong and ruddy profile. Lovely.

I'd never been in a Land Rover before and it was entirely different to what I would have expected. It was a bit like being in a car when car thieves had stripped out all the interior furnishings. And raised it about a metre off the ground. The clutch was a stick that came out of the floor, there were wires poking out everywhere and the dashboard looked like it was straight out of the seventies; a black plastic angular set of boxes with no-nonsense dials that told you speed and petrol. There were no thermometer or average speed displays in this vehicle. The seats were quite comfortable though, I just had to keep my legs over to the right to avoid the sharp seam where the seat cover had been ripped open and then badly mended with some duck tape. And there was a funny smell. Coming from the back…

We had arrived at the pub. Gwyn parked out at the front and escorted me inside, his body close to mine which I enjoyed immensely and I really didn't feel too scared about the cat at all now I had a strong Welsh farmer pressed against me.

It was a Saturday night and the pub was full. There were a rowdy crowd of men near the bar, talking loudly in Welsh – not German – and older men and women sitting at the tables elsewhere. I scanned round the room quickly and was relieved to see Tomos in the seat that he'd occupied the other night; by the fireplace, head down, absorbed by his pint. I tapped Gwyn on his shoulder. He followed my line of sight and nodded, and then led me to the bar. A few of the burly Welshmen at the bar slapped Gwyn on the back, greeting him in Welsh. I just smiled and hoped my mascara hadn't run after the crying earlier on. Why hadn't

I checked my appearance in the wing mirror? Did Land Rovers even have the luxury of wing mirrors? Probably not.

"What do you want?" Gwyn asked.

"Lemonade?"

"Really?"

"My liver will never forgive me if I have any more alcohol."

"Fine, then. Lemonade it is," and with that he turned back to Angharad who had come over to us, all winks and smiles.

They talked in Welsh, which I couldn't make any sense of, even though I'd been exposed to it for a couple of years now. I think I caught the name "Tomos" somewhere in their conversation. It must have been a question about what Tomos was drinking as Angharad pulled a pint the same colour as the one that was before the old farmer.

Gwyn and Angharad rattled on so I dipped back from the bar and surreptitiously watched Tomos from across the crowded, smoky room. It seemed ridiculous now to think that I had once entertained the notion that this little old man with a weather-beaten face and hunched shoulders might be going round the countryside with a bread knife doing the attacks on animals himself. But then, how much more of sensible was it to suppose that he was keeping a puma locked up in a dog kennel or wherever it was and using it to do his dirty business? Either way it seemed crazy to associate this rather sad old man who was quietly minding his own business with that befanged wild animal lurking outside that tore sheep in two. Perhaps the whole thing was just a load of nonsense? Maybe I was just too eager to get one up on Marcia and do something exciting this weekend and was looking for an adventure when there wasn't one to be had? Tomos' injuries could well have been the result of a farming accident and as for the cat I'd seen on the road half an hour ago – well, it could have been just a large domestic cat that some farmer's wife had overfed. Couldn't it?

No.

Not unless the farmer's wife had slipped the animal muscle-enhancing power drinks beloved of bodybuilders. No, that was definitely an exotic animal out there. I wondered where it was right now, prowling around outside, recognising Gwyn's Land Rover and trying the door handles. Sniffing the ground and knowing that I was inside the pub. Then it would be waiting for someone to push open the pub door and it would be inside, hunting me down, padding silently on the pub carpet, slinking beneath the tables and chairs. The one that got away wasn't going to be so lucky next time…

Gwyn was kept talking at the bar but I couldn't join in as I didn't understand what they were saying. The words came out so fast it was a wonder that anyone ever understood each other.

I glanced over at Tomos. He was nearing the end of his pint. We should make a move over there before he either left for the night or bought his own pint.

Gwyn turned to me and his friends all looked in my direction. "They want to know what you think of Tretower?" he asked.

"Oh. I like it," I said. Did they not speak English? That was crazy.

"It's not the best of times to be yer though, is it?" one of the men said to me laughing into his pint. "Have you seen our wild cat then?"

Oh. They did speak English.

"Erm, no," I said, glancing quickly at Gwyn who was almost imperceptibly shaking his head.

"Well, it's a nasty business, see," another was saying, still in English. "It's Elijah I feel sorry for; the animal has clearly got it in for him. I wonder what it is about his animals that make them so susceptible, like. Must have the tastiest Welsh lamb in the valleys, I reckon!" More laughter and "oh aye-ing". "It's like this, see – his farm isn't the most remote, and it isn't the only one to back on to woodland. And we all know his walls and fences are in good shape after last year. Remember that, lads? Building up those walls over a weekend!"

There was more laughter and they slipped back to Welsh again.

"Come on," Gwyn said quietly, picking up Tomos' pint. We threaded our way through the pub towards the old hunched farmer.

"Mind if we join you?" Gwyn asked him. Tomos raised his eyes briefly, frowned and then went back to staring at his pint again. He mumbled something, which can't have been in English because I didn't even catch one word of it.

"Well, my friend here," Gwyn replied, pointing to me, "doesn't speak any Welsh and she'd like to talk to you too."

"*Saesneg!*" spat the old man, still not looking up from his pint.

Saesneg. I'd come across this before in Cardiff; you couldn't well avoid it if you were English and living in Wales. It was the Welsh equivalent of the Scots and Irish Sassenach. It still meant "Saxon", that is English, but whereas the Scots term had a certain negative connotation the Welsh word didn't. Apparently. Still, it was the way he spat the word out that gave it its full meaning in this instance. I'd only come across a handful of anti-English Welshmen (always men) but they'd certainly left an impression.

"Yes, I'm English," I said defensively, "but I live in Cardiff."

"Cardiff," he laughed. "That's not Welsh! So you think you'll be understanding some of our words then." He smiled meanly and took a sip of the pint that Gwyn had brought him, without uttering one word of thanks for it.

"What's Welsh for miserable old racist with a chip on his shoulder?" I asked, looking Tomos in the eye.

Tomos laughed and pulled out a stool. "Come on then. Sit your English-self down!"

I had no idea what to make of him but I did as Gwyn did and sat down, putting my drink on the table before me.

"So, Tomos, how are things?"

"Same as ever Gwyn. Same as ever."

"Not sold your farm yet, then?"

"No." He looked at me. "And not to a Saesneg either."

"So the Englishman's still interested in buying, is he then?"

"Upped his offer yesterday. Still said no. Not having the valley overrun with the damn English. This isn't bloody Herefordshire. The great Owain Glyndwr didn't fight for this beautiful old country of ours just to let us hand it to the enemy a few centuries later for hard cash."

"So English people aren't allowed to hold land in Wales then, are they?" I asked, rankled.

"Not if I can help it." He turned to Gwyn and added, "Do you know the Englishman actually had the cheek to tell me that Monmouthshire was the new Gloucestershire? Up and coming! That's what he said it was – up and coming! What am I supposed to do with that, I ask you? Daft idiot."

"What did you do?" asked Gwyn, suppressing a smile.

"I did what any good Welshman would have done, young Gwynfor. I hit him with my shepherd's crook and didn't stop hitting him until he climbed back into his city car and drove out the gates. Bloody English."

I gave him a sarcastic smile and before he could get any more pointed comments into the conversation, I said rather spitefully, "You will never guess what I bumped into on the way up here tonight."

Gwyn put a hand on my arm. "Steady," he said, but I'd hooked the old farmer's attention. He sat up and looked to Gwyn questioningly.

"Tomos…" Gwyn put his pint down and softly continued, "Why don't you tell us about the puma?"

For the briefest of seconds the old man dropped his guarded and miserable expression and looked plain shocked. Quickly recovering, he fiddled with the beer mat in front of him. "So it's a puma then, is it? Didn't know that."

Gwyn nodded. "Yes, it's a puma. And did you know they've got a team of police marksmen and a professional game hunter going over the valley trying to find it?"

"No. I didn't know that either." The old man raised his eyebrows and carried on feigning indifference. We weren't getting very far.

Gwyn tried a different tactic. "How's your dog? I heard that Old Shep got attacked by the puma, is it true?"

"Who told you?"

"One of the lads over at Caerwent Farm mentioned it."

"Well he's got no business…"

"So was Old Shep attacked by the big cat?"

Tomos shrugged. "May have been. May not have been." He carried on fiddling with the beer mat, turning it one way and then the other. But never looking back up at Gwyn or me.

Gwyn was a marvel at interrogating the old farmer. From my super-experienced position in the art of interrogation – having watched nearly all the police programmes from *Bergerac* right through to *Midsomer Murders* – I knew that Gwyn was probably doing the right thing by not jumping straight in and accusing him of keeping a puma. Which is exactly what I would have done if I were in his position. I'm sure that I would naturally default to being the bad cop, slamming my hands down on the beery table and shouting, "Show us the cat! Show us the cat, you racist Welsh bastard, before I throw you in the slammer and toss away the key!" Maybe it was the whole "*Saesneg*" thing. I'm not usually prone to violent talk.

As it was, there was no slamming of hands down on beery tables. I just watched the two of them and sipped my lemonade, playing the silent bad cop which from my TV-cop experience was often more intimidating. Who knows what lurked beneath that smooth untroubled surface? Dressed in my gold party frock and with hair in ringlets I looked about at bad-cop as Little Miss Muffet but still, I tried to affect a tough façade.

"OK, Tomos." Gwyn held his hands up. "I'm not going to play games with you, I'll speak plainly. You've got the puma, haven't you? Somehow or other you've gone and captured a wild animal and now you're using it against Elijah's stock. That's how you got the scratches on your arm and that's how Old Shep, who we all know barely leaves your farmyard let alone your house, came to be attacked. The cat's on your property and under your care."

Tomos considered for a moment before slowly looking up at Gwyn and me and shrugging.

"Well," Gwyn pushed, seeing he was winning Tomos round.

"You're half-right, young Gwynfor," Tomos relented, eventually.

"Go on then..."

"It's like this, see," he began, leaning forward conspiratorially and looking at us both for the first time since Gwyn had talked about the cat. He sighed, "I've known this cat for a long time now. Years, you might say. She's lived down yer in the valley by Coed y Brenin and she's never done me or my animals any bit of harm so I just let her be and things carry on day to day. Just treated her like a foreign neighbour." He looked over to me. "Like an Englishman."

He winked. I found myself smiling.

"Anyway," he continued, "I suppose I gets it into my head that perhaps I can use it to upset the boat a little for Elijah. You know how things are. You're not stupid, Gwynfor Jones. That man had all the good luck in the world. He got her." He nodded his head towards Angharad. "Got the best farm in the district, best flock at the best price. And six months ago would you believe it the man has not one but three healthy male grandchildren from his son's wife. Male triplets! The man never put a foot wrong in life, did he? Where as I? I just struggle along and keep my head down and no one thinks about me. No one cares about me. Well, I don't know, call it what you will – jealously I suppose, but I got to thinking. And the idea just pops into my head."

"To use the cat."

"If that's what you want to call it."

"You starved it?"

"Not starved. Let's just say I didn't let her feed for a while. Sharpened her appetite so she went for the bigger plates of food." He shrugged again. And then I saw that look again, the one I'd seen earlier in the evening when I'd been talking to Joe the policeman. The look that said, *I have more to say but don't know whether I should tell you.*

"How on earth did you capture it?" I asked, wondering how this rather doddery old farmer caught a very wild animal. Half-picturing him standing in his knackered old Barbour swinging a lasso around his head and hauling the writhing and howling beast in.

"That was easy enough to do, my young English friend," he replied, "the animal's obviously been someone's pet or something. There's not much wild about her. Anyways, she lived with me for a little while, bedded down near the sheds at the back of the farm during the winter and taking scraps of meat every so often, so we'd just sort of got used to each other, I suppose."

"Where do you keep it now?" Gwyn asked.

Tomos looked hesitant again. Now I was sure that there was something he was withholding from us. But he'd been so candid up to now how could he possibly have anything more shocking to add?

"Where do you keep the puma, Tomos?" Gwyn asked again, leaning towards him, just like a policeman in an interview on TV.

"That's the thing, isn't it," the old farmer began, slowly, going back to fiddling with the beer mats and running his thick calloused fingers along the edges. "It's like this. I don't have her any more, see."

Gwyn and I looked at each other.

"What?" I said.

"Well," Tomos sighed, "she got away, didn't she?"

"When?" we both said in unison.

"A few days ago…"

"Bloody hell! That explains why the sightings have gone up all over the valley!" Gwyn leant back and glanced around, aware that he'd been too loud.

"And why I saw it on the way up here," I volunteered.

"She's here?" The old farmer's eyes lit up and he looked towards the window expectantly. The poor old man. He must really care about the puma, however he'd mistreated her. Perhaps that lonely wild animal was the only friend he had? An abandoned cat and an abandoned old farmer, keeping each other company in this hidden valley.

"We were having this party at the Hen House, Ty Mawr…" I began.

"Party, eh?" Tomos' eyes twinkled. "I don't recall seeing an invite."

"Well, we're all English, Tomos. You'd hate it. What would Owen Glendower say?"

Tomos shrugged. "I could have put that behind me."

I laughed. "Next time maybe. Anyway, there were all these police marksmen that my friend invited and a big game hunter from Kenya…"

Tomos sat back, alarmed. "So there really is a hunter? Here?"

"At Ty Mawr. Fifteen minutes walk away."

"My God." He downed his pint and sat back, arms

crossed. "So what happened at the party? Why are these men in the valley again?"

"Like Gwyn said, they're here to get your cat. I was talking to one of the marksmen earlier this evening and he said that it was common knowledge a big cat lived round here, but it's only since it started attacking people's property that it's become an issue." Tomos was shaking his head. I continued, "I started to think about everything I'd seen during the few days I'd been here and, well, I got to making a connection between you and the cat. I saw the cuts on your arm the other night at the pub, and I saw you the next day walking towards the village with blood on the front of your jacket." Tomos self-consciously drew the sleeve of his checked shirt further down his hand.

"You're very perceptive," he acknowledged, begrudgingly.

"It was luck really, and when I thought about it all it became obvious. When I got to talking to one of these marksmen who told me that they had a theory the cat was being manipulated, well, I knew it had to be you. I set out to see Gwyn and talk to him about it. And that's when I met it. Her. On the path between Tŷ Mawr and Gwyn's farm."

"At what time?"

I looked at my watch. "Half nine?"

Tomos rose to his feet and pushed back his chair. "You're a brave girl," he said, "English, but brave. And smart too, coming up here to find out the truth for yourself before sending in those muscle-heads with their guns and their noise."

I smiled, happy to take the scraps of praise.

Tomos continued, "But now we've got to take action. We have to catch her. She's a trusting soul and not at all afraid of people. She'll come up to those policemen or that hunter chap as bold as brass to make friends. What did they say they would do with her once they've got her?"

Gwyn and I looked at each other for a second.

"There's talk of putting her in a zoo," Gwyn said, sparing Tomos the details.

"Never!" Tomos was grabbing the table now. "We've got to make sure they don't get her. We have to do something and save her from them. My poor girl!"

"You're not going to get her now?" I asked.

"Of course we have to get her now. She could stroll up to those policemen this very evening and then what would happen to her? No, we should definitely get her this evening. We should make the most of the policemen and the hunter being occupied by your English friends over at this party you didn't invite Gwynfor or me to." He nudged Gwyn, who looked plain embarrassed. "We'll need something to entice her to us..." He looked around, as if the solution lay in the main bar area of the pub.

"Oh my God." I slapped my forehead. "What on earth is happening? There's a puma on the loose and we're going to catch it? We're going to go out there this evening and look for it? There are trained professionals down the road who could do a proper job – if they weren't too pissed. If we amateurs start having a go, God knows what will happen! Surely you can leave it up to them? We can tell them that she's tame and you can help them out?"

"We're hardly amateurs," Gwyn objected, looking offended. "Tomos and I are more than used to dealing with animals. And we have the right equipment to capture it."

"What, an exposed neck and some tender flesh?" I asked, remembering how vulnerable that part of my torso had felt on the road earlier that evening.

"She's tame," Tomos argued, "she's a lovely character when you get to know her."

"Such a lovely character that she tore your arm up?"

His face softened and he put his hands out in front of him on the table. "I was provoking, wasn't I? I'd kept her cooped up all day and had to get her into the trailer. Turned out she wasn't having any of it."

"And trying to capture her now when she's broken free isn't going to provoke her at all?" I asked.

Tomos ignored the sarcasm and shrugged his shoulders. "Not if you give her a good reason to go into the trailer. Gwynfor, do you have any meat in the house? A hunk of beef? Some lamb? Chicken?"

"None." He looked sheepishly. "Does she like bread and cheese?"

Tomos smiled again. His face cracked around the mouth area and his eyes went a bit twinkly which was probably as good as a smile ever got for him, probably not having much practice. For a split second he looked a bit like a nice old granddad, before assuming his gruff old-militant-Welsh-farmer-look again. "Let's see now…" He looked around the pub again before his eye caught the chalkboard menu and he stared at it for a moment. We followed his gaze, trying to see what had interested him. This was surely no time to be thinking about ordering profiteroles and a coffee?

"Right." He slammed his hands down on the table and made me jump. "We need fifteen pounds! Do you have any money, young Gwynfor? I've got –" and he emptied his pockets on the table, counting the coins – "eight pounds."

"I'm sorry," I said, "I came out in a bit of a hurry. I

don't have my purse on me."

"It's OK." Gwyn jumped to the rescue. "I've got the rest."

"Good man!" Tomos slapped his money down in Gwyn's hand. "Now, my young friend, go and order a very rare steak from Angharad. She hardly ever cooks the steak even when it's well done, so a rare one probably means she's just walked it past the oven."

Gwyn dutifully went off to the bar and left me with Tomos, who looked, for the first time I'd ever seen him, rather animated and, well, happy.

He winked at me. "We can have the chips before we go," he said, "shame to waste them."

I smiled at him and took another sip of lemonade. Really, he wasn't that bad. Once you got past the hardened Welsh exterior. Maybe it was a defence thing? Maybe having endured a lifetime of knocks, and having seen someone near you sail through their life with the best of luck, you were left hardened and forever embittered?

Had he really never met anyone after Angharad? Had she been the one true love of his life who was stolen away from him on the very brink of their marriage and then remained in the same village as he did, so he could watch her marry her new love, raise a family and grow old together, while he lived alone and watched from the sidelines? Now that put all my worries about a Dull Life Crisis into a perspective; some people had a much tougher life than I would ever have. So I didn't go horse riding? At least I wasn't condemned to a life of solitude while my true love cavorted around the neighbourhood with another man.

"You and Gwynfor then, is it?" Tomos brought me back to the present, looking at me meaningfully.

"Oh. Oh no!" I said, putting my drink down hastily and suddenly going very hot. "No, I've only just met him."

He just nodded. "Shame," he said eventually. "Nice man, Gwynfor. Had a terrible rough one from Merthyr a while back. Awful scraggy thing she was. No, you're much better. So you're not…"

"No!" I said, with pantomime gusto, now aching to ask about the terrible scraggy one from Merthyr. How long ago was that? What was she like exactly – what does scraggy mean? Did she not wash her hair very often or something? Or did it mean she was very thin. How thin? Thinner than me? Did he like thin women? And how long had they been seeing each other? Did she have a name? Was there a photograph?

I didn't ask him any of the questions. I just smiled and nodded and pretended I was completely uninterested, ferociously gripping the edge of the table with the effort of restraining myself from launching into so many questions.

Fortunately, before I had chance to break down and beg Tomos for information, Gwyn came back from the bar and all talk returned to the puma and what we ought to do with it once we'd caught it.

Assuming that we caught it.

We all agreed that it had a right to its freedom. We didn't want it to go in a zoo and spend its life padding round a small wire cage and being shouted at by obnoxious sugar-crazed school kids. And we didn't want to leave it on its own out there, with a good chance that a pack of hung-over marksmen might maim it in the next few days.

"So you think there's no possibility that this puma of yours will escape the hunters and eventually things will die down a bit? No prospect of her going about like before?" Gwyn asked, playing with his empty pint glass. "I mean, if you say she's been living here untroubled for years now…"

"I don't reckon she's got much of a chance, to be honest," Tomos said, sadly. "I've seen to that haven't I, fool that I am. No, I think now that livestock have been affected she stands the best chance if she were to be taken somewhere else where she can mind her own business and not get into trouble."

"But where?" I asked. "Where can she go where it doesn't matter what she kills to eat?"

Tomos thought for a moment.

"England?"

"Tomos!"

"OK, OK, only joking. I reckon we should drop her in to Mid Wales," he said slowly, thinking it through. "I've got a brother up there in the Carrog Valley with acres and acres of land. She would be fine with the rabbits and the birds to catch, just like she used to be. Plenty of woodland, the river. I even recall him saying there was a sighting of a big cat or something up there a few years ago. My cat might have company, which would be nice for her…"

"Yes, but they don't like company, do they?" I said, the voice of knowledge since I'd spoken to Joe the policeman who had boastfully told me everything Josh had told him. "That police marksman I told you about earlier was saying that big cats' territories are really important and they don't overlap them with other cats. Suppose we put her in another cat's territory? The other cat would rip her limb from limb. She'd be torn in two. And the original cat would have the advantage because he'd know the terrain and he could…"

"But it's a female," Tomos said. "Shouldn't be so much

of a problem. Although it's a good point you're making there, miss. But I don't think we need to worry ourselves about it. Ahh lovely, steak!"

Angharad bought the dinner over and for a moment there was an awkwardness as she and Tomos looked at each other but said nothing. He still loved her. It was so sad.

We tucked into our chips and surreptitiously Tomos wrapped the steak in a clean white handkerchief and put it in the satchel he always carried with him. I saw Gwyn eyeing up the steak – honestly, did the man never eat? What he needed was a good woman...

Within a few minutes the chips were finished.

"Come on then," Gwyn said, getting up. "Let's go and bag us a puma!"

27

"**Go** on, go on!" Marcia clapped her hands together in excitement, eagerly leaning towards me. She was leaning so far towards me, in fact, that she was almost falling off her seat. I was so enjoying the moment, taking my time and sipping my wine while her eyes, wide like saucers, were imploring me to hurry up and tell the story.

"This wine is really lovely…"

"Oh come on, come on, Rachel!" Marcia slammed her manicured hands down on the table. "What happened next? Oh my God, I can't believe what you're telling me!"

"Well," I said, slowly putting my wine glass back on the coaster, "after the pub we took Gwyn's Land Rover and went down to Tomos' farm. The men thought it was best if we split up and looked for the animal separately…"

"And you were OK with that? Going out there on your

own?"

"I had no choice," I said, savouring the look on her face. "Besides, I already knew what I was dealing with. I'd fought the puma single-handedly on the lane earlier that evening and managed to stun it, giving me just enough time to get to Gwyn's."

"Oh my God, you're just so brave!"

I laughed modestly. "I did what I could. Anyway, we were determined to rescue that poor animal so we split up and I was assigned the track that led down into the valley and to the river. It was dark, really, really dark, but Tomos had given me a torch. It was powerful enough, but it meant that I could only see straight in front into the beam so for most of the time I had no idea what was lurking in the woods on either side of the track."

"You must have been terrified!"

"Well, you know, not really." I examined my nails. "You do what you have to do. Anyway, I'd been on my own for about ten minutes or so when I saw it, straight in front of me in the torchlight. I don't know why, but I crouched down and with my third of the steak I lured it up to me and managed to tie some rope around its neck."

"No way!"

"Oh yes. I just sort of knew what I had to do and I did it. I wasn't the least bit frightened. All I had to do then was to call Gwyn and Tomos on my mobile to say I had it, and walk it back to Tomos' farm. I must have looked extraordinary, emerging from that wood with a puma straining on a lead, still dressed in all my party gear – gold dress, kitten heels and curled hair. Huh, I guess that's what drove Gwyn to do what he did next."

"I so wish it had been me!" Marcia whined miserably, throwing herself back in the chair. "All I did last weekend was swim the channel in a record time, but that's really lame in comparison to your weekend…"

I replayed this triumphant scene over and over in my head as Gwyn manoeuvred his Land Rover down the muddy track from the pub to his house.

"Are you all right?" he asked, glancing briefly in my direction before turning back to concentrate on the road which was treacherous to say the least, twisting left and right, plummeting sharply with no warning and rutted with potholes.

"Who, me?"

"Yes, you. You keep sighing."

"Oh. I'm fine. Don't worry about me."

"Maybe we should take her back to Tŷ Mawr," said Tomos from the back seat. "This is no place for a woman."

"NO! I'm fine. Honestly. And I want to be here. I've already met the puma once, so what's the big deal?"

I didn't want to be sent back to the Hen House and miss all the excitement. What would I have to tell Marcia if I went back now? That I stayed safe inside by the fire while a handsome farmer lassoed himself a puma in the Welsh countryside?

"Well, here we are, anyway." Gwyn pulled up at what must I assumed was Tomos' farmhouse. In the beam of the headlights I could just make out a tiny crooked building, timber framed with small leaded windows and a bent and bowing roof. There must have been a fire on as smoke was coming out of the chimney. Probably for his dog, Old Shep, curled up in front of it, waiting for his master to return from the pub.

Gwyn turned off the engine and we sat in silence for a

moment. I looked over to him but could barely make out his expression in the thin moonlight coming in through the windscreen. Tomos, sitting in the back, was completely in the dark.

"So what are we going to do then, Tomos?" Gwyn asked.

"I reckon it should be me that goes out with the meat, looking for her. She knows me, she trusts me."

"Trusted," I corrected.

"OK, call it what you will, but she knows me. Gwynfor, you stay by the trailer and when I bring her in – if I bring her in – you be ready to close up the doors once she's inside. Be sure to stay downwind of her, though. We don't want her to know you're there."

"And what shall I do?" I asked in my bravest voice. There was a long pause. It answered my question without them needing to say another word.

It was Tomos who finally spoke up. "I reckon you should stay in the house."

"WHAT?" I cried. "That's not fair! What's the point of me being here if I have to stay in the house? I won't even see what's happening! Can't I at least stay in the Land Rover and be a lookout? I won't make a noise, I promise. Please don't leave me in the house. I want to see."

"Oh for the love of God!" I could make out Tomos holding his hands up over his ears. "Stop your whinging, for God's sake, woman! You can stay in the vehicle if you like, but no sudden movements. No noise. And no more whining!"

I nodded, still put out that I wasn't going to be on active service. Still, a lookout was important. I checked my phone – I still had plenty of battery left and there was one tiny bar of signal. I should be OK.

"Phone OK?" Gwyn asked, seeing me checking it.

"Fine. Is there a phone in the house just in case I don't have enough signal?"

"Go in the front door, straight ahead on the left," Tomos said. "I keep the door unlocked so go right in. Shep won't bother you – he'll be by the fire all night."

I nodded. Now I was beginning to feel more involved. If this were a film, I would be kitted out with one of those silver headpieces that people have in call-centres, with a little microphone attached that I could talk to the boys on. I would be dressed in close fitting black stealth clothing, a bit like Catwoman but without the tail. Or the ears. And I'd be the key to the success of the whole scenario. If this was a film, I would be the first to spot the puma and have to direct the men to the animal so the whole success of the mission would be down to me. Really I was the key to the whole thing.

Tomos and Gwyn continued to work out a foolproof plan for rounding up the puma without being pounced on, clawed, bitten or generally savaged to death.

I turned to the dash and carefully positioned my mobile for quick-access. My command centre was up and running. I peered out of the windscreen into the moonlit farmyard to the left of the house; the concrete ground was a dazzling white rectangle in the black forested landscape. It was spooky to know that out there, probably not far away, the puma was prowling around, looking for food. I shivered. So much for my big plan to emerge glorious from the woodland with a puma on a leash and make Gwyn hot under the collar. But the realisation was beginning to dawn on me that exposing myself to mortal danger was not the only way to put an end to my Dull Life Crisis. Surely it was enough just to be here, sitting in a Land Rover in the remote Welsh hills late at night and playing lookout on a puma-hunt? This on its own proved that I was, in fact, leading a very exciting life. It was a Sunday night and there wasn't a Domino's pizza box or rented video in sight. I wondered, fleetingly, what was happening back up at the Hen House. How was the party going on? Had Louisa pounced on Josh the Hunter yet? Would he stab her with a sedative dart and make a quick getaway?

Tomos and Gwyn had begun speaking in Welsh now, but every so often they would slip in an English word, sometimes an innocuous word like "see?" or "yes". But just as I was slipping back into my daydream telling Marcia about the weekend, I was horribly brought back to the present when they unmistakably used the words "muzzle" and "neck hold". Hmm, this was definitely a job for the boys. And farmers at that. But was Tomos right to think that firstly she'd remember him and secondly, if she did remember him, she would forgive him for what he had done, keeping her cooped up and hungry? Could the plan really work? Could we actually capture the animal? Christ, what if it all went wrong? What if she turned on him, with her pointed fangs and razor-sharp claws? What if Tomos stumbled out of the woodland ripped to pieces and bleeding everywhere? Who would I call? How would I direct the ambulance to the farm? Where the hell were we? Near the Crossed Keys pub in the Brecon Beacons but down the valley a bit. Shit, I should get directions from them before they went off.

"Rachel, Rachel!" Gwyn hissed at me, trying not to make too much of a noise. I should really stop daydreaming.

"Sorry, miles away. What?"

"We're off now. Did you hear what we had planned?"

"Erm, yes. Absolutely." It was probably best to sound

like I knew what he was talking about.

"Good. Well, you stay in the vehicle. Don't get out. Not even if you hear us shouting."

"Fine," I said, smiling with pursed lips. Suddenly I wanted my contact centre headgear and Catwoman outfit. Then I'd feel more the part.

"Is there anything you want to ask before we go?"

"Erm." I thought hard. Nothing. My mind was blank. "No?"

"Right then, come on Tomos, let's get this cat into the trailer." And with that the two farmers silently got out of the vehicle, pushing the doors gently closed and disappeared round the farmhouse and towards the barn.

The address! That's what I needed to ask them. How would I direct the emergency services to the scene of mutilation if I didn't know where we were? Did we turn right or left out of the Crossed Keys? Maybe while they were still in sight I should get out and go to Tomos' house to get the address, he'd be bound to have some post somewhere. Then I could work out where we were to send the paramedics.

I went to open the door and then thought better of it. Can't they do satellite tracking of mobiles these days? They'd know where I was. Surely? But then do satellites pass over Wales? They must do.

I checked my mobile again. No signal! How? I hadn't moved. I had one small job to do and I'd not been at all prepared for it.

I checked my mobile again – one bar of signal! Someone at Vodafone was having a laugh at my expense.

I sat back in my seat. How long would it take to catch a puma? Days and days if the police marksmen were anything to go by. How long were Gwyn and Tomos going to give it before they gave up? It was nearly midnight. Midnight! How had it got so late? But then, now I started thinking about it, it did seem a long time since I had been sitting on the sofa with Joe the policeman and learning all about pumas. In fact, it seemed more like days than just hours ago. Five hours ago I was taking the rollers out of my hair, for goodness sake. Five hours ago I had no idea I was going to come face-to-furry-face with the puma, find out the secret of the sightings and go big game hunting in the Beacons. I just imagined I was going to get off my trolley on cheap wine and have a bit of a dance. Funny how things turn out.

Had anyone from the party even noticed I was missing yet? Was anyone concerned? Perhaps they just thought I'd gone to bed early. Perhaps my Dull Life Crisis aura was enough to convince them I'd just left to get a good night's sleep. I wonder how the party was going? Had Henna worked her charms on the policeman? Maybe I should give them a call, tell them I was OK. Would they even hear the phone though?

I checked my phone again. The single bar of signal had gone again now and the display was void of any network. Shit. Why should signal suddenly disappear like that?

I put it back on the dash.

Remembering what Tomos had said about no sudden movements I stealthily wound the seat back to make myself more comfortable. After all, I might be here a long time.

I looked out. Nothing.

I hadn't even seen Tomos leave the barn and go into the woodland. Was he still with Gwyn, setting up the trailer?

Quarter past twelve.

He must have gone into the woods by now. Surely?

Perhaps there was a route into the woodland via the barn that I couldn't see.

"Ouch!" I'd moved my leg onto the rough seam of the seat. I shuffled across and examined the rip in the moonlight. It must have been made a long time ago as I could see in the dim light that there had been at least three attempts at patching it with tape. Not a vehicle for women; perhaps the rough one from Merthyr had said the very same thing to him. Had tried to get him to buy a white BMW to take her round the shops? I had to concede that however knackered and unbelievably filthy the Land Rover was, it was such a very suitable vehicle for here and I couldn't imagine it down in the city, crawling along the main roads in nose to tail traffic jams. Up here, covered in mud and dented and scratched, it didn't look out of place but if it was parked outside the offices where I worked it would instantly be towed away for looking like an abandoned vehicle. The only off-roaders I ever saw were the ones with leather seats and tinted windows.

It was getting cold. I looked around and saw an old blanket on the back seat. Slowly I reached back to get it, but shrank away when I caught a whiff of it. It was absolutely disgusting. I left it where it was and rubbed my arms instead, trying to restore some heat. What time was it now? Twenty-five past twelve. Still no sign of the puma.

The rug really stank. How come I hadn't noticed it before? What on earth had Gwyn kept wrapped up in it? Did he keep his torn-in-two sheep in it? Had he never heard of washing powder? All my womanly instincts, which up to now had been entirely non-existent, were overflowing. The man had no food in the place, was disorganised and lived in a sparsely furnished, although quite homely, house. How long had it been since the scraggy Merthyr girl?

And just what did scraggy mean, anyway?

I stared out of the windows, gazing into the blackness around me. Something scurried across the yard and my heart leapt but it must have been a mouse. I could understand now why Joe the policeman had shot a squirrel by mistake – once you're wound up and expecting to see a puma, that's all you will see.

An owl started its spooky hooting from the woodland right beside me.

Then some birds near the house started squawking. I sat up, stiffened in anticipation. Had the puma disturbed them? Or Tomos?

I angled my wrist to check my watch in the moonlight.

One o'clock.

I was really cold now, and there was no way I could warm myself up. Holding my arms wasn't working, nor was drawing myself up in the seat – it just made my back ache.

Gwyn had left the keys in the ignition and I was sorely tempted to turn the heating on. It wouldn't make much of a noise to have the engine running for a little while, would it? But then maybe it would. And it would be pretty bad to jeopardise the whole evening by starting the engine up. The farmers would more than likely be very cross with me.

So there wasn't much I could do, bar going indoors or putting that stinky blanket around my shoulders.

I looked back at it on the back seat. It looked very thick and warm. Tentatively I reached out and bought it to me.

URGH!

It really did smell very, very bad indeed. Now that it was near my I knew there was no way I was prepared to cover myself in that smell. It would never come off my clothes. Or my skin.

Throwing the rug onto the driver's seat, I huddled back and put my arms around my waist, resolutely staring forward into the night.

At half past one I put the blanket round me. It was warm.

At thirty-five minutes past one I stopped feeling nauseous from the smell of the blanket.

The moon had moved over to the mountains in the distance and a different set of shadows were cast onto the moonlit yard. The trees looked as though they were actually creeping slowly towards me, the black branches scratching long shadows reaching for the Land Rover. There was now less visible distance between the black gloom of the woods and me. Even less chance to see anything.

Oh my God.

She was watching me.

Even wrapped in my blanket safe inside Gwyn's Land Rover, I thought my heart was going to give way it was banging so violently in my chest. The puma was standing a metre away looking in at me.

I didn't move.

Crap. Was my presence going to jeopardise the whole thing? Where was Tomos? WHERE WAS TOMOS?

I turned my head slowly to look into the woodland while keeping the cat firmly in view. I couldn't see anything. No sign of the farmer. Maybe Gwyn could see what I could see – maybe he was going to come round and entice it in to the trailer?

I turned back slowly to the animal, standing right in front of me and looking right at me. She was a beautiful thing. Lit by moonlight, her coat was wonderfully soft-looking, with a white nose and chest. She had a way of looking very calm and her eyes were almost docile.

I looked at her mouth. I couldn't see any blood. It was a good sign; hopefully Tomos wasn't lying bleeding anywhere clasping the back of his neck, taking his last shaky Welsh breaths. I stayed absolutely still, hardly breathing, clutching my stinky blanket closely around me.

Then, from beside the puma, I saw Tomos emerging from the black woodland into the moonlight, so slowly, hands held out at his sides. It barely looked as if he were moving.

He was saying something to the puma, which turned to him now and watched with such a casual, disinterested expression it was hard to imagine there was any real danger involved. But I'd seen those wildlife programmes where a perfectly docile-looking lion yawns, stretches and then rips apart a bouncy gazelle without batting an eyelid.

Tomos, still holding out his hands beside him, spoke to the cat again. It began to move gradually towards him and the pair inched towards the barn. It was working!

I stayed frozen still, scared stiff in case I ruined the whole thing.

They disappeared from view.

Sinking back into the seat I took a few deep breaths. Tomos had been right, the cat must be really tame, judging by the way she followed Tomos' directions. Poor thing – to think of all those men with guns hunting her down. We were definitely doing the right thing.

I think.

I threw the stinky blanket back on the seat behind me. I'd generated enough heat to last until daybreak.

I kept my eyes fixed on the corner of the farmhouse where I'd last seen Tomos and the puma disappear. No one emerged. I stared and stared until I knew the shape of each cornerstone of the house perfectly, but still neither Gwyn nor Tomos appeared from behind them. I checked my watch. It was now ten minutes since Tomos had walked round the corner with the cat. I gingerly reached out and took my phone. No signal. Damn. Replacing it, I paused, still leaning forward. Had I just heard something? The faintest of clicks? I couldn't be sure.

"All right there?"

"Fuck!" My hand flew up my chest. Gwyn was right outside my window. How had I not seen him walking towards me? Tomos was coming up to the Land Rover and within a moment they'd both climbed in.

"Bit jittery?" Gwyn grinned and flicked on a light.

"Bad language never did any lady any credit," came the quiet reproach from the back.

"You scared me!" I defended myself. "So how would a lady deal with being terrified?"

Tomos thought for a moment. "She'd come over all faint, I reckon."

"Anyway…" I decided we should move on. "Well?"

"She's in the trailer having her steak." Gwyn smiled and then yawned.

I clapped my hands together in excitement.

"Oh sorry, I didn't mean to make you guys jump. That's amazing though!" I turned to Tomos. "She just walked alongside you like a dog! She must really trust you."

"Yes. Yes she does." The old man nodded, lips pursed tight and head bowed. He took a deep breath in and clapping Gwyn on the shoulder said, "You two ought to be getting back. I'll keep her in the trailer tonight – she'll be safe there. She's got food and water, and Gwyn put straw in for her to sleep on so she's got it good. Come back tomorrow and we'll take her away."

And with that the old farmer shook Gwyn's hand and muttered a few words to him before getting out of the Land Rover and heading indoors.

I buckled my seat belt.

It was over!

The cat was captured and we were safe. I yawned. Gwyn wearily started up the vehicle and we left Tomos' farm and headed up the road again. I turned to wave at Tomos, who was standing in his doorway, watching us go.

"Are you sure he'll not let it out into the wild tonight?" I asked as we turned a corner and he disappeared from view.

Gwyn yawned again and rubbed his tired eyes – no mean feat when you're trying to manoeuvre a four-wheel drive up a potholed twisty road at two in the morning. I gripped the dash.

"Absolutely sure," he said. "I think Tomos is rather attached to that animal, and if it stays out in the wild here it's bound to get caught. He's a sensible man, is Tomos, when it comes down to it, and he knows he's doing the right thing by letting her go."

"Poor Tomos," I sighed, my thoughts filled with the image of the old man waving us off from his front step. "First he lets Angharad go, and now he has to let his beloved puma go. It's just not fair, is it?"

Gwyn looked over at me, the Land Rover juddering into a pothole. "Who said things are fair?"

"I know that. It's just … well, he deserves a break doesn't he?"

"Rachel, Tomos hasn't suffered too badly."

He said my name! "Yes but…"

"He still sees Angharad you know."

"Yes at the pub but…"

"No. He *sees* her."

I looked straight at him but his eyes were fixed to the road. Surely not? Surely not in the sense of "seeing" someone?

"Do you mean –?"

"Yes," Gwyn laughed, wrenching the wheel to avoid us plummeting into a steep wooded ravine.

"Oh good God," I laughed, despite the terror of the drive.

"And not just Angharad either. There's Gwenda: she works over at the post office. He's been seeing her off and on for years now."

"No way!"

"And another woman over at the market but we haven't worked out her name yet."

"Now you're joking! You must be."

"Not a word of a lie, Rachel. The lads round here call him Casanova Bach; it means 'little Casanova' in Welsh. Right old dark horse, he is. He'd be after you if you were up here any longer."

"I wish I was."

"What, with Tomos?"

"No! Gwyn that's just – just wrong! I mean, I wish I was staying longer."

The words hung in the air and there was nothing more to say. We bounced round a rough corner and I settled back into the seat and let Gwyn concentrate on the difficult drive. I surreptitiously looked at him as he drove me back to the Hen House. His hair was ruffled and pulled, and his shoulders were slightly hunched with tiredness and concentration on the road ahead. He still looked devilishly handsome. Should I invite him in for a drink? Surely at 2 am some of the girls would still be around? It would be a pretty poor party if it had finished by now.

28

$\mathcal{A}s$ we neared the Hen House I began to realise just how tired I was. Wound up and nervous in the Land Rover waiting for the puma to appear, I hadn't given much thought to dozing off, but now that I was safe, the heating was on and the Land Rover was rocking backwards and forwards on the bumpy track, I realised I was actually completely exhausted.

Still, I must have used up a lot of calories with all that muscle clenching, heart pounding anxiety. Maybe putting myself in terrifying situations was yet another solution to a newer, slimmer me. What with that and the lusting, I would soon be one of those size zero women and I could sit next to Marcia and make her look like a hot air balloon in comparison to my newly trim frame.

We pulled up at the house.

"Looks like that party's still in full swing," Gwyn said without much enthusiasm. And really, I couldn't blame him. The wine and policemen had definitely lost their appeal and there hadn't been much more to the party than that. What was more appealing was the thought of my newly acquired king-sized bed in my newly acquired king-sized bedroom. Sleep…

The lights were all on, and as we watched the front door was pulled open and a figure lurched outside, hanging on to the doorframe for support.

"That's odd," I began, yawning and peering out into the night, trying to make out who had just left the house. Being so tired was like being drunk; things blurred and distorted and nothing made much sense any more.

"What?" Gwyn asked.

"I don't recognise him."

"Who?"

"That person." I pointed in the direction of the man that had gone outside and was now throwing up violently, leaning for support against Laura's car.

Something was definitely not right.

"Eurgh!" Even though it was truly appalling, I just couldn't take my eyes off the vomiting man. Now he had partially turned to Laura's car and was covering that. God, she was going to go ballistic.

"Who is it, then?"

"I have no idea." I watched the man sink lower and lower. His knees buckled and in one movement his hand slipped off the puke-covered bonnet and he fell face down into the pile of vomit on the ground. Silence again.

"Isn't it one of the policemen or that big game hunter chap?"

"Josh? No, I don't think so. The men who arrived when I was at the party were all pretty stocky chaps, but Mr Vomit here is really skinny. Urgh!" I held my head in my hands and groaned. Why was this happening? I hadn't realised that coming back to a party still in full swing would mean no sleep – and sleep was now my number one priority.

"Do you want me to come in and see if everything is OK?"

"Would you mind? I'm really sorry but..." It was probably nothing. One of the policemen had probably invited their mate or something. We walked past the man that had collapsed onto the ground. Gwyn bent down and put his hand on the man's neck.

"He's still alive," he laughed but I didn't find it very funny. Maybe because I'd come face to face with the puma that evening and death seemed a whole lot closer than it had done in my previous thirty years. Or maybe it took a lot more to shock me now that I knew Tomos was the local stud.

Inside the Hen House the smell was the first thing that hit me, which was surprising because after Gwyn's manky blanket I thought my ability to smell anything would be disabled for the next couple of months at least.

The haze of fags and weed in the air was inescapable. And worrying. Because when Laura had run through the house's Health and Safety regulations when we'd first arrived, there were pretty strict rules about not smoking in or around the premises. We'd never get rid of the smell by the time we were due to leave the place tomorrow. Today! I kept forgetting it was the early hours of the morning. If we had to leave the house by 10 am we had less than eight hours left.

There was another smell too, mixed in with the smoke. I sniffed, tentatively. It was the sour alcohol smell that hung on the breath of very drunk people. The place smelt like a seedy pub from my university days.

Both Gwyn and I were so numb from our evening that we walked like the dead down the hallway. There was no loud music now, just the noise of the TV.

We walked in to the sitting room, crisps and nuts and broken glass crunching under our feet. Bottles and cans were scattered on the trestle table, leaking their contents onto the wooden floor where it seeped down the cracks in the old boards. There were two unknown men either sleeping or passed out on the sofa, with another slumped on an enormous suede bean bag watching American football on the TV, crumpled can of Stella in one hand and the most enormous joint in the other.

Where was everyone? Where had the girls gone? I struggled to find some evidence of the room I'd left when I'd set out to find Gwyn earlier that evening. Where had our party gone?

The man watching the TV turned round slowly to look at us.

"Hello?" I said.

He looked fuzzily at me through the haze of his spliff. "Yeah." He raised a hand half-heartedly and turned back to the TV.

"Er, who are you?" I asked.

"Howie," he said, not turning from watching the game. The name was familiar but I couldn't work out why.

"Howie. Right. Why are you here?" I could feel Gwyn bristling with anger beside me. The place was trashed. One of the curtains had been pulled from the window and lay crumpled in a corner covered in cans of cider and upturned bowls of crisps. Where was Laura? She would be doing her nut.

"Fuckin' chucked us out, didn't he?"

"Who?"

"Fuckin' tight-arse landlord." Howie turned round to me, clearly pissed off at having the game interrupted. "Didn't like the drink and fags." He waved his can and his joint at me, to demonstrate what a drink and a fag looked like. He turned back to the football.

"Look, Howie, sorry, but I'm just not getting it." I'd had to deal with a puma, for God's sake. No junked-up stranger was going to get the better of me. I went up to him and stood in front of the TV blocking his view, which was something Marcia would not have been able to have done, given her skinniness. "Why are you staying here? This is a hen do. You can't stay over here."

"We're the stag do, aren't we?" As soon as he said the words my heart sank. I knew why I recognised his name now. The worst had happened. "James said we should all come and join you lot rather than try to book ourselves into some other bleedin' hotel. Anyway, there aren't any hotels round here in this wasteland. It's a fuckin' dump, this area. At least you have a pub near you. There was nothing near us."

"Where are all the girls?"

"Went to bed, I s'pose. Dunno." And he was lost to the TV again.

Where was Laura? Surely she wouldn't have stood for any of this?

I backed off and ran upstairs. Gwyn followed close behind.

I opened my bedroom door, dreading what I'd see.

From the hall light I could make out Henna lying across my bed. Henna wound round one of the policemen, semi-clothed and definitely post-coital, fast asleep.

"Oh my God," I hissed quietly.

269

"Your room?" Gwyn whispered.

"Yes. Oh, this is awful!"

I opened the door wider and surveyed the scene. Beer cans, underwear, crushed crisps. I could feel myself trembling with anger and utter despair. I was exhausted. This was the last thing I wanted. Why couldn't I just go to sleep on my own bed? I was frozen to the spot, shaking and staring at the figures on the bed. Who or what was in her room if she was in mine?

"Look," Gwyn said softly, holding my arms and standing before me, "come back and stay with me. I've got a sofa you could sleep on. You can't stay here tonight."

My lovely comfy king-sized bed was just there. It was so unfair after all I'd been through in the last few hours. I felt cheated. I could feel the tears coming down my cheeks for the second time that night, this time out of self-pity.

"Come on." Gwyn pulled me to him and I fell into his arms and against his chest, which was deliciously broad and warm. We stood there for a few wonderful seconds and I melted into him, listening to his heart beating, closing my eyes. I could sleep just here, standing up next to him. He pulled back gently. "Come on, we really can't stay here. Have you got a bag or something you want to bring with you?"

"Yes." I reluctantly left him and hunted round and found my holdall in the dark. My pyjamas were on the floor beside the wardrobe so I threw them in, shaking the crisps off first. I tiptoed around the room as softly as I could so as not to wake the sleeping bed-thieves.

We headed down the corridor towards the staircase. I paused.

"You go to the Land Rover," I said. "I just want to make sure Laura's OK. She's the one who organised the

270

weekend and I absolutely cannot believe she would have let this happen to the house."

"All right then." Gwyn crept down the stairs. I lightly knocked at Laura's door. Nothing. What had happened to her? Was she even in the Hen House or had most of the girls left? But then their cars were still outside. Cautiously, I pushed open the heavy oak door and went in. There on the bed was Laura, Joe the policeman curled up beside her and – Josh! All naked! All three sprawled drunkenly, barely covered by duvet or sheets. I grimaced, feeling sick now, and hastily beat a retreat.

Fair enough – that was why things had got so out of hand with the stag weekend boys. Laura had been otherwise engaged. With Joe and Josh! What kind of a party had it turned into? And there was me sitting in a lonely cold Land Rover further down the valley covered in a filthy old blanket and worrying whether they would have missed me at the party. What was I thinking?

Still, I reasoned as I retraced my steps along the hall and down the staircase, at least I wasn't about to get hung up on having missed all the action and living a Dull Life. I'd much prefer to have had the evening I'd had, although I would have loved to have witnessed what went off in the Hen House. What had happened to Louisa, who was presumably now somewhere with her fiancé James? What had their reunion been like? What had happened to the other policemen? Where were the other stag weekenders? I was intrigued – but only slightly. More than that, I was exhausted and ached for bed.

Dodging the passed-out puker by the front door, I climbed back into Gwyn's battered Land Rover.

"Everything OK?" he asked.

"No. It's an absolute disaster. Boys and girls

everywhere." Gwyn raised his eyebrows but I didn't elaborate. It was just too seedy to share with him right now, especially as I was on the brink of staying with him. He might think that I was that sort of girl, and he'd get completely the wrong end of the stick. Promiscuity for me these days was falling asleep clutching two remote controls, rather than being faithful to just the one.

I yawned uncontrollably loudly. "Thank you so much for putting me up tonight. There's no way I can stay there." I fumbled around with the seatbelt, too tired to know how to work it. Gwyn took it off me and clicked it into place.

"No problem," he said and we drove off.

Within a few minutes we were outside Gwyn's house. It felt like years since I'd been at his front door hammering it with a rolling-pin and screaming. Not my finest moment perhaps.

What a very, very strange night. Now that exhaustion had set in it all seemed a bit unreal. Did I really see a puma? Twice? And had we really caught it to take it to mid Wales tomorrow?

Gwyn turned the engine off and I sat in my seat, staring out in front of me in a daze. I closed my eyes for a moment, nestling in to the now familiar seat. I could happily sleep here, right now.

"Come on, Rachel." He unclipped my seat belt and helped me out. He held my hand and led me inside to his cosy lounge with an enormous sofa that looked almost as inviting as my hijacked double bed back at the Hen House.

"Here," he said. "It's not much, I'm afraid, but it'll take ages to change my bed so it's probably best if you have this. And it's very comfy. I fall asleep on it all the time."

I sank down onto the thick cushions that moulded

around me. It felt wonderful. "I can't thank you enough," I said, running my hands through my hair and holding my head which felt like it weighed a ton. "Really. I'm so grateful." I tried to stifle another yawn, but it was so enormous it wouldn't be stopped.

"I'll leave you to it then," he said. "Bathroom's at the top of the stairs on the right. Goodnight."

"G'night" I said, yawning again. I ought to find my pyjamas and my toothbrush. Surely I could have a bit of Gwyn's toothpaste. Couldn't I? But it was all too much. I was beyond all that. I pushed the holdall onto the floor and sank down onto the sofa, kicking off my kitten heels. The sofa smelt of him and I buried myself deep into it, almost as if I was enveloped by him. Within a few seconds I must have fallen asleep.

I half woke up when I felt him laying a duvet over me and I think, although I can't be sure, that he kissed the top of my head.

I drifted off.

29

That night I had the strangest dream. I don't know what it was that put it into my head – maybe having gone through such extremes of terror yesterday, my brain had been temporarily rewired or something, trying to make sense of what had happened.

I dreamt I was back in the office, working away on a report. It was all pretty normal. Except that all my colleagues were pumas. They were dressed in puma-shaped suits with shirts and ties, all busy working away at computers and printers, typing up memos with their great sharp claws tap-tapping on the keys. I'd been so engrossed in my report that I hadn't noticed I was surrounded by them straight away, but when I did notice, and screamed, they didn't react to me at all. They just carried on stapling their bits of paper and chatting on the phone, hind legs crossed and up on their desks, twirling the phone cord through their paws.

And then the office doors opened and Gwyn strode in to the department, except Gwyn wasn't a farmer any more he was dressed just like Peter The Sandwich Man who always sold me my lunch. In his enormous wicker sandwich basket, there weren't the usual egg and cress sandwiches and tuna mayonnaise wraps; instead there were hundreds of tiny multi-coloured rolling-pins. I peered in and stepped back in horror – each of the little rolling-pins had faces and they were laughing and talking with each other while they were being jostled about. In Welsh.

I woke up with a start.

It was already light. For a split second, I wondered where on earth I was, but then I remembered. Urgh. I buried my head underneath the thick duvet and scrunched my eyes closed – however late it was, I still hadn't had enough sleep.

And what the hell was that smell? Was that smell coming from me?

Memories of last night came back to me: the puma with the big round eyes, hammering the rolling-pin on Gwyn's door, and confronting Tomos in the pub. Then the long cold vigil in the Land Rover with the mangy blanket.

Ah! The blanket – that would explain the smell on my clothes.

No wonder I felt so awful. Last night I must have lived three years worth of excitement in one evening. Maybe four years, given the whole Dull Life Crisis thing.

Perhaps I could go back off to sleep again and wake up much, much later. Maybe September. From the very small movements I'd just made, I could tell that things hurt; my legs and my arms had pulled muscles which ached as I shifted around, presumably from being so tensed up around the puma yesterday evening. But really, I thought as I lay buried beneath the duvet trying not to smell the mangy blanket smell, I ought to be getting up. Gwyn would no doubt be awake now, and if not now then soon, and it wouldn't look very good lazing around on his sofa for hours. And as for the smell, I definitely needed to have a wash and get changed into something that hadn't come into contact with whatever I'd put around my shoulders last night.

But even though I knew I had to get up, I stayed exactly where I was, under the duvet snuggled up on the sofa and thinking of all the things that needed to be done today.

One thing was for certain: the hen weekend hike was going to be called off. Not just because the girls were going to be too hungover to hike as far as the kitchen in search of a bucket, but also because the state the house was in after the party meant it would be an enormous job just to get it remotely presentable. I'd already mentally said goodbye to my deposit when I'd got as far as the hallway last night. And then, of course, there was the puma. She needed to be taken away to safety; deposited somewhere in mid Wales.

So much to do – but actually all I really wanted to do was stay under the duvet for a while, even though I smelt so bad, and then maybe lounge around with a cup of tea for a while. With Gwyn.

Maybe have another manicure.

That would be nice.

I must look a real state. I peered down under the duvet to see. I was still wearing my party dress, which, thankfully, being velour was relatively uncrumpled. What an absolute brilliant buy it had been. Who would have thought it could be used as sleeping attire? How versatile

– I was a bit like Day to Night Barbie where you flip her skirt round and she transforms from pinstripe office-chick to pink tulle party girl. Here was I without the need to turn anything inside out going from party girl to Wee Willie Winkie in one easy step.

But it was my make-up that I knew I really ought to check. I hadn't taken it off last night when I'd flopped onto the sofa, so now I probably had panda eyes at the very least. I should hunt round in my holdall and find a mirror.

I lay under the duvet still, enjoying the warmth. It was just so damn cosy.

I must have nodded off because the next thing I knew there was a low buzzing noise. I poked my head above the duvet and listened. It was a helicopter.

I really should get up.

I kicked off the covers and immediately regretted making a sudden movement. Everything hurt. How could I have forgotten the pain?

There was no sign of Gwyn and I couldn't hear anything from upstairs so I gingerly padded over to the window, stretching my aching leg muscles as I went. I pulled aside the curtains. It was a beautiful, sunny day and I winced as I looked out.

When my eyes got accustomed to the light, I could make out two tiny helicopters circling over to the west. Were they up there hunting for the puma? They must be. I yawned and checked my watch which I hadn't taken off my wrist last night. It was eight o'clock.

I put a hand up to my hair, tentatively. It felt as though a gaggle of small puppies had made a nest on top of my head, the hair was so knotted and fuzzy from sleeping on the sofa. My God, I must look like a complete freak with blackened panda eyes and ten-foot tall bouffant hair, still dressed up in my party gear. Who was it that my mother used to like – Dusty Springfield? Did I look like the trampy version of Dusty Springfield right now?

I really needed to find that mirror and make-up bag. And a bathroom.

"Morning!" Gwyn suddenly breezed in through the front door looking fresh as a daisy.

Hastily I turned back to the window so he couldn't see my face, desperately trying to smooth down my hair so I didn't look as unkempt as the slumped, begging vagrants that I used to skip over when I lived in London. At least, unlike them, I hadn't wet myself. Although actually thanks to the Land Rover blanket it smelt as though I had. What a nice touch.

"Hello," I said, wishing I were presenting a better image of myself than I currently must be. What on earth would he be thinking? "Thank goodness nothing happened last night – look at the state of her this morning."

"Do you want breakfast?" Gwyn asked cheerily. How come he was so alert? It wasn't fair.

"Erm, yes, is that OK?" I said, still avoiding looking at him by concentrating on the view from his window.

"Sure. But there's only toast, I'm afraid. I never seem to have anything in. Sorry."

"Toast is fine. Can I go and have a wash?"

I turned round cautiously and he pointed out the bathroom and I grabbed my holdall and ran up the stairs, two at a time, keen to be reunited with my long neglected friends Mr Soap and Mrs Water. Me! Me who every evening before turning in for bed had always stood dutifully in front of my well-ordered bathroom cabinet and carefully cleansed, toned and moisturised. Always so methodical and so in control of everything. To not even have brushed my teeth last night. Now that was really living! So even though I smelt bad, even though I did have panda eyes and it did indeed look like puppies had set up a home for themselves in my hair, I felt just a little bit pleased with myself. I felt a bit slutty. A bit decadent. Look at me – partying in the evening then gallivanting about at night with no time to cleanse, tone and moisturise.

Put that in your pipe and smoke it, Marcia.

I dug out some clothes and arranged them on the hooks behind me. Gwyn had definitely been cleaning the bathroom that morning, there was an overpowering smell of pine forests, and the basin and bath were gleaming with that just-cleaned look about them. Bless him. I wondered what time he got up? Farmers usually got up at four in the morning, didn't they? Or was that dairy farmers because of the milking? Would a sheep farmer need to get up that early? Did he milk the sheep? No! Although goats were milked, weren't they? Why was I even thinking about this? What did it matter? What mattered was the state of my face.

Stuffing my stinky gold dress as far down into the holdall as I could, I had a quick wash in the basin before putting on my jeans and a cherry coloured T-shirt. Then I washed my hair using a bottle of Fruits of the Forest shampoo I found on the side of the bath. (Really, Gwyn? Fruits of the Forest?) I towel-dried it and managed to drag a comb through it so I looked a whole lot more groomed. Lastly I delved into my make-up bag and put on some concealer, a stroke of mascara, a dab of blusher and I was ready to be seen.

Skipping down the stairs, I heard Gwyn clattering around in the kitchen. I dumped my bag and went to join him.

"How long have you been up?" I asked him sheepishly, sliding into a chair at the kitchen table and wincing with the agony of using another muscle group I'd strained last night.

"A couple of hours. You were fast asleep though so I left you to it. I've already been over to see Tomos and we've agreed that I'll take the cat up to the Carrog Valley in the next hour or so. You do still want to come with me?"

"Absolutely!" I bit into the buttered toast in an effort to not sound too desperate. There was no doubt in my mind whatsoever that I should be going to mid Wales with Gwyn. After all, the alternative to spending a day with a handsome Welsh farmer was going back to the Hen House and hosing someone else's sick off the gravel. No contest.

Gwyn made a cup of tea and brought it over.

"Sorry, there's no milk…"

"No milk? But you're a farmer!"

"So?" he laughed.

I shrugged my shoulders. "I thought farmers had loads of milk."

"Dairy farmers maybe. I have sheep."

"Sheep's milk, then."

"You want me to milk a sheep for your tea?"

I chewed my toast contemplatively, trying to keep a straight face. "Another time maybe."

"Fine. Fine." He walked back to the loaf and started cutting again, still laughing.

What on earth did the man survive on? He must spend his days being half famished.

I helped myself to another slice of toast. "Thank you

so much for putting me up last night," I mumbled, my mouth full. "I'm so grateful. There was no way I could have stayed in the Hen House, it was awful, wasn't it?"

"It wasn't great. Do you need to go back for anything?"

"No. Do you think I ought to go and say goodbye though? Oh pants!" I slapped my forehead. "I do have to go back. I left my laptop there! Damn, damn, damn."

"What time do you have to leave the property?"

"Ten this morning." I looked at my watch. "An hour's time!"

"There you go, then. You'd better go now."

"Urgh. They'll try and rope me into cleaning up."

"Just say you're helping me with something and you have to go straight away."

I laughed. "Yeah, like they'll all be really understanding about that."

Gwyn shrugged. "I find the truth is usually best."

"Yes. I know. You're right. And I ought to go back because they might be wondering where I am."

Gwyn raised his eyebrows. "You think so?"

"Yeah. Probably. If they're up yet. Anyway, if there's going to be any showdown about not helping in the clean up then it's best done now and not at the wedding. Do you want me to give you a hand with the washing up before I go?"

"Yeah. Great."

We stood side by side, me washing, Gwyn drying. So much more civilised than last night when Henna and Laura were washing up and I thought plates were going to fly. I couldn't help smiling at the thought of them bickering, with Henna trying to hide the dirty plates in the cupboards.

"I'm glad you're coming up to Carrog with me," Gwyn said quietly, interrupting my thoughts.

I glanced sideways. He was looking immensely uncomfortable, drying a plate with a furrowed brow belying his deep concentration on the task in hand.

"Me too," I managed; sounding really cheesy and wanting to come up with something better, but failing completely.

I wished I didn't feel so awkward in front of him. I wished I could take my hands out of the soapy water and put them round his neck and pull him to me. But it would have been wrong, I don't know why. There was a restraint between us this morning. A natural hesitancy. But then we'd only met a couple of days ago so perhaps it was to be expected.

I wondered whether I'd wasted an opportunity with Gwyn last night. The man had invited me back to his place, for goodness sake, had come downstairs and laid a duvet over me. Had maybe even kissed me, I couldn't quite remember. I should have pulled him onto the sofa with me – what had I been thinking, going back to sleep? Surely the mood would have been more conducive to action last night than this morning? How could anything possibly happen in the bright light of day? Maybe if I had taken the lead last night then things would be different this morning. But then, I had been extraordinarily tired. And extraordinarily rough-looking. And smelt pretty bad too. And however perky Gwyn looked this morning, I was pretty sure that he had been as tired as I had been last night. So perhaps making a move last night would not have been the most appropriate thing, given the circumstances. Still, it was pretty frustrating to think that last night might be all we had, apart from a few hours journey babysitting a puma.

"Are you OK?" Gwyn bought me sharply out of my reverie.

"Fine. Fine," I said, focusing on scrubbing the already very scrubbed butter dish.

"It's just you had a really strange expression just now."

"Oh!" I tried to affect being all bright and breezy. "You know, just thinking about the cat."

Gwyn nodded and went back to concentrating on his drying. "Yes, it's a tricky one. I must say that I don't feel entirely happy dropping it off in mid Wales. But like we said last night, leaving it here is not an option. It's going to get caught and it's going to get killed. At least in mid Wales it's got a chance."

"But what about the locals? Will they have a chance?"

"Tomos was saying it's hardly populated around there, and the cat's not going to actively seek out humans, so it should be fine. Did you hear the police helicopters this morning?"

"Is that what they were? Police helicopters? I saw one the other day."

"There are three up there this morning. Two police and one media helicopter. The big cat story's all over the radio this morning too. I reckon our cat got up to mischief just before Tomos caught her last night and the police have upped their search. I wonder how your policemen were when they reported for duty this morning? Did you see any of them when you went back to the house last night? Except the one in your room, that is."

"Erm, yes, but they were catching up on their beauty sleep too," I said euphemistically, still not wanting to reveal the sordid details to Gwyn, "so I'm sure they're in fine form this morning for some big game hunting. Do you think if the policemen have dogs with them then the dogs will pick up the scent and trace the cat to Tomos' trailer?"

Gwyn shrugged his broad shoulders. "It's a possibility, I suppose. That's why we need to get moving. Are you ready to go down to the house now?"

"Sure." I let the water drain out and dried my hands on Gwyn's tea towel, my fingers just brushing against his. "So I'll see you back here in half an hour?"

He smiled and my heart leapt. I quickly stopped myself from gazing at him in adoration and went to get my holdall, waving goodbye before heading out into the cat-free outdoors with a spring in my step.

30

The sun was already hot and I turned my face up to catch it. I felt exhilarated and refreshed – I felt, in fact, exactly how I should have felt after my beauty treatments, if the blurb on the booking form had been anything to go by: I was "rejuvenated". All the petty worries about my Dull Life Crisis, about my work and my social life, boyfriends (or lack of) and friends (ditto) evaporated for the time being and I just enjoyed being. Walking along and listening to the breeze rustle the treetops and the birds singing and the occasional faint bleating of a grazing sheep. No gales, no black rustling woodland and absolutely no toothy animals lurking in the hedgerows. Just sunshine, birdsong and the promise of a good day spent with a gorgeous dark-haired Welsh farmer. And a vicious puma locked in a trailer. Maybe this euphoria I was feeling was what Marcia felt when she was on the back of a horse, careering across the countryside

– maybe this was what she was on about when she was talking about "being at one with nature".

I walked on, finding it hard to believe that this was exactly the same stretch of path I'd walked along a few hours earlier and how differently I'd felt then. And how differently I felt about the Hen House. Last night when I'd set off to Gwyn's farm the Hen House had been a sanctuary, somewhere safe from the scary outdoors. I remember the feeling of despair that descended when I turned the corner and the yellow lights of the Hen House disappeared from view; how lonely and isolated I'd felt when I couldn't see it anymore. But now, as it emerged from the woodland when the track curved sharply, my heart sank. The spell had been broken. I could no longer think of it as a bohemian backdrop to my exciting weekend.

Now all I could think as I crunched my way down the gravel driveway was the smell of fags and booze, the orgiastic sleeping arrangements and the man passed out in his own pool of vomit by the front door.

How would the house be this morning? Would anyone be up? Had they made a start on cleaning yet?

Well, the man had gone, and so had his stomach contents. I walked up the steps to the front door, hesitating for a moment, dreading what I'd find when I walked in. I turned the knob and pushed open the door, slipping into the hallway.

It still smelt like a student union on a Saturday night. Urgh. I walked in to the lounge and there was Laura, mop in hand, cleaning the floor where the sticky cans had dripped last night. She had a thunderous look on her face, scowling in the direction of two ashen-faced blokes I'd never seen before, who must be from the stag do. They were trudging round the room putting cans and fag ends into black bin liners.

"Rachel!" Laura stopped mopping. "Where were you last night? No one knew where you'd gone."

"Was I missed?" I asked, half hoping that I actually was and that they cared.

Laura looked slightly awkward for a moment, examining the handle of the mop. "Well, not exactly. One of the blokes said they saw you arrive with another man in the middle of the night so we just thought you'd left with your farmer bloke. Was it Gwyn?"

"Yes," I said sheepishly.

"Oh bravo you! I didn't see him arrive. What time did he turn up because no one else remembered him being here at all?"

"He wasn't here at the party exactly," I said, not wanting to tell her what happened, "it's a long story…"

It was a risk but Laura didn't look like she was the type of person that enjoyed listening to long stories. Fireside yarns were all well and good for some, but this girl needed a short succinct briefing and she was done.

"Yes, well, never mind that, Rach. You will never guess what happened to one of the stag boys last night!"

"Go on," I said, perching on the arm of one of the sofas. Surely Laura wasn't about to launch into a story about her sordid threesome? I really didn't want to hear it and, looking at the grandfather clock still tick-tocking away in the corner, I had to make a move.

Laura came over and sat on the other arm of the sofa. "One of the stag do lads had rather a lot to drink and went and threw up outside. Hah!" She shot a look at the lanky red-headed boy that was collecting beer cans and he visibly shrunk away from her, head bowed. "At least someone had the sense to go outside to throw up. Anyway, apparently the lad passed out on the driveway and when he came to…" She paused and looked at me.

I shrugged. "Go on."

"When he became conscious there was a puma! Seriously! A puma, standing right in front of him."

I stood stock still. What do I say? "Oh her, yes well, she's really quite tame."

"Don't you think that's shocking?" Laura prompted, clearly looking for a response.

"Shocking? Yes. Absolutely! Was he all right?"

"Yes. Managed to get himself up and go indoors without being attacked. Most of us were in bed by that time and didn't hear him. One or two were around and he told them, but by the time they went back outside to check the animal had gone."

"Golly," I said, sounding all Enid Blyton in my phony surprise. So that's what the puma had been up to before Tomos had caught her. Gwyn had been right, she had been busy before she went in the trailer. No wonder the police were all over the valley this morning if she'd paid a visit to the Hen House and its police occupants.

"Well," Laura was saying, "all the policemen and Josh stayed over last night and this morning as soon as everyone heard the story of the puma at the front door the policemen and Josh were off to the police station in an instant. I mean, can you believe it? This animal really exists! And it was here, right outside the house."

"Incredible."

"You said you heard something the first night, didn't you, after Gwyn had gone off with his vet chap to check on the dead sheep? Maybe it was the puma that you heard too. To think how much danger we'd put ourselves in. Christ, we were lucky. To be honest, I didn't believe that it really existed, I thought it was a bit of a hoax or something – just a fox up to some tricks."

I nodded, lips pursed.

"Howie!" she suddenly barked and I leaped in the air. The bloke who had sat in front of the TV a few hours ago with his spliff and his Stella sidled over to us, bloodshot eyes and grey skin testament to his hard night. I had to hand it to Laura, she must have had her fair share of drink at the party and yet here she was looking alarmingly fresh and in command. And not only that, but she'd managed to get this wasted bloke up and about at just after nine in the morning, and here he was sporting a really quite fetching pair of yellow rubber gloves and carrying a bucket filled with cleaning products. The girl worked miracles.

"Have you cleaned all the bathrooms now, Howie?"

"Only the upstairs ones. I've still got to do the downstairs toilet," he croaked, eyes fixed to the floor.

"Hurry up. You're emptying the bins after." She glared at him and he slunk off. "Sorry, Rach, you have to keep these boys in hand. Anyway, where did you stay last night?" She went back to mopping the floor.

"Oh at Gwyn's," I said as lightly as I could, not wanting to make a big thing about it. "I got back to the Hen House but my bed was already taken and I didn't fancy trying to kick the residents off it so Gwyn offered me his sofa and I accepted."

"Oh, that would be Henna and one of the policemen I suppose," Laura said with a smile on her face.

I nodded.

"Well, it was some party last night," Laura admitted, and I half-waited for her to say something about her own remarkable private gathering, but she didn't. "Louisa is really pissed off about the stag boys gatecrashing her night.

Well, we all are." She glared once again at the two boys clearing the cans away and they scurried out of sight out towards the kitchen like cockroaches fleeing the light.

"Did you stay on the sofa?" she asked, watching the stag boys scuttle away with a look of deep satisfaction.

"What?"

"On Gwyn's sofa. Did you stay there or was there a better offer once you got to his house?"

I laughed. "No, I stayed on the sofa. I'm not sure if I should be offended that there was no better offer, but what with one thing or another we'd had a hell of a night and it was about two in the morning when we got back to his farmhouse so we just crashed."

"What happened? Why was it a hell of a night?"

I bit my lip. "Oh … you know … just something at the pub…"

"Sounds like a long one, so you can tell me later. Right now there are things to do and now you're back you can make a start on the kitchen. I've drawn up an informal list of things that need to be done and when Louisa comes down she can help you with the list I've assigned you to do. I told her this morning that hen or no hen do she has to chip in on this one. Most of us are the worse for wear and we need to pull together to get this house in a fit state to give back. I've already called the caretaker who's given us until midday to clean up after ourselves, but it's going to be a tough mission to get it in a good enough state for us to get our deposit back. You can see the new rota on the kitchen next to the old one. I've called in Sunday Emergency Rota 1. It's informal because I haven't had everyone sign it off but I'm sure that they'll all agree to it. They should do, they trashed the place."

I stood there. Looking at her. Half of me, the self-righteous half of me, wanted to say a firm, "No, I will not clean up your mess," and explain that I had a legitimate reason for being elsewhere as I was going to help a friend with a problem. A furry problem with many pointy teeth. And that the state of the Hen House was not my problem: I hadn't got drunk and trashed the place. I hadn't let the stag men in. I hadn't been entertaining two men up in my room when I should have been keeping an eye on the party downstairs.

And then there was the part of me that desperately wanted to avoid any confrontation. Especially confrontation with a Hackney-trained TA-loving hardcase. And besides, I'd had my fill of confrontation for the weekend. How much could a girl reasonably be expected to take? The various courses of action – stay and clean, stay and explain myself or just scarper without a word played out in my head and for a couple of seconds I stood and smiled inanely at Laura. What should I do? What should I do?

Laura was frowning now – quick responses were the order of the day with her, none of this "making your mind up" business.

"Right," I said brightly, "better get the rubber gloves on. I'll just go upstairs and check my laptop's not been damaged first, then I'll get right on to that kitchen list. Version number one, did you say?"

"That's right," she said, looking at me rather suspiciously and then shrugged her shoulders and carried on mopping. I bounded up the stairs, past Henna who was hunched on the landing looking very green and gingerly sweeping up the fragments of what had been a porcelain candlestick. She nodded at me, too ill to talk.

"Just going to check my laptop's OK." I bounded past her.

I knocked tentatively on the door to my room and hearing nothing I went in. That bed had really seen some action over the course of the weekend. Only not when I was the occupant. Ahh well…

I saw my laptop on the window seat and grabbed it. I checked my watch; it was almost ten. Gwyn would be wondering if I was staying at the Hen House to clean up. Maybe he'd be starting to think about making a move on his own if I wasn't back soon. After all, with so much police interest in the cat he'd have to move quickly. If he or Tomos were caught harbouring the animal then they'd been in all sorts of trouble.

I sneaked down the hallway clutching my laptop. Louisa's door was open and I could hear muttering coming from inside her room. Really I ought to go and explain myself to her. I owed her that.

I knocked. The muttering stopped.

"Yes?"

"Lou, it's Rach! Can I come in?"

A few seconds later the door opened and a red-eyed James smiled weakly at me and walked out. I went in. Louisa was sitting on a window seat staring out over the valley to the river beyond. She was still dressed in last night's party dress and I was pretty sure from the look of her that she hadn't slept at all.

We sat in silence together on opposite window seats, watching a large brown bird circling near the valley floor. I surreptitiously checked my watch. It was five past ten. I ought to get moving.

"Listen hon, I'm really sorry things haven't worked out quite how they were planned to," I began.

She continued staring out into the distance. "S'OK."

"Were you up all night talking to James?"

"Yes." She sighed. "And listening to everyone shagging."

"Yeah." I nodded. "I noticed that last night."

She looked up from the window. "I thought I heard you talking to someone in the middle of the night. Were you with Gwyn?"

I nodded.

"Where did you guys go? Did he come over to the party? I didn't see him."

I took a deep breath. "I went over to his farm." I watched her expression to see if she'd be cross, betrayed, disappointed or glad, but she remained impassive; in all likelihood she was emotionally spent from having talked to James all night.

"Don't worry," she said eventually, examining her nails, "I don't mind. So why were you over there? If that's not a stupid question?"

I leant forward. "Well, promise you won't tell anyone what I'm about to tell you?"

She still looked on, expressionless. "Jesus, what did you get up to with that man? Go on then, I promise I won't tell a soul."

In a voice barely above a whisper I revealed my weekend's secrets, from noticing Tomos' wounded arm in the pub to spying him covered in blood walking away from the direction of a cat attack. I told her what I'd learnt from Gwyn about Tomos' past, and what the policeman had told me about the cat being manipulated. Then I described that terrifying walk up to Gwyn's farmhouse once I'd pieced everything together.

"Fucking hell Rach!" Louisa was staring at me agog, a pinch of colour now in her cheeks. "What happened at Gwyn's?"

She actually laughed when I told her how we went up to the pub and interrogated Tomos, and her eyes widened when it came to the bit about capturing the puma in the trailer. It was an ideal time for me to run through the slightly improved scenario that I was planning on delivering to Marcia in a few days. But I just couldn't do it, not to Louisa. Instead I tried to describe to her the smell of the blanket which made her laugh.

The door creaked open and James crept in looking hopeful at the sound of laughter. He walked over and carefully laid a black tea on the seat beside his fiancé. Ex fiancé? Louisa stopped laughing and turned to face the window again. He grimaced and walked out.

"The thing is, Lou," I whispered when I heard him go down the staircase, "we actually caught the puma and she's currently in the back of a trailer waiting for us to take her to somewhere safe."

"No way!"

"I know. And I said to Gwyn that I'd go with him to help him."

"Help him?"

"Yeah, I know. I can't drive the Land Rover, I can barely navigate and I'm certainly not getting involved in the cat. But I'll be a sort of trucker's mate, keeping him company. And I can always call for the ambulance if he gets hurt. Suppose he gets attacked when he lets the cat out in the middle of nowhere? At least I'll still have fingers to dial for help with."

She nodded. "You'd better go, then."

I put my hand on hers. They were icy cold, clenched in her lap. "Oh hon, I'm so sorry that I'm going now and not helping with the clean-up. Are you going to be OK?"

She nodded. "You go. And it's fine. Honestly. At least

it'll be one of those weekends to remember. I certainly haven't had a dull hen weekend."

I smiled and stood up, picking up the laptop. "Don't say a word to the others though."

"My lips are sealed. Talking of which, give Gwyn a kiss from me. You lucky thing."

I walked towards the door. "So I'll see you…"

"At the wedding. Yes." She sighed. "Probably."

I blew her a kiss and shut the door behind me.

Henna was still huddled on the same stretch of landing, poised with a dustpan and brush in her hands, delicately trying to sweep up the same bits of china without moving too much. In the cold light of day her face looked very, very bad with the oozing toxins adding a horrific dimension to her hung-over appearance.

"See you at the wedding," I whispered to her. She looked up, half-drunk, trying to make sense of what I'd just said.

"Oh. Right. Still on, is it?" She stared at me blankly. "Oh! What? You're not going are you? What?" she mumbled, putting her dustpan down and scattering china all over the floor. "Oh fuck."

"Yeah. Someone's in trouble and they need my help."

"Does Laura know?"

I winked. "Anyway, sorry to leave you."

"Ah, don't worry about it. You weren't even at the party, were you? Where did you go?"

I waved my hand and walked down the stairs. "I'll tell you another time. See you soon."

She held up a hand in a sort of salute and turned to her sweeping again. I trampled down the stairs, glancing at the grandfather clock. It was half ten.

"Rachel! I need you to get that red wine stain out of the curtains." Laura appeared from nowhere, brandishing the mop.

"Mm yes sure, I'll get right on it. Just let me pop this laptop in to my car so it doesn't get in the way of all that cleaning." I bounded past her, heading outside into the clean air and brilliant sunshine, heart pounding with the guilt of my deception. I would make a crap spy.

Once out in the driveway, I opened up the car, threw the laptop on the passenger seat, jumped in to the driver's side, gunned the engine and in a dramatic wheel spin, gravel spraying out just like in the films, the car screamed out of the driveway and up the track. Before I reached the gates I saw Laura leap out of the house and sprint towards me, still gripping her mop.

"RACHEL!"

Shit! I dropped down a gear and tore up the lane.

31

I pulled up abruptly round the back of Gwyn's house. I checked my rear view mirror. No Laura. Should I try to drag hay over the car or was there some camouflage tarpaulin lying about that I could use to disguise it? Laura would now be on some sort of mission for me, undertaking a reconnaissance of the area looking for the deserter. And when she found my car God only knows what she'd do with it. I could see her now, like a Terminator she wouldn't stop until she had hunted me down and made me pay for not having fulfilled my duties as listed in the Sunday Emergency Rota 1.

"Don't worry about it," Gwyn said, laughing rather unkindly, when I told him what I wanted to do, "your friend won't come looking for your car."

"She's not my friend. And she will. She'll hunt me down! She'll hunt me down and then she'll exact some sort of revenge on me for not helping to clean up at the

Hen House. You don't know her. She's in the TA. She scares me."

"Rachel, calm down, you're being ridiculous. She won't come looking for the car or for you."

"Please can we put some hay over it?"

"No!"

"Just a bit?"

"No," he laughed, "but if you're that bothered about it why don't you park it in the barn and I'll close the barn doors?"

"Can you lock the barn doors?"

"For goodness sake!"

"Territorial Army…"

"Is this the girl I met in the pub the other night? The one with the very short hair?"

"Yes. That's Laura."

"She doesn't look scary to me."

"Which barn is it?" I said, deciding to distract him, as I just wasn't going to convince him about Laura's inevitable settling of scores. I parked the car in a vast empty barn and pulled the doors to, Gwyn slotting a bolt through the latch and looking at me, amused. I shrugged my shoulders. He would never understand.

"Are you ready now? Shall we go?"

When we arrived at Tomos' farm, Gwyn drove round the back of the yard and reversed until he was tight up against a knackered old shed.

"Shouldn't you leave some room behind the Land Rover to attach the trailer?" I asked, unclipping my belt and opening the door.

"This is the trailer."

I slammed the door shut. "No. Seriously?"

"Yes, of course. What did you expect?"

Something roadworthy? Something at least remotely capable of holding a wild animal? This wheeled shed had to be the oldest most decrepit trailer I had ever seen. Did they make trailers in the sixteenth century? It certainly looked that old, and was battered and banged with deep dents along the left side and a gap along the right side. The thing was an antique.

Suddenly I had a bad feeling about the whole escapade. Suddenly it didn't look like such a good idea any more containing a highly vicious animal in an Elizabethan casket on wheels.

"It'll be fine, Rachel." Gwyn opened his door and got out before coming round to my side and opening my door. "It's sturdier than it looks."

"Morning, young Gwynfor. Morning, English girl." Tomos appeared from around the corner with Old Shep limping alongside him. I took a good look at the old farmer after the revelations of last night. Was he really such a lover of women? He must be in his late seventies, if not his early eighties. Grey wispy hair, tanned and weather-beaten face. Handsome? Maybe at a stretch. A long stretch. There was something of the very aged Sean Connery about him I suppose. If you squinted.

"Yes, it is bright, isn't it?" Tomos looked at me. "Lovely sunny day. I've got some old sunglasses if you want to borrow them for your journey."

"Oh. No thanks."

"Is she all ready to go?" Gwyn asked, patting the trailer. I jumped back, expecting it to collapse into matchsticks at any second.

"Yep. She's had some more food and water in there this morning and she's as quiet as a little mouse. You won't have any trouble with … her…" He sucked his lips and turned away from us.

"Now, Tomos, don't you worry about her. She'll be fine." Gwyn laid a reassuring hand on the old farmer's shoulders.

Tomos nodded and walked round to the trailer, eyes averted from us. "Better help you fix it on then," he said in a small tremulous voice.

I stood around watching, stroking Shep who had come for some attention. His left ear was badly mangled, presumably from the cat attack. He seemed remarkably calm considering the animal that recently attacked him was a few feet away. Or maybe when you get as old as Old Shep then nothing really bothers you too much any more.

A couple of minutes later and the trailer was as secure as a knackered old trailer could be.

"Cup of tea?" Tomos offered.

"No, we'd better be off," Gwyn said.

There was a pause.

"You know maybe…"

"No, Tomos. We're doing the best thing for her." Gwyn got into the driver's seat.

Tomos nodded. "Right you are. Right you are. Well, goodbye, Rachel." He held out his hand and I shook it. "Are you sure there's no Welsh blood in you? You seem a nice girl."

"No. None. Although I'm a quarter Scottish on my father's side, I've been told."

Tomos frowned. "Best keep that to yourself then. The Scots are as bad as the English. No, I'm convinced there's a Welsh past to you." He patted me on the back and leaning forward he said in a quieter voice, "Now, you look after young Gwynfor, won't you? He needs a good woman does Gwynfor. Someone to look after him. Feed him up a bit. He's looking thin. Anyway, no doubt I'll be seeing you around here again very soon."

I didn't know what to say. So I nodded and gave him a kiss on the cheek. "Don't worry about the cat. We'll see she gets to her new home safely."

We pulled away and drove off leaving Tomos behind, watching us go. He raised his hand in a wave and just as we made to turn into the corner and disappear from view, he pulled out a large handkerchief from his coat pocket, blew his nose and wiped his eyes.

32

"**How** long will it take us to reach our destination?" I asked, and then added, "actually, where is our destination?"

"It'll probably take around three hours to get there, given the speed we can go at with this trailer in tow. And we're heading to an area north-west of Newtown. Do you know around there at all?"

"Not so much."

"Montgomery?"

"No," I said again, rather embarrassed at my poor geography. Were these big cities? Should I know where they were?

Gwyn searched his brain for somewhere I might have heard of. "What about Birmingham?"

"Yes, Yes! I've heard of Birmingham."

"OK, well, you go west of Birmingham and keep going west until you hit the Cambrian mountains."

"Oh, OK," I said. How was that supposed to help me work out where we were going?

I was about to say something, but as we turned the corner and reached the brow of the hill Gwyn slammed on the brakes and the trailer groaned ominously behind us.

"What?"

There were people everywhere. Milling in the streets, sitting on the walls, crammed into the tiny post office, the convenience store and the pub. The laid-back locals were jostling with suited media men and the armed police, all of them talking, shouting and gesticulating to each other, trying to get themselves heard over the commotion. There was a man with a News Cymru jacket who was interviewing two old men beside the bridge and over by the pub a man with a microphone branded with the BBC logo was talking to Angharad.

"What are we going to do?" I looked despairingly at Gwyn. There was no way through the crowds.

He bit his lip, thinking. "We can't turn back now. The trailer would come unhitched if I tried to reverse and besides, we haven't room to manoeuvre. We'll have to press on through the people here. We have to go through the village, there's no other route that the trailer could take."

"But what if the puma starts yowling in the back?"

Gwyn started to inch the Land Rover forward towards the crowds. "Best get her out of here, then."

I wound down my window as we made our way slowly down the main street, sticking my head out to get the breeze; it was hot in the cab. Two old men were talking to a policeman.

"I saw it the other day."

"Well I saw it twice last week."

Meanwhile the man from the BBC was asking Angharad, "So if you knew it was here all along, why did you tolerate it?"

"You know –" I settled back into my seat – "it's actually quite funny when you think about it."

Gwyn looked round at me briefly before focusing back on the road. "Why is it funny?"

"All these people are here because of the puma and not one of them knows that it's right here in the middle of them! Come on, you must admit that it's rather funny how tantalisingly close they all are to her."

"I suppose so," he acknowledged, easing the vehicle into first gear again and edging towards the mass of people in the road, who one by one started to make way for us to pass. "I just hope to God that she doesn't give us away. There would be hell to pay if we were found with her."

"Oh I forgot to tell you!" I turned to face him but he was concentrating fully on the road, his black brows knotted in a frown of concentration. "One of those guys we saw at the party last night met the puma face to face!"

"Really? That explains all this sudden interest then."

"He wasn't hurt or anything. Actually, it was the guy that we saw throw up and collapse in front of the house. He passed out and apparently when he regained consciousness the puma was standing right over him."

"Oh him." Gwyn momentarily ground to a halt as an old man inched his way across the road. "She's a tame little thing, isn't she?"

I slapped my hand over my mouth.

Oh!

Oh my God!

"What is it?" Gwyn looked over at me, suddenly worried. "Is something wrong?"

"Nothing's wrong." My mind was working furiously. "It's just that – we both saw the guy walk out of the Hen House and collapse last night, didn't we?"

"Ye-es," Gwyn said, turning back to navigate through the people around us.

"But by the time we got back to the Hen House and saw that happen…"

"…We'd already captured the cat!" Gwyn finished the sentence off for me.

"Oh my God!"

Gwyn started to laugh a hearty laugh.

"But does that mean there's more than one of them?" I asked.

He nodded, still laughing.

"And do you think Tomos knows that?"

"What do you think?"

"Well, shouldn't we be trying to catch the other one too?"

"One at a time, maybe," he said, looking over at me and grinning. "We could do one each weekend. You're not busy next weekend, are you?"

I smiled. "I suppose we should see how this goes first. Will your trailer even survive the trip?"

"I'll have you know this trailer is as sturdy now as the day it was built."

I laughed. "But it probably wasn't that sturdy when it was built five hundred years ago."

"Forty years ago as it happens. And true, it wasn't very clever then."

We'd come to a standstill again. Progress was frustratingly slow and I glanced back at the rickety trailer that was rocking slightly now that we'd stopped. Was she walking around back there? Gwyn wound down the window and shouted something in Welsh to a couple of middle-aged women who were chatting in the centre of the road and had refused to acknowledge the Land Rover which was nuzzling their handbags.

"That's Gwenda." Gwyn held up a hand in a wave as they eventually stood aside.

"*Diolch*!" Gwyn called out to them as we passed.

We were making it. I could see the edge of the crowds now, just passed the old red phone box that was all but covered in ivy.

Finally we emerged from the mass of people and Gwyn changed up into third gear. We pulled away just as we both heard a loud and unmistakable yowl come from the trailer. Gwyn hit the gas and away we sped down the hill the trailer clattering and crashing behind us. I looked in the mirrors and saw one journalist turn and watch us go, a look of incomprehension registering on his face.

33

We'd been driving for what seemed like hours and the weather was getting steadily worse. The road had been climbing since we'd left the Beacons and we were now in a barren landscape; the brooding low clouds and the hazy bursts of drizzle made its remoteness feel all the more overwhelming. Gone were the rambling oak woodlands and the rolling hills. This was much bleaker territory. The wipers squeaked each time they made a pass across the windscreen and the trailer had developed a worrying groan whenever we went round a bend in the road. Twice Gwyn had to stop the Land Rover and go out in the rain to check if the trailer was still holding together sufficiently, although what was deemed sufficient was gradually getting less and less, from being a roadworthy secure trailer to simply holding together without too many bits falling off.

The last time he climbed back into the driver's seat,

soaking wet, he grimaced. "Reckon we have a 50:50 chance of making it to our destination."

"Oh great. How far are we from the drop off point?" I said, not having seen a single farmstead for a good quarter of an hour. Surely this was desolate enough to release the cat? It hardy looked like we were on the outskirts of some great conurbation.

Certainly we must be a few miles west of Birmingham by now…

"We're nearly there." He pulled off again, the trailer letting out a long low whine as it jerked forward. "I think it's just a mile or so off this road and then we'll be in the woods that Tomos' brother owns. He was right, wasn't he, there's nothing much going on around here. A lot of the land is owned by the Water Boards because it's ideal for reservoirs. And what's not Water Board land is owned by the Forestry Commission. I reckon she'll have a fine old time out here. Plenty of rabbits and mice, fish in the rivers and the odd bird or two. She'll be set up."

"Do you think there are any other big cats out here?"

He shrugged, slowing down to take another corner, the trailer groaning more loudly than it had done yet. "Well, there were reported sightings a few years back, so Tomos said, but they could have been hoaxes, and if they were real the animals could have died or moved on to new territories. But who knows?"

"I'd like to think there was someone out here for her," I said, peering out of my side window to the river that still thundered in the valley bottom below. "I reckon there's a tasty Mr Puma out here just waiting for a wife. He's got a great den and fishing rights to all the rivers round here, and he's just looking for the right kind of girl to set up a family with."

"Sounds like you read too much of that romantic fiction stuff."

"No! It's just the way the world is. Everyone's looking for someone."

"Are they?" Gwyn raised his eyebrows but continued to concentrate on the winding road in front. We were only doing fifteen miles an hour, hampered by the road, the trailer and the weather.

At last we came to a dirt track turning off the road with a weatherworn blue sign saying "Cefyn Clawydd" that Gwyn took, slowing right down so the old trailer didn't disconnect completely from the Land Rover. He dropped down to first gear and we inched our way to the destination.

I didn't think it was possible to have a track in worse condition than the ones that led to Gwyn's farm and the Hen House, but this track made those look like newly surfaced super-highways. It zigzagged sharply through thick dense woodland, at times barely wide enough for the trailer to pass, with outstretched branches of the wet trees dragging across the trailer's sides. The Land Rover skidded on a patch of wet gravel, slipping into a deep pothole. Gwyn yanked the steering wheel and the trailer screeched.

"This is impossible!" he said through gritted teeth, leaning forward and concentrating hard.

"Can't we just pull up here and release her?"

"No. Tomos was adamant that we should do it at the end of the track. And besides, we need to turn round and there's no way that I'll be able to reverse the trailer back along the track. Hold on!" And we plummeted into another pothole. The trailer scraped against the road and yowling started up from the back.

"Sorry, old girl!" Gwyn shouted.

We turned a sharp bend and our journey came to an abrupt end at an old wrought iron gate with *PREIFAT* written on a plaque and nailed to it. The road opened out just as Tomos had predicted, allowing Gwyn to be able to reverse easily.

"Well!" Gwyn stopped the engine and sighed loudly, "This is it. This is where we say goodbye to our passenger." As he said the words the puma set up her yowling again from the trailer. The rain clattered on the roof and ran down the windows as we sat and contemplated the task ahead.

"So how are you going to let her out?" I asked.

"Me?"

"Well, I'm presuming it's going to be you," I half laughed. Did he think I was going to be the one to go round the back and let her out?

"Oh, then. Me it is. The last time I got out to check the trailer I wrapped twine round it to make sure the doors were kept closed. I reckon I could keep the twine in place while I unbolted the doors and then once I was back in the Land Rover I could release the twine, let the doors open and let her free. What do you think?"

"I think you're a genius!"

"Not just a pretty face," he answered, proudly. "Could do with your rolling-pin though. The whole thing might go horribly wrong. I can't imagine she'll be in a great mood after having been thrown around for three hours on bumpy track."

There was an old coat draped across the back seat of the Land Rover, which Gwyn now reached back for, leaning in close to me as he did so. Throwing it around his shoulders, he jumped out of the car and into the rain.

"Is there anything I can do?" I shouted after him.

"You can hold the twine tight while I unbolt the trailer. Here." He handed me the end of the cord. "Hold this and I'll feed it through the window and round the back to the other side."

I wound the window down and the rain came sleeting in. Gwyn passed the twine in and wound the window back up so there was just enough of a gap to let the cord pass through. And certainly not enough to allow a savage puma to leap in. Was the glass toughened? I looked for the reassurance of the little kite mark on the window but I couldn't see it. What if she came through the window?

Gwyn had now disappeared around the back of the trailer and I sat, listening to the clatter of the rain and the sound of my breath coming thick and fast, fogging up the windows.

Gwyn now appeared on the other side of the Land Rover and passed me the other end of the twine which was fed through the window on his side.

"OK Rachel, I'll unlock the back doors now. Make sure you keep that twine really tight. I don't want to come face to face with her." Pushing the wet black curls back off his forehead he gave me a quick thumbs up and I smiled back weakly.

Suddenly my hands had become useless clammy rubbery appendages. My palms were glistening with sweat and with it my twine-gripping ability weakened dramatically. I had to hold on to this thin blue cord otherwise the door that Gwyn was unlocking would swing open and out she would pounce, straight at Gwyn's throat with all those white teeth. I was, quite literally, holding Gwyn's life in my hands.

No pressure then.

I wound the cord round and round my damp rubber-like hands, cutting off the blood to my fingers. How tight would it have to be? Supposing she threw herself against the doors when she heard the bolts being pulled across? Was I holding the twine tightly enough to keep the doors closed or would my arms be ripped off my shoulders as the doors flew open and the twine was pulled tight? And how long could I suffer bloodless fingers for? And shouldn't I stop moaning about it because at the end of the day wasn't Gwyn's life more important than having the use of my fingers?

Hmm...

Gwyn disappeared round the back. I sat and watched my fingers turn various shades of white and blue.

I heard the ancient bolts of the trailer being drawn back.

Within a second, Gwyn had jumped into the driving seat, ducking below the twine that was running through the slightly open window. He slammed the door behind him.

"Oh thank God!" I said and let the twine unwind from my numb hands, laying them on my lap, massaging the blood back into them as best I could. They were stinging with pins and needles.

Gwyn was breathing heavily through his sudden exertion and, probably, nerves. I looked over at him.

"Well?" I asked, feeling a whole lot perkier now we were both safely in the vehicle again.

"Well, I guess we just sit and wait for her to come out."

"What if she doesn't want to come out?"

"Oh she will. I suppose she just has to get her bearings. Have a sniff around, that sort of thing. You know what cats are like," he panted, wiping the rain off his face and running a hand through his wet hair.

Not really. I'd never had one and, thanks to this weekend, I wouldn't be getting one any time in the near future. The pet food aisle at my local Sainsburys would now forever be a mystery to me.

The ends of the twine sat in my lap as I kneaded and massaged my tingling fingers.

"Here." Gwyn took my hands in his own broad hands and in big strong strokes he massaged them back to life. I looked up at him, heart racing. He was leaning towards me so that he could hold my hands and I was leaning in towards him. So close. He sat forwards, now holding my hands still beside his knees and pulling me towards him…

Slowly the blue twine began unravelling from my lap.

We both saw it happen and pulled apart. One end of the twine slithered right off my lap, up the door and disappeared out of the gap in the window. The other end of twine swept over Gwyn and out through his window. Outside the back door of the old trailer banged open ominously. Gwyn dropped my hands and both of us wiped the condensation from the windows so we could see outside. My window faced down through the dense dark woodland towards the river below, while Gwyn's window looked towards the wooded private estate beyond the gate. Nothing. All I could hear was the door, banging against the trailer. I couldn't see her anywhere. I felt clammy and cold with fear, half imagining her prowling around to the front of the car, working out how she would get in to this old tin box and eat the meat inside.

"Here," hissed Gwyn. I scrambled over to his seat, almost sitting on his lap in a bid to get a look. And there she was, as graceful as ever, slinking slowly down the road and towards the river below. We watched as she stalked off, her coat quickly becoming soaked in the rain before she disappeared into the thick ground cover and was gone.

We stayed still, watching for her. Perhaps she'd return? But no – we must have sat there for a full ten minutes, my legs becoming numb with the effort of perching on the very edge of Gwyn's seat. She didn't come back. And now, suddenly, I felt rather sad, to my surprise. That was it – she'd gone. We'd released her into the wild and wouldn't be seeing her again. The end of the adventure.

Poor cat. She can't have had a very happy life and I wondered what her story was. Probably captured when she was young in her native country (which was where exactly?) and then put in a circus or a zoo or something before being left to fend for herself in the wilds. I really hoped that she'd find a home here and not be bothered by people again. It was certainly remote enough here...

"Rachel are you crying?"

"NO!" I said, face turned resolutely to my window, wanting to blow my nose but having no intention of doing so in front of Gwyn. I wasn't one of those 'dab it and have done' girls, I was a 'honk and blow' kind of a girl, and that would so ruin the moment.

"You are crying – I can see, you've made the door wet."

"Well, I'm sorry," I said, sniffing and wiping my face with my sleeve, "it's just so sad, that's all. I hope she'll be OK out here. Not lonely or anything."

"She's not human. She doesn't need friends."

"I know that! It's just, well she's had a rough time of it, being thrown out from wherever she came from, then

314

being taken away from the village. Always moved on. I just hope she'll be happy and she can stay here."

"I'm sure she will. Look, use this hankie."

"Thanks." I blew my nose.

He laid a hand on my shoulder as I blew my nose again. I felt as though I were five years old and had grazed my knee.

"Shall we go?" he said gently.

"Yes," I replied in a small voice, "let's."

34

We edged down the track, the trailer bumping and rattling behind us; less stable than ever now we didn't have our feline ballast in the back. I wondered how she was doing, slinking into the woodland, exploring her new home.

"She'll be fine, you know." Gwyn cast a glance over at me.

"How did you know what I was thinking?" I smiled. "Am I that easy to read?"

"Like a book!" he laughed.

"I could be thinking about anything else. Work, going home, anything…"

"Were you?"

"No. I was thinking about the cat," I admitted, a little sullenly. Cross that I was so easy to read. Did he also know how I felt about him? And if he did, was that so much of a problem anyway? Besides, it was all for nothing, we were pointing in the direction of home and this evening I would be driving off back to the city…

"Now what are you thinking?" he asked. "Now you look even more down in the mouth."

"Will you stop analysing me, Mr Psychiatrist! I thought you were a farmer, not a head doctor."

"Maybe I'm just in tune with the female mind."

"Are you?"

"No."

"Well then, you concentrate on the driving, and I'll concentrate on my very important thoughts, thank you very much."

And then the trailer broke.

There was a sharp crack followed by a dull scraping noise. Gwyn stopped the car and got out. I sat in the front and watched him go round to the back and examine the damage. He came back in a minute or so, soaked to the skin, his long-sleeved t-shirt sticking fantastically to his broad chest. I looked away, hoping I hadn't been too obviously leering at him.

"Well," I said, diverting my attention by closely examining the dashboard, "is the trailer broken?"

"Yup. I knew I should have fixed it before we left, but there you go – there was no time. At least we got the cat into the countryside. If we still had her in the back we'd be in real trouble."

"Are you with the AA?"

"Not as such."

"The RAC?"

"Not really."

"Are you with any recovery people?"

"No."

"Oh. Well, can you mend it yourself?"

"No." He started laughing. "Have you finished your interrogation now?" He looked at me, waiting for the next question.

I shrugged, lips pursed.

He leant forward, eyebrows raised, waiting.

"OK then, yes, I've finished."

"Good. Anyway, I've patched it together with some of the twine..." He began to explain what had broken but I tuned out, preferring instead to concentrate on the beads of rain dropping from his hair down his neck, to run in tiny rivulets down his chest. More than anything at that point I wanted to be reincarnated in my next life as Gwyn's favourite towel.

"So," I said, going back to examining the dashboard again, "do we have to leave that pile of kindling here or can we get back to your place with it as it is?"

"I can't leave it here. The Water Board would probably have something to say if I abandoned a vehicle on their property."

"Yes but it's not technically a vehicle, is it?"

He laughed. "What would you call it, Rachel?"

"I don't know. Nailed together bits of wood?"

"OK, I can't leave my bits of nailed wood here. And besides they might find traces of big cat in it – you never know. Then where we would be? And we can't go all the way back to the farm because there is no way that the trailer is going to last the long journey home. We'll have to find a nearby garage and see if they can fix it. There should be an old road map in the back somewhere. Can you find the nearest town?"

I hunted, leant round and picked up a battered old road atlas. "It's a bit old. It's a 1982 map of Great Britain and Ireland. What good is that?"

Gwyn shot me a bemused look.

"What?" I said, leafing through the pages.

"Do you really think this area has changed much since 1982?"

"How should I know? Anyway, shush, it's not easy to read all these place names in your foreign language."

I managed to find Tretower and traced our journey to here. And felt quite proud of my orienteering skills.

We were, it turned out, in the middle of nowhere.

Which had been exactly the point of our journey.

"No. There isn't anywhere near. We're miles away from any towns. Especially Birmingham," I added, just to let him know I'd found my bearings.

"What about villages then? We passed a couple on the way here. Do you remember seeing a garage when we drove past?"

"No. Oh, there's a place just north of here called Waenfach, it's got a little black square on it, what does that mean?" I went to the key on the back cover. "Village – that might be good. It was a village in 1982, so maybe it's a small town now? The other places we passed only had a round dot which means –" I flipped to the index again – "Other Settlement. That sounds smaller than a village, don't you think?"

"OK, the black square it is then. How do I get to Waenfach?"

"You go right at the bottom of the track. It's in the opposite direction to going back, but only by a few miles. Is that OK?"

"It'll have to do. I didn't see any garages on the way either."

I was over the moon. Now we were a team, because I had a job to do! Now I was navigating while Gwyn was driving – he was relying on me. And here we were, travelling together along the roads to get to the place with the black square.

The road wound down into a heavily wooded valley with a few houses dotted along the roadside. As we kept our descent there were more and more houses, which boded well; Waenfach was looking like a sizeable place for mid Wales.

"This is it!" I said, putting the map down as we turned a corner and the sign proudly announced we'd arrived in the village of Waenfach, regional finalist for Wales in Bloom last year.

"Oh it's lovely," I said, and it was. A mish-mash of red-brick Georgian townhouses, white painted cottages and Victorian bay-fronted terraces lined the streets.

"But does it have a garage?" Gwyn asked.

"It has a hairdresser's," I said, peering out through the rain-streaked window.

"Yes, that's not much good," he laughed. "I don't think we can perm our way out of this."

"A greengrocer's?"

"No."

"Garage!"

"Where?" He slowed down, if that was possible as we were only doing about twenty miles an hour, and looked where I was pointing. On the left just after the row of shops was an old garage with an ancient petrol pump standing outside. The wooden sign on the corrugated building read "G Mason, Mechanic".

"*Da iawn*," he said, "perfect, well done," and pulled in to the forecourt. He came to a stop beside the pump, the trailer rattling and clanking before finally heaving to a standstill.

"It doesn't look very open," I said, ominously. It didn't look very twenty-first century either. Had they ever mended anything later than a Model T Ford? Would they take one look at Gwyn's T-reg Land Rover and marvel at the alien space-wagon that had just landed on their premises?

"You stay here and I'll go and see if anyone's in."

"No, I'll come too. I've been sitting down since we left Tretower."

I jumped out, glad to stretch my legs. It was true, I'd been sitting for nearly three hours now and was probably well on the way to getting deep vein thrombosis.

It was pelting down with rain so we dashed for shelter beneath the roof of the garage.

"Hello?" Gwyn called. "Anyone there? Hello?" It looked deserted.

"Shall we try the butcher's next door?" I asked, peering into the gloom but not seeing anyone there either.

"Sure." We dashed out again and into the butcher's.

And had a shock.

I don't know what I was expecting really. It's not as if I haven't been in a butcher's shop in my life, but it was very different to the ones I'd been in during my nice suburban upbringing. My kind of butcher's shop had sausages and steaks arranged in white plastic trays with green plastic grass separating each red line of meat. And there were usually posters up on the wall of a housewife having raptures holding a fork loaded with sausages, with a caption "Make Mine British Pork" or something along those lines.

This butcher's, though, was the real thing.

I could feel my mouth gape open at the sight of pheasants hanging limply from big metal hooks in the ceiling and, worse still, rabbits dangling from string with their heads in plastic bags, with what was clearly blood pooling at the bottom.

The cat would like it in here.

I hid behind Gwyn and tried not to look too horrified by the carnage, adopting what I hoped was an "oh-yes-I'm-quite-comfortable-with-this-level-of-gore" look. Honestly, this house of butchery should have an eighteen certificate outside it.

Gwyn and the slaughtermonger with the horribly bloody apron were talking in Welsh so I couldn't join in. I stood behind and smiled, staring at the packets of gravy mix resplendent with pictures of happy cows and happy hens on the front winking at me. Why do the manufacturers do that? It's sick.

"OK. *Diolch*. Thanks. Come on then." Gwyn turned to me and out we went, to my huge relief. Once back in the rain again, I took a deep breath in, filling my lungs with good clean air that didn't smell of dead animals.

"He said that the garage is open on Tuesday. The mechanic is his brother so he told me that I could leave the trailer on the forecourt today and give them a call on Tuesday morning."

"That's very trusting of you. Are you going to do that?"

"Of course! Who would steal it anyway?"

"True. And I suppose you haven't got much choice, have you? But what about getting back here tomorrow? It's a long journey to have to make three times."

"I asked about that too," he said lightly, "and there's a bed and breakfast place just down the road apparently…"

He left it hanging in the air. We stood in the rain facing each other. I could feel myself smiling.

"I don't know whether you have to get back to Cardiff tonight, with your work and everything?"

"Oh that." I waved it away. "I can take a day off. It'll be fine."

"Well, I don't want to inconvenience you by making you stay up here…" He was grinning now, his face shiny in the rain, his hair plastered to his head. He was so absolutely gorgeous standing there in front of me that I just couldn't help myself any longer. I took a step towards him and as I did he took a step to me, cupping my face in his warm hands and kissing me softly on the lips. I responded, kissing him back, gently at first but as he pulled me to him there was more urgency. We stood there, pressed tight together, the rain falling all around us but I didn't feel it.

"Come on," he said, pulling away gently and running a hand through my soaked hair. "Let's get out of the rain and see if there are any vacancies."

I nodded, heart pounding away in my chest, and we headed back to the Land Rover. But not before I glanced over at the butcher's shop and saw the butcher watching us, grinning, with a plucked chicken dangling limply in each hand.

35

We walked back to the Land Rover, Gwyn holding my hand and making me feel more rapturous than the woman with her fork full of pork sausage.

Together we managed to disentangle the battered old trailer from the Land Rover, our fingers touching every so often as we unwound the twine from the tow bars. Neither of us said anything, too caught up in being next to each other and enjoying the moment.

Within a few minutes we were back in the vehicle and heading further north to the bed and breakfast.

I checked my watch – it was three o'clock. The Hen House would be vacant now, just a lone cleaning woman no doubt cursing us for trashing the place, shaking her duster in anger. The girls would have gone their separate ways home: Louisa going back to more long, arduous conversations and a possible wedding, Henna returning to write a very entertaining article for her paper on big cats, Laura probably berating herself for failing to take charge sufficiently, but no doubt entertaining herself by coming up with various elaborate ways to discipline me. The police marksmen would be stalking through the valley, guns held out in front of them, radios at the ready, paracetamol and alka seltzer close to hand. The media would be busy asking everyone about their experiences with the big cat – and Tomos? Who knows where Tomos would go to look for comfort in his hour of need?

And where was the girl with the Dull Life Crisis who had driven up the road from Cardiff a few days ago? What had happened to her? Well, she had gone on the adventure of a lifetime. She'd helped farmers in distress, she'd braved horses and big cats and anti-English Welshmen and now here she was, somewhere in mid Wales with her lovely farmer heading off to a B&B. As Santa so aptly put it, ho ho ho.

I could start to worry about things like toothbrushes, pyjamas and other practicalities, but really, that was so DLC. Far better to sit back and enjoy the scenery – albeit rather wet – and hope the place didn't disappoint.

36

It didn't. Myrtlewood Grange was a beautiful three-storey Georgian house set just off the road in the next village we came to. It must originally have been some sort of a watermill, as a giant wooden wheel was suspended on a whitewashed building beside it. A rambling honeysuckle climbed over the front porch and twisted around the wooden sign, which announced we'd arrived at the B&B and that there were vacancies to be had.

Gwyn pulled up in the car park to the side and we sat for a moment, the rain still beating down on the roof.

"OK?" he said, looking over at me.

"Absolutely," I said, and leant over to kiss him again. Now that I'd started I just couldn't stop myself. The man was fantastic.

"Shall we go in?" he said after a few moments of sheer bliss.

"Sure." I composed myself and hopped out. Gwyn

went round to the back and got my bag out of the back.

Hold on.

Why was that here?

I looked at him, nonplussed.

"Well," he said, shrugging his shoulders, "I worried that something like this might happen and thought, you know, you'd probably like to be prepared…" He petered out and hid his sheepish grin by diving into the back and getting out another bag. His bag.

I nodded, suppressing a grin and grabbed the bag from him in a mock-angry way.

"You were presuming an awful lot!" I said as we headed to the porch.

"Do you mind?" He suddenly looked uncertain.

"Not at all!" I laughed. "Very sensible."

The owner of the B&B was a short, stocky, ruddy-faced woman called Mrs Jones who smiled a lot and was enormously cheerful. She welcomed us in straight away and sat us down by the fire in one of the large sitting rooms while she went to get us cups of tea.

"But you're soaked!" she said, coming back with a tea tray laden with scones and jam and cream. "Here's a couple of towels for the worst of the rain." She handed over two towels after she'd put the tray down on the sideboard. "Well, it looks like the weather's set in for the next couple of days, the way its going. I hope you're not planning on spending much more of your time outdoors?"

"Oh no," Gwyn said without batting an eyelid. I tried to cut my scone to disguise my embarrassment, but my hand was shaking and the knife kept wobbling. Gwyn explained our circumstances with the broken trailer.

"Old George'll have it mended no problem," she said. "Clever man. Anyway, I've got to go and get dinner ready

– there's another couple from Oxford staying tonight and I guess you two will be wanting dinner here too?"

We nodded. This place was heaven.

"So let me show you up to your room now then before you make a start on those scones." And with that we got up and followed her upstairs, trying not to look each other in the eye.

We'd been given a room that faced out over the fields behind the house. It was gorgeous, painted a deep russet red with an enormous sleigh bed opposite the sash windows.

"There's your en suite just here." She held the door open for us. "And there's tea and coffee making facilities just here on the chest. Anything you need then just come down to the kitchens. I'm usually to be found there."

"Thanks," I said, hoisting my holdall up and turning to throw it on the bed.

"Wait!" She ran over to me and I froze, mid-swing.

"Sorry, it's just old Smog here, she's made a home on your bed," she laughed and I suddenly saw an old grey striped cat lying curled up on the coverlet. "I'm sorry, I don't usually let her up in the guest rooms but I must have left the door open by mistake and she came up here. You don't mind cats, do you?"

"Oh no," I said, "we don't mind cats at all!"

Gwyn laughed out loud.

37

I was dying to tell Angela everything. Absolutely aching to tell her. It was a bit of a miracle, in fact, that she didn't already know about my weekend because I almost blurted it out when I was on the phone to her arranging the night out.

But I managed to keep it to myself.

Just.

I wanted to tell her that, after last weekend, I had someone else I wanted to invite to her barbeque, if it was all right with her? Who? Oh, his name is Gwynfor and he's all man. ALL man.

We'd only just settled down in the City Bar and Canteen and ordered the wine and tapas. I'd already told her I had some news and besides, she could probably tell there was something up with me by the way I was looking eager and impatient, perched on the edge of the bench and completely unable to relax. Well, either I was eager and impatient or I had cystitis.

"OK, what's your news?" she said.

Thank God! I thought I was going to explode with having to restrain myself. I opened my mouth, took a deep breath –

And then Marcia walked in.

"Marcy!" Angela stood up to greet the bony-bottomed one and got the usual mwah mwah kiss on each cheek. I still had my mouth open, ready to launch into the story of my weekend. I closed it and smiled tightly at Marcia. Ngh.

"Hi Rachel," Marcia said breezily, "it is just so nice to see you again! Have you lost weight – you look different!"

"No, Marcia, I'm still fat."

"Oh." For once she was lost for words. It was priceless. "Well, I can see you've already got your drinks, so I'll just go and get a wine. No talking behind my back when I've gone," she laughed and shimmied over to the bar.

"I'm sorry, Rach. Marcia mentioned that she really wanted to come along tonight, and I thought that it would be a great opportunity for you two to ... well, you know, kiss and make up and all that. Anyway, can you tell me your news now while Marcia's at the bar – is it secret?"

"Oh everybody can hear it!" I said enthusiastically, quite glad now that I'd have a bigger audience. "Marcia can hear it too. In fact, I'd really like her to hear it."

"Hear what?" said Marcia, flouncing down on the sofa beside us. "Anyway," she flapped her hands excitedly, "before you tell us what you have to say, I just have to tell you about my weekend. I had the most amazing weekend ever!"

"So did Rachel," Angela said, seeing my crestfallen

face, "she was just going to tell us."

"Go on then." Marcia sat back and crossed her arms, clearly a bit pissed off that the spotlight was off her.

"No, no, you first," I said graciously, holding up my hands and seeing her check out my manicure. Ha! "I'm sure my weekend will just pale in comparison to yours." I sat back and helped myself to the olives.

She beamed and sat on the edge of her seat. "Oh well, if you're sure then. My weekend was brilliant – just fantastic. Girls girls girls! You should go orienteering! Seriously! It's such fun! Toby and I joined a few friends from London, you remember Ed and Milly? Dean and Becks? Anyway, we went on this organised orienteering weekend where a team of you have to get to all these points by a certain time. And our team won! Of course! Toby was such a whizz at navigating. Well, it was so much fun we booked another weekend straight away – we're going back to the Carrog Valley in mid Wales in three weeks time, it's just perfect for that kind of thing, so remote, so wild! Rachel, are you OK? God, did that olive go down the wrong way? Here, have a drink."

Other work by Claire Peate

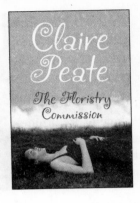

"I guessed that I was in for a treat, and I was not disappointed... Claire Peate... kept me turning the pages and laughing." *Hilary Gibson*

The Floristry Commission

There are some things in life you'll never forget – or forgive – that mean flinging your lime green kitten heels into a bag and leaving without a backward glance... and most of your wardrobe. For Rosamund it was the sight or her erstwhile boyfriend making love to her swine of a sister in front of the fridge.

She's nowhere to go but the Welsh Marches and her old schoolfriend Gloria – after all, she could hardly run home to mum.

But if Ros thought the City was full of intrigue and betrayal, it's got nothing on *Kings Newton*. Before she knows it, she's up to her eyes in trouble with the testily pre-nuptial Gloria, planning floral subterfuge with a camp and gossipy colleague, and covering for all and sundry in a desperate attempt to survive the battle between the swoon-inducing lord of the manor and his unruly townsfolk.

ISBN: 978 1870206 747   £6.99

Forthcoming titles from Honno

About Elin
by Jackie Davies

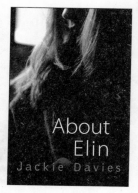

A haunting novel of love and loss

Elin Pritchard, ex-firebrand, is back home for her brother's funeral. Returning brings all sorts of emotions to the fore, memories good and bad, her own and those of the community she left behind.

September 2007
ISBN: 978 1870206 891
£6.99

More than Just a Hairdresser
by Nia Pritchard

A cut above the usual shampoo and set...

Mobile hairdresser Shirley and sidekick Oli use the tools of their trade to covertly trail a client's philandering hubbie...

November 2007
ISBN: 978 1870206 853
£6.99

Other titles from Honno

Hector's Talent for Miracles
by Kitty Sewell

Mair's search for her lost grandfather takes her from a dull veterinary surgery in Cardiff to the heat & passion of Spain.

ISBN: 978 1870206 815   £6.99

Facing into the West Wind
by Lara Clough

Jason may be lost and friendless, but he has a gift. He has a face people confess to.And those confessions are going to change everything ...

"A deeply felt and accomplished first novel" *Sue Gee*

ISBN: 978 1870206 792   £6.99

Girl on the Edge
by R.V.Knox

Just how did her mother die and what did Leila witness on the cliff top, if anything? A compelling psychological thriller set in the moors of North Wales.

ISBN: 978 1870206 754   £6.99

All Honno titles can be ordered online at
www.honno.co.uk
or by sending a cheque to Honno

FREE p&p to all UK addresses.

About Honno

Honno Welsh Women's Press was set up in 1986 by a group of women who felt strongly that women in Wales needed wider opportunities to see their writing in print and to become involved in the publishing process. Our aim is to develop the writing talents of women in Wales, give them new and exciting opportunities to see their work published and often to give them their first 'break' as a writer.

Honno is registered as a community co-operative. Any profit that Honno makes is invested in the publishing programme. Women from Wales and around the world have expressed their support for Honno by buying shares in the co-operative. Shareholders' liability is limited to the amount invested and each shareholder has a vote at the Annual General Meeting.

To buy shares or to receive further information about forthcoming publications, please write to Honno at the address below, or visit our website: **www.honno.co.uk**.

Honno
'Ailsa Craig'
Heol y Cawl
Dinas Powys
Bro Morgannwg
CF64 4AH